OPERATION NIGHTFALL

Also by John Miles

THE BLACKMAILER

THE SILVER BULLET GANG

THE NIGHT HUNTERS

OPERATION NIGHTFALL

A Novel of Suspense

by John Miles and Tom Morris

THE BOBBS-MERRILL COMPANY, INC.

Indianapolis/New York

ISBN 0–672–52085–0
Library of Congress catalog card number 741–7665
Designed by Winston Potter
Manufactured in the United States of America

Third Printing

OPERATION NIGHTFALL

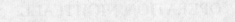

PRELUDE

Friday, May 17, 1974

The tension—unexpected and painful—hit Keel hard as he nudged his Camaro into the parking slot beside the metal hangar. He paused for a moment and left the engine running, for the air conditioning, while he adjusted.

Under the circumstances, he realized, the tension was normal enough. But they had not been caught up till now, and there was no reason to expect disaster at this late date. It was just that this visit to the field, after all the others, was a final one: everything was changing now, ending, and if they were not caught right now, they would not be caught at all.

They would not, he thought, be caught at all.

Shutting off the ignition and unbelting himself, he left the car. The blinding South Texas heat enveloped him immediately. He put on his sunglasses against the pavement glare and walked briskly around the building, glancing as he often did at his reflection in the blank office window. He saw a tall man, slender, sandy-haired, wearing beige slacks and a lemon-colored sport shirt open at the collar. There was nothing wrong with the reflection; it did not, after all, reveal that he was a failure.

Beside the office entry door on the south side of the hangar a workman was nailing a painted wood slat under the company sign that was already mounted there. Both the old sign and the new slat were red-on-white, so that they could be read easily together:

Alpha Aviation
Galveston's Finest!
Flight School—Rentals—Charters
CLOSED

Inside the hangar it was dim and hot and deserted. The old Cessna 150 stood off in a far corner, engineless. The building smelled faintly of oil and gasoline. Keel walked through quickly, going to the windowed door that led into the office.

With most of the furniture gone and the venetian blinds closed, it was a barren, dusty little place under the buzzing fluorescent lights. Even the Piper pictures had been removed from the walls, leaving darker rectangles of unfaded paint around the tacks. At the counter bisecting the room, a squat, fat man with fading red hair was counting out money for a younger man with modishly long hair and a mustache. Both looked up as Keel entered.

"Tom," the older man said. "Good."

"Everything all right?" Keel asked casually.

Hank Cline was sweating profusely in the stuffy office, but the experience of his business going under had not entirely erased his sense of humor. He mopped a pudgy hand over his bald spot and smiled grimly. "Under the circumstances, I suppose so."

Keel nodded to the other man, Jack Abercrombie, but said nothing. Abercrombie had already turned back to watch the money on the counter top. He was busy being solemn; he looked a little like Larry Csonka.

Hank Cline slapped a few more twenties onto the counter. "That's it, Jack. Six hundred."

Abercrombie gathered up the wad of bills and started to put it into his wallet.

"You'd better count it," Hank Cline said with that little well-meaning frown.

"It's right," Abercrombie said. "I watched you."

"Sorry it has to be cash. You know what happened to the checking account."

2

Abercrombie touched a fingertip to the end of his mustache. "I know, Hank. Cash is fine."

"Maybe," Hank Cline said with a ghastly smile, "better?"

"I'm damned sorry it had to turn out this way, Hank."

"I know. Anyway, thanks. You did good work for us. It wasn't your fault."

The men shook hands. Then Abercrombie turned, hesitated, and walked over to where Keel waited. Abercrombie extended his hand. "Luck, Tom."

"You too," Keel said, shaking his hand. "Try to keep in touch."

Abercrombie's smile was rueful. "I'd say I might drop you a line—"

"But neither of us knows where we might end up."

"Right."

They looked at each other.

"Anyway." Abercrombie's hand dropped to his side.

"Take care."

The dark-haired man walked to the door, raised a hand in a half-salute, and went out. The door closed gently behind him.

Hank Cline sighed audibly in the silence. "It wouldn't be so bad, going out of business, if people didn't get hurt. That's a good man who just left here."

"He'll come up on his feet," Keel said.

"I suppose so." Cline sighed again. "Well. Let me pay you off, too, Tom. You're about the last. The people and the cash money are going to come out just about even."

Keel watched soberly as Cline counted it out. The man's hands were shaking slightly and he was very pale. The months of decline and struggle had been very, very hard on him, and Keel felt a certain amount of distant sympathy. Failure was never pretty. He knew: he was an expert.

"You were a good chief flight instructor," Cline said when the money was pocketed. "I want to thank you."

Keel shrugged. "Alpha Aviation still went down the tube."

3

"It was economics . . . the gas shortage . . . too many things. You did your part. Everyone did."

"What are you going to do now?"

Cline's eyes were vacant. "I don't know. I've got the fishing boat. We didn't come out too badly on selling the planes and equipment, you know. I've got to go through the bankruptcy thing, but almost everybody will be paid. I'll . . . think about it. I don't know."

"I enjoyed working for you."

Cline frowned. "If we had just gotten a few more charters . . . a few more students. If just that single charter deal in Oklahoma City had worked out like we hoped, we could have gone maybe another year . . . got through this bad spell."

"The charter thing was bad luck," Keel agreed carefully. "If they had used the Aztec as many hours as they thought they would—"

"We would have cleared at least five thousand dollars," Cline finished for him. "I know. God knows I've thought about it enough. But they didn't fly seventy or eighty hours a month; they flew twenty in *two* months. And we didn't make any money—we didn't even break even." He sighed again. "Nobody's fault. Just more bad luck, the last straw."

So it was all right. Relief flooded warmly through Keel. "I'd better be going," he said.

"What are you going to do? Do you know yet?"

"No."

"I hate it, seeing things break up. You and Jack Abercrombie were good charter pilots for us—good flight instructors. I'll miss you."

"I'll try to keep in touch," Keel lied.

"Think you'll be seeing Abercrombie or any of the others again?"

"It's a small world, but I don't know about that. I'll miss them. They were good guys to work with."

Hank Cline looked at him, and for an instant Keel was afraid the man actually was going to cry. "Luck, Tom," Cline said finally and held out his hand again.

4

Relieved to be finished with it, Keel left the hangar and drove around the perimeter of the airport. Galveston's skyline was hazy in the distance, and the day was getting even hotter. Keel hoped the next job would be in a cooler climate; not the north, with its really bad winters and with flying constantly fouled up by industrial haze and scum, but a little farther up, anyway. Oklahoma City?

He had enjoyed Oklahoma City during the two months he was supposed to be flying charter. The girl he had spent most of his time with had been fantastic, good therapy for the breakup of a marriage.

But the girl, he thought, was probably behind him for good. Like Alpha Aviation and Hank Cline and a lot of other things. And what did a failure try next?

Nudged by the old bitterness, he finished the circuit of the airport and pulled into the parking lot near the commercial terminal. The car he was looking for, a gray Peugeot, was not hard to locate because the lot was not crowded. Keel pulled in beside it and looked across at Jack Abercrombie through the opened window.

"You get it?" Abercrombie asked.

"Yes."

"I had to leave. I thought you and Hank were going to start playing violins or something."

"Hank's not a bad guy."

"My heart bleeds. Now what about the split?"

The question did not surprise Keel. "How about tonight at my place?"

"Your new apartment, you mean?"

"Where else?"

Abercrombie nodded and touched his mustache in a characteristic gesture. "All right. Ten?"

"Eight."

"Won't a meeting be obvious at that time?"

"Visitors won't be noticed as much at eight as they might be at ten."

"All right. Will anyone else be there?"

"Phil Lester."

Abercrombie thought about it. "All right."

"See you then." Keel rolled the window back up. He drove away.

Tom Keel's apartment consisted of two rooms and a dining alcove tucked into the garage corner of a singles apartment complex. His furniture consisted of a Sears sofa-bed, three director's chairs, some odds and ends his ex-wife had allowed him out of the attic, and some planks on bricks that formed shelving for magazines and flight manuals. It was depressing. Jack Abercrombie and Phil Lester seemed not to notice.

Possibly they were cheered by the Jack Daniel's that Keel poured. More likely, they were buoyed up by the four neat stacks of money he had placed on one of the wall shelves.

"Just so we understand each other," Keel told them, "I want to review the thing briefly."

"No need for that, old buddy." Phil Lester smiled. He was a small, slender, fox-faced man of about fifty whose drawling good nature might have really bothered people like Keel if he had not also been an exceptional aircraft and power plant mechanic. "We trust you."

"So did Hank," Keel retorted.

Lester smiled and nodded agreement. Abercrombie, also amused, raised his glass in a mock salute. The take had been astonishingly easy. They had persuaded Hank to rent the Aztec to Joe Donovan in Oklahoma City. Hank believed the whole story—how Donovan would job out the aircraft to an oil company for charters and make a little profit by charging more per hour for the plane than Alpha Aviation was charging him flat-rate, by the month.

The lease to Donovan had been for two months, for $1,200 a month, plus $40 an hour of flight time, pilot—Keel —included, but not fuel or oil. Hank Cline had expected about eighty hours a month from Donovan, or $3,200 a month for hours flown, plus the $1,200 base fee.

What he got was a tachometer reading showing that Donovan flew ten hours each month.

What Donovan and Keel had done was disconnect both the recording tach and the engine tachs to prevent flight time from registering on the aircraft. They went to Oklahoma City and dropped Keel off, to be around in case Hank Cline called, and Donovan took the plane on to Denver. He flew seventy-nine hours one month and eighty-one hours the next. The difference in rates charged and hours actually flown had provided their neatly illicit profit of $6,300, net.

"Our shares," Keel reminded them now, "came to $1,575 apiece."

Phil Lester grinned. "And can I use it." He went to the shelving, carefully selected one of the stacks of money, and began counting it.

"We can all use it," Abercrombie said, getting his share.

"I'm taking Donovan's share to him in a couple weeks," Keel added.

"Where is he?"

"Memphis, at the moment."

"Working?"

Keel was faintly amused. "At some kind of confidence game, maybe."

Abercrombie and Lester finished counting their shares and went back to the sofabed. Abercrombie picked up his glass. "What's amazing is how easy it was."

"We told you at the start it would be easy."

"I had my doubts."

"Once Phil, here, had disconnected the tachs, how was anyone to know the actual flight time on the aircraft?"

"Of course. But there were the traffic movements—the tower contacts, the instrument flight plans, all the other records."

"You know most of those records don't last," Keel retorted. "And Hank didn't have any reason to doubt us, did he?"

"No need to lose your temper," Abercrombie said,

"I'm not," Keel said. But his face was hot.

7

"After all, we are home free now."

"Right," Keel bit off.

"And I wasn't criticizing you. Far be it from *me* to criticize *you.*"

"I can do without your sarcasm, Jack."

"And I," Abercrombie responded intently, "can do without any more of your eternal supersensitivity. No one criticized you. I wasn't even implying that the plan wasn't good. Obviously it was. We have the money, right? Get off your high horse for once, Tom. Jesus Christ!"

"I'm not on a high horse," Keel said stiffly.

Abercrombie was grinning at him, but there was anger behind the eyes. "You're on one half the time. You're too damned sensitive, always looking for offense when none is there. You're practically a perfect pilot and this was a perfect little operation. All *I* was trying to say was that I'm glad we got away with it. All right?"

Keel watched him. Keel's pulse thudded heavily in his skull. Surprisingly, he was suddenly very angry.

"I make very few mistakes," he said, not knowing why.

"Right," Abercrombie said. *"Right."*

Phil Lester hummed tunelessly for an instant. "Maybe we ought to split, boys. I know we all got a lot to do."

"Like count our money," Abercrombie said.

Keel, still watching him, said now, "What was wrong with the operation, Jack?"

"Nothing! Good God, get *off* of it, will you, Tom?"

"If there was something wrong with it, I planned it. It's over, so now you can let me know."

Phil Lester said quickly, "I only wish it had been a lot more, personally."

"It couldn't be more. You know that."

"Sure. Just wishing, man."

Abercrombie added, "As easy as that was, it sort of makes a man wonder why he isn't stealing a *big* chunk of loot."

"Especially now," Lester agreed.

"You're already hooked on with the Airmen, aren't you?"

8

"Oh, sure. Can't keep a good A&P mechanic down, man. But that's just a living. I'm talking about getting rich."

"Getting rich," Abercrombie mused. "That's not so easy."

"It could be done," Keel said. He was still feeling belligerent.

"Think so?"

"Yes."

"How?"

"We were inexperienced, and this worked. If a man had above-average intelligence, plus an original scheme, he could probably make off with a lot of money and never be caught."

"Glory, hallelujah," Phil Lester said. "That's for me."

"And me," Abercrombie said.

"You've agreed to that job with Shell," Keel pointed out.

"I'm not going to get rich at it."

Keel felt a new kind of pulse. "You mean if a truly clever scheme did come up, you might be interested?"

"Truly clever?" Abercrombie frowned at his glass. "Why not? This one worked, didn't it?"

"We could come up with something," Keel said.

"What?"

"I don't know. But we could."

Phil Lester said, "With our savvy, it ought to be around aviation, somehow."

"Probably," Abercrombie agreed.

"It would have to involve money, directly," Keel said.

Abercrombie studied him. "As opposed to dope or merchandise or something like that, you mean."

"Yes. If you steal anything but money, you have the problem of fencing it."

"Even with money, you'd have to have a plan for spending it a little at a time, or in scattered locations. A man can't just dump several big ones on the local car dealer and expect to get away with it."

"One thing I liked about this deal," Phil Lester interjected, "was the way we had contingency plans. I mean, we

9

could have pulled out before I pulled the tach cables, or if Mack had gotten suspicious, or even when the first monthly payment came in. We had options, see? Any plan has to have a lot of 'em."

"I don't like the idea of sweating it out a long time, though," Abercrombie added.

"Right," Keel snapped. "Hit and get away with it. That's the only way."

"Hit and get away with *what?* And where?"

"I mean," Keel said, "it would want to be a paramilitary operation. Waylay a Brink's truck or something like that. Perfect timing and execution. Then prearranged escape routes for each of us separately. Plans for unloading the money carefully. Everything phased and worked out *perfectly.*"

Abercrombie studied him with a little smile. "Have you got something in mind?"

"Not really," Keel admitted.

"But you've been thinking about it."

"I'm past the point where I can ever hope to have a career with the airlines, I think. I've tried the corporate scene and don't like it. I'm not crazy about being a flight instructor all my life."

Abercrombie grinned again. "Especially with those alimony payments, eh?"

"Is that anything to you?" Keel flashed.

Abercrombie raised his hands in mock surrender. "Okay, okay."

"I don't like cracks like that, Jack."

"I'm *sorry.*"

Phil Lester put down his empty glass with a smack. "No perfect plan in sight, huh? Oh, me, oh, my. I better blow."

"We could come up with something," Keel insisted.

Phil Lester's uneven teeth gleamed. "If you do, call me fast."

Abercrombie got to his feet. "Tom, it's been a kick." He extended his hand.

Keel shook it. "Maybe I'll be in touch."

"Yeah. Why not?"

10

The two men left. Keel locked the door behind them and stood quite still until he heard their car engines in the parking lot. He felt the dingy little apartment behind him, but he could not turn to face the reality of it.

This kind of reality he didn't need. There had been far too much of it already. He might have had his break with Braniff just before being called to Vietnam duty. Even afterward, with his gunship experience, he might have had a chance if his return had not coincided with personnel reductions being made by several airlines in financial trouble over spending too much for the 747. He had gone into life as a corporate pilot with his hopes still undimmed. But dreams had a way of fading; they died a little with every stupid flight, every case of Cokes you broke open for asshole executives, every cigarette you lit for some so-called secretary whose eyes challenged you, over the match, with the mutual knowledge of what you were really flying her off to do with the boss all weekend.

There was so much money *out* there! That was what drove Keel wild. He had seen executives spend hundreds of thousands the way he might spend fifty cents. He had flown million-dollar airplanes to billion-dollar resorts for a crummy $10,000 per year. It was crazy, all of it. There was nothing fair about anything anymore. And now his marriage was over, and the alimony payments would start backing up before too long unless he found another rotten job.

So he could slave away to pay an ex-wife.

And have *nothing*.

But the money was out there, waiting. He was a very intelligent man. Abercrombie's wry smile might have indicated that *finding* a plan was a virtual impossibility, and yet . . . *and yet* the money was there, and he deserved it; he had it coming. If he could just find the right target—the right plan.

Mentally he ticked off the basic aspects in his mind:

1 *Cash as a target;*
2 *Paramilitary operation and strike;*
3 *Thorough planning;*
4 *Precise execution;*

11

5   *Flexible escape routes;*
6   *Alternate plans in case of trouble;*
7   *Methods of spending the money without detection.*

Restlessly, Keel's mind prowled for ideas. He remained standing by the locked door of his little apartment for a very long time.

Sunday, June 2

It was hot and windy in Oklahoma City, and the sky over the motel pool area was blinding blue. A few kids were splashing in the pool; two pretty young secretaries were sunning themselves in tiny bikinis on the sun-glaring pavement on the far side. Joe Donovan, stretched out almost flat in a beach chair shaded by a huge pink parasol table, looked fat, hairy, and contented as he raised his wide-brimmed straw hat just enough to sip his Collins and eye the girls. Then he sighed and lay back down.

"That," he said judiciously, "is real nice."

Sticky and uncomfortable in his street clothes, Keel nudged the envelope on the edge of the table. "Maybe you'd better count it."

"Not necessary."

"No. Maybe you'd better."

Donovan looked at him from under the brim of the hat, which was of the type that had stray pieces of straw sticking out here and there as if the maker hadn't quite finished before going off to a luau. Donovan was in his forties and somewhat overweight. His pale red hair was thicker on his chest than on his head these days, and his eyes had a tired, milky quality. He kept trying, though.

"You're uptight," he said soothingly. "Consider the lilies of the field. Consider yon girls. Why should I count money when all these good things are at hand?"

"It's all there," Keel said. "The money, I mean."

"I know that, friend. Relax."

Keel grimaced. "Yeah."

12

"You found gainful employment as yet, friend?"

"I think I'll be working as a flight instructor in Memphis."

"Oh?" Donovan was still covertly eying the girls. "Good deal?"

"It's a paycheck."

"Too bad we couldn't get to old Hank for a few more bills."

"That's what Jack and Phil said, too."

"Ah, well."

"There's a lot more money out there."

Donovan eyed him again. "Am I about to get felt out on something?"

Keel was sweating more heavily now and was painfully tense. "I've got a little idea, as a matter of fact."

"Is that a fact."

"Bigger than the other one."

"Really?"

"It would take all four of us," Keel said.

Donovan was still more interested in what was happening across the pool. The brunette had turned over to sit up and was holding her untied bra to her breasts with one careless hand. The hand almost slipped. Donovan muttered pleasurably.

Keel got to his feet. "I'll see you around, Joe."

"Wait a minute, wait a minute! You said you had a plan."

"I'm not sure anybody is interested."

"You take life too *seriously*. Sit down. There. Good. Relax. Tell me the plan. What the hell. It ought to be good for laughs."

"It would take all four of us," Keel repeated, teeth close together.

"You, me, Jack, Phil?"

"Or you and me and two others."

"What's the deal?"

"A Pan Am flight to Honolulu."

Donovan studied him. "What about it?"

"We hijack it."

Donovan chuckled, and the chuckle became a laugh.

13

His sweat-glistening belly bobbed up and down. "That's a great one! That's really a good one!"

"I'm serious."

Donovan waved his hand. "Forget it. That's a big offense. And they're wise to anything—*anything*—anybody could come up with. Forget it!"

"I've got a plan that would work."

Donovan chuckled some more and returned his attention to the girls.

"It *would* work."

"Forget it, man."

Keel studied the other man's averted face, mostly hidden by the ridiculous hat. Keel was having a hard time holding his temper. He had expected any number of things, but not to be dismissed.

He pushed back from the table. "I'm going up to my room, take a nap."

Donovan waved lazily. "Check with you later."

Simmering, Keel went to his room.

At supper in the dining room, he was eating with Donovan when the two girls from poolside entered, again with no male escorts.

"There are your girls," he told Donovan.

Donovan, who looked like nothing more than a sunburned old sailor in his pale slacks and open-necked shirt, looked up and then twisted his lips in derision. "Them?"

"You were more in favor of them earlier."

"Ah, so. But I put a little move on 'em after you went to your room. Froze me off solid."

"Maybe it's just as well you're moving on to Dallas."

"Yep. Another job, another dollar."

Keel thought about it. "You in Dallas, me in Memphis, Phil still in Galveston, Jack in Houston."

"Hard to pull a caper, spread out like that."

Keel said nothing.

"All right," Donovan said after a while. "Tell me."

"About what?"

"You know about what! The job."

"Not here," Keel said.

14

"In my room when we're through, then."

"If you think you might be interested."

"I'm asking, right?"

Keel felt a renewed pulse of excitement. He had worked very hard on the plan. He had confidence in it.

In Donovan's room later, he outlined it.

Donovan listened attentively, seriously.

"So what do you think?" Keel asked finally.

Donovan walked to the window, parted the heavy draperies, looked down at the fairy-tale lights around the pool area for a moment, then turned slowly. His eyes seemed older, turned down at the corners, and very weary.

"It won't work," he said.

"Why?" Keel demanded.

"There's too much risk every step of the way."

"When? Where?"

"Every step of the way, I said."

Keel's face heated. "Tell me where. Explain. I've worked hard on this."

"I know you have," Donovan said seriously.

"Then tell me what's wrong with it."

"All right." Donovan walked to the couch, sat down, stretched his legs out and locked his hands behind his head. "Number one. You assume we can smuggle guns into the plane through the catering-service trays that go on board. That means we have to find an accomplice inside the catering company's service kitchen. We don't have any such contact."

"We find someone," Keel argued doggedly. "It might take a while, but we could find someone."

Donovan studied him. "And smuggle the guns into the kitchen, and then hope the guy can smuggle them into trays, somehow? Okay, okay. Maybe it can be done. *Maybe* we could even get to the trays and get the guns after we're in the air, without tipping the stewardesses off. It would be tricky—"

"I told you how we—"

"Okay. Fine. I'll grant you that, too. So now we're standing in the aft kitchen area with our guns, right?"

15

"Right," Keel said.

"We make the girls take us up front. We tell the captain to orbit right where he is, and we tell him to call LA and tell them we want a million bucks waiting for us at the LA airport, and we'll be back in one hour to pick it up. Right?"

Keel felt sweat streaming down his face. He was caught up in it. "Yes," he said.

"We fly back, we land, we pick up the money on the runway. Right?"

"We send a girl out for the bag of money," Keel corrected him tautly. "No FBI sharpshooter is going to get a crack at us."

Donovan sighed.

"Anything wrong with that?"

"Nope. I'll even give you the odds on that part. We'll say nobody overpowers us on the airplane, nobody shoots out the tires and traps us on the ground at LA, and somehow we get it back into the air again. There are holes there, buddy, but I'll give them to you."

"So there's no problem," Keel said.

"We fly back out to sea," Donovan said, reviewing. "It's dark by now. We make the captain put the plane down on the deck to avoid radar pursuit—"

"Right, right."

"We make him fly to a prearranged spot, which we can check by electronic devices just as well as he can, and we bail out."

"With the chutes we picked up along with the money," Keel agreed.

"What makes you think those chutes won't be stuffed with newspapers instead of good, strong silk and neatly folded shroud lines?"

The thought hit Keel with paralyzing force. He stared.

Donovan shrugged. "I mean, if I were an FBI man and somebody asked *me* for a million dollars and two parachutes, I'd give the man the lousiest, most rat-eaten chutes I could dig out of the trash can. Then, when he jumped, he'd have a nice two-thousand-foot free fall, and end up as nice chunks

16

of blubber floating around for the sharks and Charlie the Tuna."

"We could figure out a way to pack small trick chutes in suitcases," Keel replied, ad-libbing swiftly.

"They'd let them go by the on-board search?"

"They don't search anymore. They X-ray."

Donovan unlocked his hands. "I don't think it would work. But I'll even allow you *that*. Now. We hit the water safely, let's say. We've got flares. Here comes Phil Lester with a power boat. Right?"

"Right. We—"

"By careful enough planning let's say he actually finds us. He buzzes off as fast as the damned thing will go. It's pitch black. Even if there are some military aircraft in the area, which there will be by now, maybe we get out of the immediate area. Right?"

"Right."

"In comes Jack in a helicopter. We rendezvous. We ditch the boat, climb into the bird, buzz back, low, to the coast of northern California, land at a prearranged spot, pile into a couple of cars and split. Later we meet again somewhere else—*far* away—split the cash, and go our merry ways." Donovan paused again. "Right?"

"That's it," Keel said stubbornly. "And I don't see what's wrong with any of it."

Donovan grimaced. "Man, there are just too many *if*'s!"

"We could work out every detail . . . every angle—"

"*Maybe* the guns could be gotten onto the plane," Donovan said, ticking off a point on a blunt finger. "*Maybe* we could get to the guns. *Maybe* we could get to the front without somebody trying to jump us. *Maybe* we could get on the ground at LA, and back off again, without being reduced to hamburger meat. *Maybe* we could be sure the captain flew to the right spot. *Maybe* we could get out of the airplane—"

"He's low and slow," Keel cut in, unable to restrain himself on this point, at least. "We could safely pop a side exit."

"*Maybe* we don't get smashed by the empennage as we dive out. *Maybe* Phil finds us. *Maybe* we get away from the area. *Maybe* we rendezvous with the chopper all right. *Maybe* we sneak back to land. *Maybe* we land unobserved. *Maybe* we get out of the area. Then, for Christ's sake, *maybe* we can stay in hiding, meet again safely later, and figure out how to spend the money. Which is probably thoroughly marked by the FBI in the first place."

Keel tried to hide the disappointment that had begun to spread, sludge-like, through his body. The "maybe's" had hit him like rocks. There were so many. He was not ready to give up, but he could see, for the first time, how many places the luck had to be very, very good. He felt like an idiot.

Donovan got up, went to the dresser, got a glass and a bottle of scotch, and poured a drink. He glanced at Keel and poured another drink without asking, then brought it over.

"And finally," Donovan added softly, "where do we get the money for the boat and the chopper? We may have to buy both, under assumed names, well in advance."

Keel looked at the glass in his hands. He raised it and drained it.

"Sorry," Donovan said.

"I'm not going to give up."

"Nobody should try something quite this reckless. Besides, the airlines have had whole think tanks of experts working on hijacking situations. They've even got that hijack emergency center in Washington. You know that. They've thought ahead to virtually every kind of airplane hijacking. They'd be a step ahead of us most of the time with all their contingency plans. They could overwhelm us with sheer technology: radar, jet fighters, destroyers off the coast, you name it."

"And yet," Keel muttered, "a hijacking is so good because we know they have that policy: give them what they want, don't risk the plane or the passengers."

Donovan drained his glass and went back for the bottle. "You've given this a lot of thought."

"And work."

Donovan nodded thoughtful agreement.

"We could make a haul," Keel told him angrily. "If not with this, then with something else."

"It's finding the right deal," Donovan said, surprisingly.

"You don't think the whole idea of a carefully operated scheme is crazy, then?"

"My friend," Donovan said, "you are a man after my own heart. I've been looking for just the right plan for years."

"And the right help?"

"I think you and I understand each other."

They drank in silence. From the pool area came the muted sounds of canned music. Even recognizing its cheap quality—the make-believe aspect of this whole cabana-like atmosphere around a cheap motel pool in Oklahoma City— Keel found himself longing for something like it—something real and exotic and expensive and *his.*

"What," Donovan asked after a while, "do you make of these new regulations on controlled airspace? They're sure making it more complicated for the little guy, aren't they?"

Keel hesitated an instant before responding. *Change of subject: change of interest.* End of hope. He was bitterly disappointed.

Tuesday, June 4

Keel was getting acquainted with the new flying service at West Memphis airport. The manager met him at the office door as he returned from a walk through the hangar area. "Somebody wants you on the phone. Long distance."

Surprised, Keel picked up the telephone on the counter.

"Donovan here," the familiar voice said over a scratchy connection. "Listen. Is there a place where you have a secure phone? Where you could call a number I'll give you?"

"What's going on?" Keel asked. His heart moved a little. He wondered . . . discarded the hope. It was too soon, too good.

"Tell you tonight," Donovan drawled. "Call me at eight, your time. Okay?"

"Okay," Keel said, swallowing.

"Here's the number."

Keel dialed it promptly at 8 P.M. from a telephone booth. It took a while to push in all the dimes and quarters. When he was through, the operator got off the line.

"Listen," Donovan said, and Keel could hear the suppressed tension in his voice. "You had an idea about an airplane. How about the same kind of operation against an entire damned airport?"

Sunday, June 30

Keel was awakened early by the sound of some kind of big engine, and for an instant he stared at the water-stained wallpaper of the little room, disoriented and not remembering where he was. Then he saw the cheap dresser in the corner, the picture of two of his brother's children on the wall, and the opaque gray of the window, with a fruit tree beyond. He remembered.

Swinging his legs out of the bed to the cool linoleum floor, Keel reached for his slacks and pulled them on. He padded barefooted to the window, which was fully raised to combat the fierce heat-humidity characteristic of nights as well as days in this part of Kentucky. He looked out the window, trying to locate the engine noise.

There was a dirt driveway from the narrow road, several fruit trees, a chicken house, a ramshackle old barn, a fenced cattle pen. Beside the pen he saw an old Ford tractor. His brother Richard was on the high seat, alternately pumping and retarding the throttle. The tractor engine belched and snorted coldly, the hollow sound racketing off the walls

20

of the barn. A mist of oil smoke formed a thin bluish line in the air all around the tractor.

Keel hurriedly pulled on a tee shirt, his socks and his shoes. He left the bedroom and went down the narrow upstairs hallway to the stairs. His watch said 6:30. He had arrived the night before after eleven, having had a bad time finding the place. There had been an hour's excited talk, with Richard, his wife Cindy, and all five of the kids taking part. But Keel had been too tired and it had been too dark to see much of anything. Going past the living room, with its shabby lounge chairs and antique black and white television set, he felt like a stranger.

The kitchen was ablaze with light from a too-large fluorescent fixture, obviously purchased secondhand and hauled in to be bolted to the high ceiling. Cindy, still in faded pink robe and corduroy slippers, was at the rust-stained sink. She turned, smiling with surprise.

"You're up awfully early, Tom."

"Richard's tractor makes a fine alarm clock."

She studied him with a moment's concern. She was a small woman and had once been enormously attractive. The blonde hair was faded now, lopped off rather too short. Her face was lined; her mouth and eyes seemed to turn down at the edges from perpetual strain. She was, Keel knew, only thirty. She looked much older.

She said, "The bed wasn't too uncomfortable?"

"No, it was fine."

She gestured. "It's not the best bed in the world. I'm sorry—"

"I slept soundly. I heard the tractor, that's all."

"I wish those kids of ours would hear it. Honestly, they're the worst sleepyheads. If I didn't get after them, I think they'd sleep till eight o'clock some days."

"What's Richard up to out there?"

"There's some fence down," she said apologetically. "I know he really didn't want to have to do anything while you were here, it being such a short visit and all. But some of the cows got out last night and he said he wanted to get out

21

there and haul two new posts in. He hoped he could have done it before you woke up."

"I'll go out and give him a hand."

He went out through the closed-in back porch with its collection of buckets, brooms, mops, shovels, milk containers, empty clay pots, hose, and everything else, and down the shaky wooden steps to the back yard. The earth underfoot was wet, spongy. It had rained a little in the night and the air smelled warm-wet and green. He walked around a little pump shed that had no roof, crossed the bare dirt of the side yard and skirted the barn.

Richard had the tractor idling now and was behind it, struggling with a length of heavy, rusty chain. A man of Keel's height, he was slightly heavy, bald on top, with the rest cropped close in the old-fashioned style. He wore bib overalls, the top of some long-handle underwear, and heavy, yellowish boots. His face, partly averted, was intent on the work he was doing. A stubble of beard grayed his cheeks, but it was a good face, square, intent, honest, with evidence of considerable pain.

Keel got close enough for Richard to see him in his peripheral vision. Richard straightened up with a surprised grin that only changed one side—the good side—of his face.

"Expected you to sleep till noon!"

"You know I can't do that, Richard. I've got to get back."

Richard nodded, stepped heavily onto the side of the tractor, and cut the engine off.

"Why did you do that?" Keel asked in the sudden silence.

Richard shrugged. "I can do it later. If you're up—"

"Cindy said you have some fence down."

"Well, yes, but it's nothing important."

"Damn it, Richard, she said your cows are getting out. You need to fix that fence."

"I can do it later, bud. Not every day your brother comes to visit."

The kindness, so quick and obvious and consistent, troubled Keel. "I can help you if we do it now."

22

Richard shrugged and walked around to the tractor. He opened the switch and adjusted the throttle, then went to the front and reached down and jerked a crank. The tractor rocked but would not fire. He repeated the process four times. The tractor started. He hurried around to the seat and adjusted the throttle slightly. He grinned at Keel again, although sweat had popped out on his forehead and he was ghastly pale.

"Come on, then!"

Keel climbed up onto the side rail of the tractor and hung on. His brother engaged the gears and slowly released the clutch. The tractor lumbered across the bare yard, out behind the barn and through a gap in the fencing. The field beyond was rolling, soggy under the great wheels. Mist hung in the low spots, and off in the distance were trees along the fence lines. The first crimson disc of the sun peeped out beyond the hills to the east.

They lumbered across the field. At the far end a few minutes later they came into brush, where this section of the field was being reseeded by the woods that rose up, shaggy and mysterious, just beyond. Cattle—about twenty head— stood in a corner of the fence some fifty yards away, watching.

"There it is," Richard yelled, pointing.

Just ahead, there had been a natural wash down out of the field into the woods. Two fence posts lay almost flat on the ground, and as they pulled nearer, Keel could see that the earth was chopped up where some of the cattle had gotten out.

"This ought to do it," Richard said, throttling the tractor back.

The new fence posts were already nearby, part of a stack evidently kept ready at intervals along the fence. Working ponderously but quickly, Richard hooked the tractor chain around one of the downed posts, which Keel now saw had rotted. Richard got wire tools from a metal box on the side of the tractor, cut the wires, lashed the pull-chain to the broken posts one at a time, and pulled them out. Keel watched this.

23

"Get the new posts now," Richard said, heading for the stack, "and we've got 'er whipped." He picked up one end of a heavy post and started dragging it across the mud.

Keel hurried forward. "Let me get the other end of that."

"No. Hell. No sense in you getting yourself all dirty."

"I've been dirty before, you asshole."

Richard grinned and let him help. The post was very heavy with moisture, and its surface was slick with rich gumbo mud. They wrestled it together to the hole, and then the hole wasn't deep enough. Richard got a spade and attacked the hole with furious competence.

"No sense"—he gasped, whacking at the hole for punctuation—"putting in a new post that's just—going to fall—over." Dirt flew. Richard's face was bathed in a sickly sweat and his color was terrible again.

He got the first hole done and leaned on the spade. "Whew! Let me catch my breath!"

Keel took the spade. "Let me work on the other one."

"No sense you—"

"Come on!"

The ground was richly soft, and although Keel was badly out of condition for this kind of work, it was not hard for him. He made short work of it. Walking back to where his brother squatted beside the first hole, he was again alarmed by the pallor, and made it a point to squat down in a similar position as if he, too, had gotten worn out.

"That's hard work," he grunted.

Richard put a work-horny hand over his chest. "The damned thing just don't work like it used to."

"Do you have pain?"

He had asked it too sharply; Richard made it a point to grin again. "It lets you know when you try to overdo."

"What's the doctor say?"

"Well, I gave up on the son of a bitch."

Keel looked at his older brother. They had grown up on a farm not unlike this one. Richard, eight years older, had always been the teacher. There was still that old feeling in Keel right now . . . the same sense that Richard knew best

24

and would show him what to do. After all these years that was unchanged.

But everything else had changed. He had been the one who managed to go to college, to learn to fly, to go into the army and learn multi-engine transport and helicopter skills he might never have learned any other way. Richard had stayed on the land, first the old home place, and then, after it was lost, the little place near Circleville, Ohio, and when that too was lost, this place here. While Keel had always known a lust to escape from this kind of life, Richard had stubbornly stayed with it, almost as if to prove that a man *could* improve himself by his own effort, *could* make a go of it the way his father, and his father's father, had.

Looking at his brother now, however, Keel saw what a terrible toll the effort had exacted.

There had been two heart attacks, one four years ago, one just last year. They had both been severe. They had bracketed something else, the onset of some disease that Keel could never remember by name. That little added touch by Mother Nature had caused the unbearable pain, had finally led to a surgeon severing certain nerves in Richard's face, so that now the pain was not so bad, but half the face was dead.

Since Keel had last seen Richard, something else had happened, too. Richard had always been tremendously active, whip-thin because of it. He had changed now. His body sagged with extra fat and his face carried little folds of fat under the jawline and eyes.

He was *old*, Keel realized. Richard was old. At forty. Just as Cindy was old (with the help of the children and the fear) at thirty.

"You need," he told his brother seriously, "to take it easy. And you need to keep seeing that doctor."

Richard shrugged again. "A lecture I can get at Sunday school. Which I got to be at in three hours or so, incidentally. So let's get these posts in, bud."

Later, back at the house, the kids were up, noisy and excited about Keel's visit. Keel and Richard washed up in the bathroom together.

25

"Might be a real good year," Richard, lathered to the elbows, told him. "If we can get the soybeans to make, we've got eighty acres I'm sharecropping with the owner down the road a piece, corn, and it looks good. The garden is coming along. We'll get the cellar full of stuff. And we can sell a couple of beeves. With milk prices going up, maybe some of the profit will trickle down to us farmers someday soon.

"Yes sir," he went on, drying hands and arms carefully, "if nothing more goes wrong with the tractor or anything, I've got a deal on some alfalfa that looks good, too. I might get that new roof on the barn this fall."

"If your health holds up," Keel said, not knowing why he was so angry.

"Nuts," Richard said. "I'm in good shape."

They went in to breakfast. The kids talked a blue streak all the time. When breakfast was concluded, the two girls automatically began cleaning things up. The boys drifted outside for chores or something, and Richard said he had something in the barn that would just take a second. Keel went into the living room and smoked a cigarette. It was full daylight now and he sat looking at the frayed rug, the family pictures hanging crooked on the walls, the Motorola TV set.

Cindy, dressed in jeans and a pale sport shirt, came in and joined him. She curled up in one of the recliners. "I wish you could visit longer, Tom."

"I've got to get back," Keel told her with regret.

"You really have a business meeting in Memphis to-night?"

"Yes."

"And you can get that far that fast?"

"I'll turn in the rental car at the airport, climb in the plane, and blast off. I'll be in Memphis before five."

"Blast off," she repeated with a smile. "Golly, I've never been in an airplane."

"Next time I'm here, I'll take you for a ride."

Her tired eyes lighted for an instant. Then she said, "I wish you could take some of the kids. The kids would really enjoy it. I don't have to go. I'm a little old anyway, I guess."

Keel looked at her and wanted to cry out. *God damn it,*

Cindy! You're not too old! You're not old at all! Why do you think of yourself as old and why do you have all those lines? What's life done to you in ten years to dry you up and wither you this way? It's wrong!

But all he said was, "Maybe everyone can go."

"I hope you like your new job, Tom."

"Cindy, forget that. What about Richard?"

She looked at him.

"I mean," he said, "his health."

"It's all right," she said vaguely.

"I'm his brother. I want to know."

She shook her head. "I don't know."

"We went out there and dug those post holes, and I thought he was almost going to faint, or something."

"He has before."

"Fainted?"

"He won't do as the doctor says. Twice this summer, already, we've missed him. I've sent the kids looking. Once, down by the creek, and the other time out behind the barn, there he was on the ground."

"He's got to take care of himself! He's not an old man! He's only forty! Nobody's old at thirty or forty!" He was dimly conscious that he was intent on making *her* realize this, too.

"I think he wants it this way," Cindy replied. "He'd rather do that—just die out there—than lie around, be sick. He's powerful stubborn, Tom."

"You ought to be able to get some help somewhere."

"Welfare? Ha."

"As sick as he is—"

"Somebody trying to give him welfare wouldn't think he was sick. He'd *kill* anybody who tried to give him a handout."

"Handout?" Richard's voice came from the doorway. "Who's got a handout? If it's more of those soft rolls from breakfast, I'll take ten of 'em."

He came into the room slowly, easily, smiling, and sat in another of the recliners. He leaned back and took a deep, slow breath.

27

"Are you all right?" Keel asked.

"Never better. —Sorry about that little dizzy spell out there in the field. I guess I ate something that laid heavy on my stomach last night."

Keel thought, crazily, of a television commercial: a farm woman, or a truck driver, telling the camera, *"We don't have much, but we've got our health. And when you've got your health, you've got just about everything."*

And another commercial: Merrill Lynch is bullish on America.

What brought these to his mind at this moment, Keel did not know. But they fed the rage.

Yes: feed the poor of America this story that health was enough, that the future was bright, the way of life good. Give them a little bit—not much, but enough to get them started. Hang the bait out in front of their noses. And then they'll run and run and run, with never a chance, never quite able to see that the gulf between illusion and reality is where almost all Americans live, with varying degrees of tinsel, with no real progress.

Richard had bought the dream. He was a Good American. Somehow, even now, after killing himself trying, he *still* believed he could make it. And poor little Cindy, destroyed by trying and by seeing her husband try and stay on the treadmill.

What, Keel thought, could a man like Richard—or himself, for that matter—hope really to win? He and his brother and the millions like them could not even begin to imagine what it would be like to be born into millions, where there was never a need to work, never a need of any kind, never a genuine survival worry, never a setback—and you took your ease at your club, while your money was lent out to lesser fools at interest, and made more money for you.

The vivid force with which the realization burst upon Keel was so intense that he was scarcely capable of carrying on a normal conversation for the next hour. When he left, on his way back toward Lexington, he was struck as always by a sharp sense of loss, and now with the sudden wondering whether he would ever see Richard again, alive. But there

28

was more than this involved. It went to the truth that Richard and Cindy and their lives had helped Keel crystallize in his consciousness.

He had always known his own life was unfair, and now he saw in broader perspective why this was so, and how far the unfairness truly reached.

Before long, he thought, as he drove toward the airport, he could have $500,000. It could be done, and for the first time he was absolutely sure that nothing, now, would turn him back from doing it.

He would make the others see. They would succeed. He would find some way to launder the money, make it safe to spend. And then he would go back to his brother and give them a suitcase—no, a bushel basket full—of hundred-dollar bills. He would fill their living room with money. He would say, *"Here. There's no charge. There's no interest. There's no obligation. There're no strings attached. It's just free, clear, happy money, to spend, the way the few who run this country have always had it, all their lives."*

Wednesday, July 3

Jack Abercrombie was puzzled. Glancing at his watch, he saw that it was already noon. He had been in the hotel room since checking in last night, and had been awake since kids with firecrackers in the alley behind the hotel had awakened him shortly after dawn. But no one had contacted him.

It all seemed very cloak-and-dagger: flying to Memphis from Houston on a commercial jet under an assumed name, registering as *James Jackson,* sitting tight to await a contact. He had no idea what it was all about. Donovan had been distinctly uninformative on the telephone, except to say that a good deal of money was involved.

It was probably illegal, Abercrombie thought, and he was not at all sure he wanted any more to do with anything like the Alpha Aviation operation. But it was a holiday from the oil company that employed him, so Abercrombie had

29

little else to do. The fact that Donovan was paying the bills for the trip was also a fascinating side benefit.

He could afford to wait most of the day, he decided, puzzled or not.

He didn't have to wait that long.

At 12:30 there was a rap on the door. Abercrombie opened it. Phil Lester was standing there.

"What the hell are *you* doing here?" Abercrombie demanded.

Phil Lester smiled crookedly as he came in. "Same as you, I s'pose, Mr., uh"—he glanced at a scrap of paper in the palm of his hand—"Mr. James Jackson, sir."

Abercrombie closed and locked the door. "Do you know what this is all about?"

Phil Lester sprawled on the bed. "Uh-uh. You?"

"How did you get here?"

"To Memphis? They flew me in, man."

"Phony name?"

"Lester Smith. Cool, huh?"

"Did Donovan set it up for you too?"

"Yep. Only the last time I had a call, it was Tom Keel."

"Keel." Abercrombie thought about it. "They've got some new deal cooked up."

"Sounds like it."

"Any ideas? Hints?"

"Huh-uh. They're real close-mouthed on this one."

"Are we going to meet here, then?"

"Dunno. Tom called me this morning at my motel, said to come here and check with you, under this classy name he gave me."

"That's all?"

"That's—"

There was another rap on the door.

Abercrombie opened it again. Donovan and Keel were there. Keel looked pale and intense, but Donovan was smiling jauntily.

"Our benefactors," Abercrombie murmured. He let them in and locked the door once more.

Phil Lester swung off the bed, and there was handshaking all around. Abercrombie mentioned the early morning firecrackers. Phil Lester said he had enjoyed the free airplane ride, and asked how Keel was enjoying his new flight instruction job. They talked about that for a minute, and then Donovan asked Abercrombie about the job with Shell. Abercrombie considered lying, but then said what he really thought: it was slightly less exciting than watching a flower bloom. Everybody laughed, but there was a strain in the room. Abercrombie knew he was tense because he wanted to know; Keel, at least, was equally tense because he probably did know, and was waiting for the subject to be broached.

Donovan, placing a small briefcase on the edge of the bed, broached it. "We could stall around," he said easily. "But you two wonder what this is all about."

"Amen," Phil Lester replied.

"Well, let's get comfortable."

Abercrombie took one of the straight-backed chairs. Donovan straddled the other. Phil Lester sat on the edge of the bed. Keel stood tensely beside the portable TV set, his shoulder just touching the wall.

Donovan began, "We did a pretty good little thing down there in Galveston. We picked up some change. For amateurs—beginners—we did a hell of a job.

"Tom, here, and I got talking about it. We agreed that the four of us—if all were willing—might make a lot more quick money. If we could come up with just the right operation."

"The perfect crime, you mean?" Abercrombie said.

"Maybe," Donovan said. "Let's just pretend for a minute. Suppose Tom and I knew a way for each of us to clear a half-million dollars in a few weeks. The actual period of danger, let's say, would be considerably less. Would you be interested?"

Phil Lester chuckled. "Who do we have to kill?"

Donovan looked at Abercrombie.

"What is it?" Abercrombie asked guardedly.

Donovan glanced toward Tom Keel. "Do you want to explain?"

Keel's eyes snapped with what Abercrombie could only interpret as nervousness. *If he's nervous,* Abercrombie thought, *it really is big. They aren't kidding.*

Keel said, "We probably need to talk about options first."

"Agreed," Donovan said. He turned back to Abercrombie and Phil Lester. "We drifted into the Alpha Aviation thing. It seemed almost to happen. Any new adventure has to be planned. We all have to be in it together from the start. Tom and I want to make it clear: we're not trying to suck anybody into anything. You hear the plan, you don't want in all the way, then it's abandoned."

Phil Lester smiled thinly. "We *that* vital?"

"We need you," Donovan said, smiling in turn. "But the point is this: if anyone doesn't like the plan, then it's ditched for everybody. None of us could go ahead without unanimous consent and participation. This is not the kind of operation we could afford to have nonparticipants knowing about ahead of time . . . or afterward."

"You don't think we'd talk," Abercrombie said, prepared to be angry.

"No, I certainly don't," Donovan said, his glacial eyes calm. "We trust you. On a more pragmatic level, we are all in the Alpha Aviation dodge together. If you, say, were to squeal about this plan, we could always implicate you in the Alpha rip-off. So we can trust one another because of the consequences any of us would pay if anyone else cheated."

"The point," Keel interjected, "is that this new plan just has to be all of us or none of us. At any step of the operation, anyone can opt out, and the whole thing is canceled."

"That puts a real burden on everybody," Abercrombie said, not liking it.

"It's the way it has to be," Donovan said.

"I'm not sure I like it even this early."

Donovan shrugged. "Do you want to forget it right now and walk out the door? No hard feelings. We won't even go on. Walk out the door."

Abercrombie didn't know what to say. He was tempted to take the option. But he was tremendously curious—his

32

interest whetted. He glanced questioningly at Phil Lester.

Lester said, "Look. If it means gettin' killed, boys, or a big risk of it, you can count me out. I'm a coward from the word go."

Keel said, "We're no good at percentages. But we wouldn't have put in all the work we've done already if we thought we were going to get killed."

"What's the risk?" Abercrombie asked.

"There's a risk."

"We *could* get killed."

"Yes, but the percentage of that happening isn't high."

"What percentage do you figure?"

"I said we were no good at that kind of figuring." Keel looked at Donovan. "Five percent? Ten?"

"Risk?" Donovan replied.

"Of a real disaster."

Donovan sighed and stretched his arms over his head. "Of failure, I suppose . . . oh . . . ten percent. Of getting caught, maybe five percent. Of getting somebody killed, very small. *Very* small."

"This is not some con job, though," Abercrombie probed.

"No," Donovan said. He seemed quietly amused. "This is all kinds of a felony. It's also a federal rap. If we get caught, it's one hell of a long term. No doubt about that. If we try and foul it up, it's the ultimate disaster. For all of us."

No one spoke for a moment. It was quiet in the room. Abercrombie heard the distant sounds of street traffic. He also heard his heartbeat.

Phil Lester broke the silence. "I'm pretty chicken," he said seriously.

Keel snapped, "We're not suicidal ourselves. Let us run over it with you. Poke holes in it. If you can tell us what's wrong with the idea, we'll be the *first* to want to chuck it."

"Well, then," Phil Lester said, raising his eyebrows. "No harm in *hearing* about it, right?"

"That's my opinion," Donovan said. He looked at Abercrombie.

Abercrombie hesitated. He knew, logically, that listening could harm no one. And yet he felt uncertainty. Even if he nodded now, he sensed, he was committed, to some degree, to something.

They were waiting.

Abercrombie thought, *What the hell.*

He nodded.

It was clear from the outset that Keel and Donovan had done their homework. Before either of them said anything further, they spread out some of the materials from the briefcase: a canvas-covered blue looseleaf book containing diagrams, maps, and plastic overlays; aeronautical area charts, planning charts, and terminal charts; instrument approach plates; aircraft operating manuals; pages from magazines and newspapers; two yellow legal pads filled with scrawled notations and diagrams; several Polaroid photographs; a hefty book of airline schedule information; a small booklet on modern firearms; a flight computer and plotter, and some other papers and manuals that Abercrombie could not identify readily. Keel, especially, arranged the materials carefully on the floor around himself, kneeling, and Abercrombie was again struck by the pale intensity of the man.

Finally Keel had everything ready. He began talking.

For the first few minutes, Abercrombie was not quite sure he saw what Keel was driving at. Keel was not being clever, trying to hide the point, but was building his case with caution, a step at a time. Abercrombie listened, watching the others, thinking he had to be misunderstanding. His mind boggled: he could not believe it.

After a little while he couldn't contain himself any longer. "Oh, listen," he said. "I've heard enough."

Keel's head snapped up.

Abercrombie waved his hands in surrender. "I give up. Forget it!"

Donovan said softly. "You've heard only part of it."

"I've heard plenty!"

"What do you mean?"

"It won't work! It's crazy!"

34

Donovan shot Keel a look that seemed grimly reassuring and said, "Tell us about it."

"Nobody's *ever* done anything like this!" Abercrombie said.

"Exactly. That's why it will work."

"Oh, no. Hell, it *won't* work!"

"Why?"

"Well, they'll just—we'll simply—" Abercrombie momentarily boggled again, stunned to see that they were actually taking the proposal *seriously.* He struggled to get hold of himself. "They'll simply shoot the planes down!"

"How?" Donovan persisted, as calmly as before.

"From the ground."

"Not likely. The planes retaliate."

"They can shoot the planes down before retaliation is possible!"

"Do they know they can? How can they be sure? Will they risk all those lives on the chance?"

Abercrombie threw up his hands. "They'll scramble some F-4s, then."

Keel snapped, "What good does that do? Can a Phantom come in a hundred feet off the deck and guarantee accuracy that won't hit innocent people?"

"And," Donovan added with the same maddening calm, "are they prepared to risk one of our planes crashing in the wrong place and killing a thousand bystanders?"

"They might risk it."

"I don't think so."

"They *might.*"

"You and I both know the official policy is against that kind of risk."

Abercrombie wheeled on Phil Lester. "Tell them they're crazy."

Phil Lester smiled, but he was pale. "Yeah, man. I hear you. But I haven't figured out what's wrong with it yet."

"You wouldn't seriously consider doing it!"

"I don't know—would you?"

Abercrombie could not believe it. He wanted to laugh, but it was not funny. "All right," he said. "I'll play the game.

35

Give me a minute to get my wits together and I'll show you why it won't work."

Donovan winked at Keel. "Take your time. That's what we're here for."

Abercrombie tried. It was unbelievable how he tried. *There were no aircraft available.* Easily answered. *Guns were impossible to obtain.* Keel already had a contact for the illegal machine pistols. *There would be no way to pick up the money.* To the contrary, there was an absurdly simple way, and it was already charted out. *They could be followed.* Pursuit would be practically impossible. *No way to spend the loot.* Donovan had worked on at least two viable options there. *The aircraft would be traced.* It didn't matter because the trace would lead nowhere. *If anyone was caught, they were all caught.* Not the way it was worked out. *Radar would detect them.* Beforehand, they would be outside the Terminal Control Area and of no concern to Approach Control; afterward they would be lost in ground clutter.

An hour fled by. Abercrombie did most of the objecting. Donovan did most of the responding, with Keel adding something now and then. Donovan remained cool, almost amused. Keel's intensity was undiminished. Phil Lester asked a question now and then and seemed almost bemused by it all.

"I still say," Abercrombie burst out finally, "they'll just shoot *hell* out of us, and that will be that!"

"And kill all those innocent people?" Donovan said.

"They might!"

"But you know the official policy: give them what they want."

"That's for a hijacking. That's not for this kind of crazy deal!"

Keel said, "We've got more people under the gun than any hijacker ever had. They'll surrender instantly."

"Maybe they will, or maybe they'll just shoot us to pieces."

"They won't run that risk!"

36

Donovan stood and stretched again. He looked at his watch. "Look. We're beginning to talk in circles. I think we need to break."

Phil Lester rubbed sweat from his forehead. "Yeah. What say we go get a hamburger or something?"

"Not together," Donovan said.

"Huh?"

"All we've done is talk. Still, from now on we aren't seen together. That's why we went to all the trouble of the rooms under bogus names."

Abercrombie stared at him. "Are we giving it up, then?"

"I'm at the Lexington; you can look it up in the book. My name is Jones, J. R. Jones, Room 128. Let's each of us think it over. If you want to speculate about it a little more, come by about three o'clock this afternoon. We can visit, talk about it. No big deal. We aren't breaking any laws. But if you want to talk more, come on by."

Keel began gathering up the pile of materials and putting things back into the briefcase. "Make sure you have the name and address right."

Phil Lester drawled, "Jones? Room 128 at the Lexington?"

Donovan's eyes crinkled. "Right."

"Rajah."

Keel finished putting things into the briefcase. "I'll go first."

Donovan nodded, walked with him to the door. Keel paused and looked back at Abercrombie. "Think about it." He waited, Donovan opened the door for him quickly, and he went out.

Donovan closed the door again and glanced at his watch. "I'll give him three minutes to clear the elevator."

"This is awfully cloak-and-dagger," Abercrombie said.

"Someone said that before," Donovan agreed pleasantly. "If you think this is a cloak-and-dagger, stick around awhile. You haven't even heard the details yet."

"I'm not sure I want to. If I drop out, the whole thing is canceled? Did you mean that?"

Donovan's cool eyes were flat and lusterless. "There's nothing to be canceled, right? We're just old friends chatting about crazy ideas. Right?"

Abercrombie looked back at him a moment, then turned to see Phil Lester's expression. It mixed surprise with anticipation, fear, and excitement.

"Jesus Christ," Abercrombie breathed.

Donovan whistled softly and consulted his watch. After a little while he waved to them and silently let himself out.

Phil Lester blew air. "Well, what do you think?"

"It's crazy. It's just ridiculous. I wouldn't touch it—"

"What's wrong with it?"

"Everything!"

"Yeah, but *what?*"

"It just wouldn't work, that's all."

"That's what I keep thinkin', too. Trouble is, I can't figure out any good reason for feelin' that way."

Abercrombie got up and paced. "Well, I'm not even going to waste any more time thinking about it. It's insane on the surface of it."

After Phil Lester left, however, Abercombie picked up the morning paper and tried to read it with interest. He could not. The sense of astonishment and incredulity kept coming back. He could not get the insane project off his mind.

The more he thought about it, once the initial astonishment had begun to pass, the more airtight it looked. He could not believe this, either. Despite the room's air conditioning, he was sweating again.

Thursday, July 4

They were in Keel's motel room, not the one he lived in but a room rented for this purpose. The atmosphere was different, and Donovan thought it was all to the good. The first three sessions had been tense, but now the feeling in the room was brisk and it was all business. Donovan could

38

scarcely believe how fast they were progressing. It demonstrated the soundness of the basic concept.

"We can't meet too long this time," Phil Lester said. "I got to haul ass and catch my flight home."

"There are a few things," Donovan said.

"There are some major ones," Keel corrected him.

Donovan nodded and gave way. Keel was pushing hard, and this too was all to the good. The man had an amazing mind for detail, a facility badly needed for an operation of this kind. He sat back and let Keel take over.

"The point about the airplanes is crucial," Keel began, locking his hands over his knee. "I think we were in agreement last night that the Cherokee Six is a better aircraft. It gives us the added range and extra space. I did some checking by phone this morning and they're available."

"What's the cost?" Abercrombie asked, his eyes bleak. He was still looking for holes, Donovan thought—almost as if he wished he could find a hole so he could stop thinking about it. But the man had been drawn in now.

"For three aircraft," Keel said, "it will cost $950 each per month. That's a special rate. It includes fifty hours of flight time, no fuel."

"That's plenty," Phil Lester said.

"We know how we can get them. The question comes back to finding two extra men if we go to the three-aircraft concept."

Abercrombie frowned. "Like I said, I think having three planes makes our chances much, much better."

"I agree," Keel said.

Donovan nodded and saw Phil Lester shrug similar agreement.

Keel told Lester, "You mentioned your friend Richard Fetzer?"

"Yeah, man. And I thought about it last night later, too. I think he's one of our men for sure."

Donovan said, "No close family ties? We agreed that's important. One of us can't be reported missing by an irate or worried wife."

"He's separated from his wife. No problem there. And

I know a couple little deals he's been in on. He's not the straightest cat in the world."

Keel said, "You can sound him out."

"Yeah."

"But on the basis we talked about. You move up on it gradually. Then, if he seems receptive, Donovan or I come down and meet with him to lay it out in more detail."

"Right. No sweat."

"He's the key," Donovan observed. "I have no doubts about the sixth man. My friend MacReady finishes up his present commitment late in the summer. I know he'll go, and I can guarantee him."

Abercrombie frowned again. "What if one of them does reject the plan?"

"Then we're back at the start," Donovan replied. "We've broken no laws and spent damned little money. We scrap it and start over on something else."

"I don't like the delay."

"Yesterday you didn't like the plan."

"That was yesterday. If we're all crazy enough to start doing it, I say the sooner the better."

Keel said, "It will take six weeks minimum to line everything up anyway. We talked about all the steps. In the meantime, we've all got details to iron out. We have to get some of the materials together and do some further checking on the site. The time won't be wasted."

"It appears," Donovan added, "that early November will be the earliest we can strike. That puts it up to each of us to figure out a legitimate excuse for being gone from our jobs about that time. Abby, you said you can put in for a week's vacation time, which ought to cover it if it runs into a weekend. I've got no problem with the charter service. If you can be sick, Phil, that just leaves Tom."

Keel said, "I'll have a charter also. We've got money to pay for it under a bogus name in our tentative budget."

"If that budget gets much bigger," Abercrombie said, "we may be in trouble there."

"We can hold it below five thousand."

"That's what we keep saying. I hope you're right."

"I'm right."

No one spoke for a moment. Donovan thought of the dozens of details they had questioned, changed, and invented in the past twenty-four hours. They were all tired now, he thought. The strain was telling on them already. They needed a break.

He said, "Just because a week or two passes and we don't hear from one another—that doesn't mean a thing. We've come to an understanding about how to proceed. November 8 is a Friday. That's the target date. Right up to that day we aren't doing anything very serious in terms of the law. I imagine there will be changes, additions, and deletions practically up to that time. Don't do any heavy drinking that might make you talk. Don't panic. Think about it, but don't worry. *Don't make notes.* This morning Tom and I burned everything that might incriminate us. From now on we work in our heads, and we don't forget anything, and we stay cool."

Keel added, "You're going to look into the T-valves, the tubing, and that material, Phil, right?"

Lester nodded.

"All right. Abby, you're to locate separation fields, and research all the area frequencies, plus making sure we know the airline schedules."

Abercrombie grunted assent.

"The guns are my problem. Donovan draws up plans for the escape routes, and so forth. The dummy corporation is no problem and we deal with that later. You're sure, Phil, there's no glitch in handling the door on the Cherokee Six?"

"It's a selling point," Phil Lester explained. "I can pull the doors at the last minute, easy."

"Fine. And checking out the site is no problem. Dynamite we take care of later. The big, immediate stumbling blocks are the additional personnel."

"I'll be in touch about Fetzer," Lester said.

Keel looked at Donovan. "Anything else?"

"We could talk all day, as we talked most of the night. I think it's time to check it in for now and go our separate ways."

Keel looked around. "Agreed?"

Abercrombie got up and slowly moved forward. He extended his right hand. Keel looked startled for an instant, then shook it. They shook hands all around in silence. Then Phil Lester left first, alone, and Keel glanced at his watch to see what time the next man should leave. They had already started to become a team.

Saturday, July 27

The long fishing pier extended into Gulf waters made blinding by the intense sun. Despite the heat and a salty wind that only added miserable humidity, there were cars everywhere along the access road, and tourists lined the pier, fishing. Some were portly men with expensive gear and, perhaps, grim expertise; but the majority were vacationers wearing floppy hats and red or yellow shorts, ridiculous Hawaiian shirts and sandals. A few of the women were pretty in swimsuits. There were small children all over the place.

Standing at the extreme end of the pier, where the planked floor vibrated with the force of wavelets against the pilings, Phil Lester talked with Joe Donovan.

"There's no doubt in your mind, then?" Donovan said.

"He amazed me, buddy," Phil Lester admitted. "He started picking up on it the minute I dropped the first hint."

"And you're sure."

"I wouldn't have waited this long unless I was *making* sure."

Donovan, who wore a pale blue shirt and slacks and a floppy captain's cap, nodded. "I ought to talk with him on this visit, then."

"I could set it up tomorrow."

"Do you know where yet?"

"We been talking at the bowling alley. Is that all right?"

"Do people know you there?"

"Uh-uh, and it's always jammed. Nobody notices nothing."

42

"All right. One thing: these gambling debts he has. They're not so serious he might get forced out at the last minute, are they?"

Phil Lester spat into the water. "He's a penny-ante gambler, man. But folks are pressing him. A few thousand and he's okay again. It ain't like he had the Organization on his tail."

"As I told you, I managed to have that friend of mine check for a past record. There's no FBI rap sheet on him."

"Richard Fetzer," Lester said, "ain't that kind of guy. I told you. Just because he's a little younger than the rest of us, that's no reason to worry. He was almost a good ball player at Houston. Since then, except for the Marines, he's been mechanic-ing sports cars and putting down bets the whole time. It ain't his fault he's a better mechanic than he is a gambler."

Donovan's cool eyes surveyed a comely young housewife whose tiny pink bikini bottoms revealed more than they covered as she bent over to retrieve a small child. "We all have our hobbies."

"Is everything else going smooth?"

"Perfectly. Keel goes to Los Angeles next weekend. I've been to Atlanta again. We'll headquarter in Memphis. There's plenty of hangar space."

"Abby hanging in there?"

"Abby is fine."

Phil Lester took a deep breath. It was still a little incredible, how they kept moving closer to the ultimate commitment. "I'll call you tonight and verify a place and time."

"Good," Donovan said, and turned and walked away.

Lester watched him saunter the length of the long pier, wending his way between the fishermen. A woman turned her eyes slightly to watch him go. He was attractive to some women, Lester thought with a tinge of envy, and he certainly knew how to use the attraction.

Of those presently involved in the planning, Donovan was the one most predictably a part of it, Lester thought. Nothing had ever been very difficult for Donovan: not becoming a Little All American at Ohio University quite a long while ago, not his flying exploits in Vietnam, not his women. Donovan was one of those men who seemed capable of handling just about anything that came along, the kind of man who might have achieved anything, even the United States Senate, if he had chosen to put his mind to it. He was attractive in a jaded, paradoxical way, and he was smart, and he had the morals of an alley cat—but with cool.

Lester wondered where Donovan might have wound up if the one woman he had ever taken very seriously, that extremely rich young woman in Florida, had not found him in a motel room with someone else and instantly divorced him. Donovan could be on a yacht somewhere right now, having a Collins and enjoying the not inconsiderable charms of that wealthy young wife. It had been the major turning point of Donovan's life. To date.

But that was the way Donovan was, Lester realized. There had never been any spilt tears over the bad luck. You did what you wanted and you took your chances: it was Donovan's credo, and he lived by it.

It was harder to figure somebody like Abercrombie, though, Lester thought. How did you figure a good pilot, a man who had had a normal family life until just a few months ago?

Of Keel, Lester was much surer. He did not pretend to understand Keel. Had anyone ever understood Tom Keel?

By this time, Donovan had vanished along the beach and into the cars parked on the access road. Phil Lester strolled back along the pier toward his own parking spot a half-mile away.

You might be crazy to get into this, buster, he told himself. *Might get caught. Might get your fanny shot off, too. You got no motivation like some of the others. You can make a fair living.*

Yes. And always stay only one jump ahead of the bill collectors, and get old and sick and try to live on Social Security.

Walking across the sandy beach, Lester remembered another beach, another time. Vietnam. And some gas in the air, sappers back in the tree line, the Phantoms coming over

44

on the deck and letting all hell loose on the sons of bitches.

It occurred to Lester that the Vietnam experience might be very important in explaining why each of them could plan to do this thing. If he could just figure it out. They had met over there, Donovan, Keel, and Abercrombie as pilots, he a dogface who had gotten recruited to help with minor mechanic duties at the air force base after a rocket attack created a severe temporary shortage of trained manpower in the hangar area.

It had been Donovan in the lead even then, Lester remembered—and Keel doing the detail work. It had required teamwork by the four of them then to get the dope out of the country in redundant control cable housings, and into Japan for subsequent reshipment to the States.

That had been so easy. Most things had been easy in Nam.

Technology and teamwork! Lester thought admiringly as he reached his car. Hell, that was what they were going to use in this operation. And it was going to be kind of fun, having some excitement again.

Saturday, August 3

The country club looked like a ski lodge built for the moon. As he walked under the cantilevered rock porch structure, Keel was very much aware of being an outsider. It seemed like a stupid place to meet his contact. But his contact had insisted.

Entering the massive building's lobby, Keel was even more aware of being an outsider, and angry about it. He walked across an enormous area of terrazzo tile punctuated here and there by an oversized potted plant. The cathedral ceiling, with great beams, lent a church-like atmosphere that swallowed up the sounds of the few people in evidence. Some middle-aged men dressed in golf clothing walked across a corner of the area toward the back, their laughter echoing faintly. Several women, some also in golfing dress, stood near the entry to what looked like a bar. Keel, momentarily confused, paused beside a rock support column partially masked by a potted palm.

"Could I help you?"

He turned toward the soft feminine voice. The woman had been standing quietly on the far side of the column, evidently alone. She was not tall, but slender, with a lovely body subtly revealed by her jersey dress and moderate heels. She might have been thirty, but something about the way her blonde hair was done—carefully atop her head—hinted that she was probably nearer forty. Her frank blue eyes met Keel's directly, with a trace of habitual irony. She was smiling.

Keel said, "I'm to meet a party here."

"Are you a member of the club?"

"No. But I'm not hired help, either."

Her eyes changed slightly, although she held the smile. "I certainly didn't mean to imply that you were. I thought I might help you."

Keel thought that she was really quite beautiful, and for some reason he resented it. He said, "My man said he would be in the practice area."

"Oh." She was amused again. "I'm sure he meant the practice tee. Do you play golf?"

"It always looked like a waste of time. How do I find the practice *tee*, then?"

She turned and pointed toward a splotch of glass toward the back. "If you go out those doors back there and turn left —shall I show you?"

"I'm capable of finding it."

"Of course you are. Go out those doors. Turn left. Walk through the cabana area. You'll pass the pro shop and find the practice tee beyond."

"Thank you."

"You're welcome." Her eyes had amazing ironic qualities.

Keel went as directed. There was only one man on the practice tee. He was youngish and tall and was methodically hitting shag balls at a little round sign poked in the ground about one hundred and seventy yards down a gentle grass slope. Keel walked over and introduced himself. The man nodded and kept hitting balls regularly, each with a nice, slight drawing action. He seemed very good at hitting golf balls. Everything about him, from his clothes to the clubs and bag and even the shag balls, looked expensive and new.

Due to circumstances beyond his control, the man said, he could not provide more than two of the weapons Keel sought. They were in mint condition, Communist-made AK-47s, clip-loaded, using the 7.62 mm ammunition one could buy almost anywhere. He was not particularly interested in selling; he made this clear, and forced Keel to pretend that he was a weapons collector interested only for esthetic or hobby reasons. Keel played along with it and said the two AK-47s would be fine, although he would prefer three. The price was ridiculously high. Keel agreed to it. The man explained how the weapons could be delivered to Keel's hotel room tonight. Keel was to pay now, in cash, by pretending to examine his golf bag and inserting the money in the front ball pocket. Keel did so and the man kept on hitting balls as if they were talking about the weather.

"I assume that concludes our chat," the man said, whacking another ball.

"The delivery will be tonight?"

"I said so, didn't I?"

"Yes, you did."

"Good day."

Dismissed, Keel walked back the way he had come. There were children and young matrons splashing in the pool, their laughter bright in the fragrant air. Beyond the pool area, people were playing tennis. Keel could also see onto the next wooded hill, where two groups of golfers tooled along a shaded pathway in electric carts. There was no sign of work anywhere. He wondered if the wealthy ever admitted to work. Perhaps it was considered unclean.

He went back inside and started across the lobby.

"You found him?"

He turned. She was seated in a large leather chair beside a huge glass office table, and the smile and the eyes were the same. Her legs were crossed. She had very nice legs.

"Yes, thank you," Keel said, stopping.

She rose. "I'm sorry about the way I spoke earlier. I didn't intend it to sound the way it obviously did."

Keel hesitated. Despite himself, he was interested in her. She was so very sleek and cool, the kind of woman who was out of his experience. "No harm done," he said.

"There! You can smile! Good. Now I feel better."

She was good at this. Keel was fascinated. *But then she never had to do anything but practice conversation,* he thought.

He turned and walked away from her.

Friday, September 6

Bill MacReady, a free man again, walked out of the front gate of the Ohio State Penitentiary in Columbus. Keel and Donovan were waiting for him and took him off in a rental car.

PREFLIGHT

Monday, October 7

The building near downtown Memphis was old, but the locater board in the dusty first-floor lobby showed that most the offices were rented by insurance adjusters, small businesses, and a sprinkling of attorneys. The office suite that Donovan had just been shown was small, two offices off a tiny reception cubicle, and it needed painting. Donovan knew, however, that it was ideal for their purposes; at the end of a dim corridor, it would not have much curiosity traffic.

The building manager, a bluff, red-faced man with thick glasses, tapped the frame of the front doorway with its thick glazed window. "And, as I said, we'll have our man paint your firm name on the glass right away. No extra charge."

Donovan scratched his cheek through the now luxuriant beard and pretended to think about it. "I think it's just about what we need."

"Good," the manager said. "Shall we go to my office and sign the lease papers?"

"We can have immediate occupancy?"

"Mr. Peterson, you sign the lease, pay the deposit, and it's all yours right of this instant."

Donovan paused, removed his wire-rimmed window-glass spectacles, polished them on his handkerchief, and strolled back through the two inside rooms. Sunlight flooded through dusty bare windows onto rotting wooden sills. There were mouse droppings in the room corners. No matter. Putting his bogus glasses back on his nose, he returned to the reception area where the manager was waiting.

"I'm satisfied. Let's go to your office."

In the first-floor room, Donovan scanned and quickly approved the lease for six months, signing *A. Peterson.* The manager gave him a notebook page on which to write the firm name as he wanted it painted on the glass door. Donovan filled in *Smith-Peterson Aerial Survey Co.*

"That will be $300, Mr. Peterson, including the deposit."

"I hope cash will be all right. As I told you, we haven't transferred our accounts yet."

The manager chuckled. "A man can still spend cash, I imagine. Here. I'll just fill out a receipt."

The transaction concluded, Donovan left the building and walked west. At the end of the next block he came to a variety store. He went inside and had a duplicate of the office key made. He then crossed the street and walked down two more blocks to a bank. He opened a checking account for the firm with $4,000 cash. He signed one signature card as Peterson, and took another card for "my associate." For a mailing address he filled in the office space he had just rented. He said his associate would notify the bank as soon as the office phones were connected. The assistant cashier treated him with proper deference.

Leaving the bank, Donovan went to the nearest telephone booth. He dialed the telephone company business office and explained. A telephone could be installed in the morning. Was he sure he did not require additional extensions? Yes, he was sure.

One more telephone call was necessary, to Keel.

"I'll meet you tonight where we agreed," Donovan told him.

"Everything all right?"

"Fine. You can go ahead on the furniture."

"I will."

"See you tonight."

Donovan did not much like the idea of returning immediately to his hotel room. A gentle cool wave had slipped through in the night and the sky was crisp, with almost a trace of autumn. It would have been nice to take a walk, see some of Memphis. But Donovan knew the risk, even with the thick, close-cropped beard and glasses: there was always the off-chance someone would see him, recognize him, and later remember. Things were going much too smoothly to allow this sort of chance if it could be avoided.

Whistling, Donovan headed directly for his hotel.

Tuesday, October 8

In the morning, the name of the company was already neatly lettered on the glass in the door, and the tile floors had been swept and waxed. Keel stood to one side in the entry foyer and watched a pair of husky men wrestle one of the secondhand desks through the narrow doorway. The men grunted the heavy wood desk through the inner doorway and set it in place. Sweating, they lumbered back through and headed down the hall for another load. Keel went to the inner office door and looked at the desk, which was too big for the cubicle. It didn't matter.

At a sound behind him he turned. A young man wearing gray work clothes, with a belt of tools around his waist and a telephone in his left hand, had walked into the room.

"Smith-Peterson?" the man asked.

"That's right," Keel told him.

"Where does this go?"

"They're just bringing in the furniture, but it will go on a desk that will sit right here, facing the hall door."

The installer looked around. "Looks like I'm in luck. Somebody had a junction here on the floorboards before. Shouldn't take long." He knelt, flipped a lid off the tiny junction box, and pulled out some wires.

The movers struggled in again, and Keel had them place the second desk in the reception area where the telephone man was working. They went away again and came back with two straight chairs each. Keel had them put one

51

behind the desk in the other room, one behind the reception desk, and two against the wall. Immediately the reception area looked crowded.

The boss teamster produced a pink delivery ticket. "I'll need your signature here."

"Fine." Keel took the ballpoint and signed *C. Smith.*

The teamster glanced at the paper. "Good enough." He pocketed it. "Thanks, and good luck to you."

"Thank you."

The telephone man had the instrument wired in loosely and was dialing things and talking to someone. Keel watched him for a minute or two, then went into the back office. He looked down at the busy street below. *Just a month to go.*

Inwardly he was tremendously excited and tense, and he amazed himself with his outwardly calm appearance. He was capable of more than he had imagined. Some of this was the touchy part, dealing with delivery people, others who conceivably might remember him. But it was a vital part, too; had to be done. All the trappings of a flourishing small business had to be just right.

There were a thousand small details in Keel's mind. He was living with the plan day and night now. The meetings with the new men, Richard Fetzer and Bill MacReady, had uncovered new angles that had to be covered. MacReady, especially, although Keel did not like him, had shown a good mind for certain kinds of detail. The details would pile up now. Some of them would be busy every day from now until the strike. The duty schedule for each of them—never written down anywhere—had someone doing something that fitted into the meticulous planning at every moment he could get free of his regular job. It was the peculiar gift—or curse—of a mind like Keel's that he was constantly aware of what everyone was doing in the entire operation. It had become true obsession.

At the moment the team was spread out: Phil Lester in Galveston, Abercrombie in Houston, Donovan probably in Denver today, Fetzer in New Orleans, MacReady at his new job in Cleveland. Keel wondered if all of them were as caught up in thoughts about the operation as he was. Then he saw that this was a silly question; of course they were; they had to be; a man did not risk his life, and hope for $500,000, without thinking about it virtually every waking moment.

The telephone man startled him by speaking from the doorway. "Looks like you're in business."

"Good," Keel said. "Thanks."

"Your number is on the instrument."

"Fine."

"I used an extra-long cord. Otherwise your secretary would be falling down over the line coming from the wall."

Keel grinned. "We wouldn't want that."

"Thanks a lot." The installer headed for the door.

Keel waited until he had gone, then went to the glassed door and made sure it was locked. Secure in the office, he went to the room that had been closed off from view and brought out a small suitcase and a fat shopping bag. Both were filled with office paraphernalia. He arranged two plastic trays, a desk calendar and penholder, some note pads and pencils, an ashtray, a small bottle of glue, a cheap stapler, and some typing paper on the top of the reception desk. He went to the other office that had a desk and spread his remaining articles around the top of that. Remembering his copy of the newspaper in his coat pocket, he unfolded it partway and put it on the corner of the reception desk. It added a nice, lived-in touch. Looking around, he realized he needed wastebaskets—and some trash to go in them now and then—plus at least one wall calendar and a couple of pictures. A typewriter and stand, and the file cabinet, would be delivered later in the morning.

He sat behind the reception desk, put his feet up, and lit a cigarette to mess up the ashtray a little. As long as they didn't hire a janitor service, and building maintenance remained marginal, a little trash would go a long way.

He dialed the answering service, was not surprised to hear there had been no calls, and gave the girl the newly installed number. Yes, he would be in and out. No, she should not contact him; he would check with her periodically.

The next call went direct long distance to the Piper rental outfit in Nebraska. The manager remembered Keel's earlier call about rates on the Cherokee Six. He was enthusiastic.

"Our company definitely has the job with the aerial mapping in the Dakotas," Keel told him. "We have a little job to do down here first, helping a firm locate some roadside restaurants; you know how they like to see the routings from the air, try to pick out choice locations. What we thought we would do, though, is rent one plane from you now, and our pilots can get a little fresh experience with the aircraft. That way we can go ahead and turn these damned Cessnas in. Then we'll want the other two planes pretty shortly, if they're available."

"They're available, Mr. Smith. Do you have some dates in mind for delivery?"

"We could have a pilot at your office Saturday before noon to pick up the first aircraft. Then, assuming all goes well, we would want the other two within a week or ten days."

"You're still thinking of a ninety-day lease?"

"That would be minimum," Keel lied. "Even with perfect luck on the weather we'll need that long."

There was a slight pause. "I'll tell you what we can do, Mr. Smith. You just give me that little additional information we'll need, and we can guarantee to have the birds ready for you."

"We're still talking about nine-fifty a month, dry, on the three?"

"If you rent three, the rate is $950 for each per month, no fuel, up to fifty hours flight time. I think I explained the added-use charges—"

"Right. And of course that's tach time."

"That's correct, sir."

"Okay, let me suggest this. We're awfully busy down here. I may have to hire a pilot to come up and get at least

54

one of the planes. You check us out, and then you call us back to verify that everything is okay. If one of us has time to come get the first plane, fine. But if we have to hire a ferry pilot, I'll have time to get the lease agreement from you in the mail. I'll sign it and give the ferry pilot our check for the first month in advance on all three aircraft."

There was a flabbergasted pause. "No need to pay in advance on all three, sir. I mean, an advance on the first aircraft—"

"No," Keel cut in smoothly, "we like to keep our books up to date. As I told you, we're small, but we're growing fast. It will make our bookkeeping simpler to pay the first month's basic lease price in advance, lump sum."

"That's great with us! And naturally the month will be calculated from the date you pick up the bird."

"Good. Now tell me the things you need to know for the firm."

It was simple enough. Keel gave their fictitious names, the false company name, the building address, the new telephone number, and the bank where they had opened an account yesterday as a business reference. It sounded very substantial and impressive. The poor guy in Nebraska was having a hard time not sounding gleeful.

"I'll be back to you within twenty-four hours, Mr. Smith!"

"Good. Goodbye."

So a major step had been taken. Hanging up the telephone, Keel could not but feel a pulse of satisfaction. It was so very easy to fool people.

With nothing to do for a little while, he thought again about the plan and the men in it with him.

The only one who gave him any worry at all was one of the new ones: MacReady. Keel tried continually to convince himself that this worry was groundless. So far he had not wholly succeeded, although he had done nothing about his lurking concern.

MacReady was not like the rest of them. For one thing, he had not served in Vietnam. This in itself might mean nothing, but Keel had fastened onto it as one of the reasons for the basic difference he felt between the rest of them and this man. MacReady was twenty-four but seemed younger. Life hadn't battered him very much yet. He was too brash and cocksure, garbage-mouthed, arrogant. And as far as Keel could determine, MacReady had not just slipped out of duty in Vietnam; he had managed so far to live his life with no sense of responsibility whatsoever.

Keel knew it was ironic for him to be thinking about something like responsibility. But he had paid his price. He had worked at something or other since the seventh grade. He had given the military everything it asked of him. He was a good pilot and he worked hard. *He had tried it their way.*

This might be the difference, he thought. MacReady had never tried at all, had never paid any kind of price. His parents were not wealthy, but they were far from poor.

The rest of them, Keel thought, might not be in the operation if there had been anyone trying to help—ever. MacReady was in it *despite* his advantages. Keel did not like that. He did not like MacReady, either. He was a punk, unstable, untrustworthy. But Keel had been outvoted, and he had decided grudgingly to go along. Maybe he was wrong, he told himself again now. He had to be.

Certainly they were lucky enough with the rest of the team. All of Donovan's detailed suggestions—the cover names, windowglass spectacles and false hairpieces and the rest of it to make later memory descriptions of them inaccurate—had all been excellent. Donovan was cool. He would be wholly dependable.

Abercrombie, too, once his initial doubts had been overcome, was wholly committed.

Keel was equally pleased with Phil Lester and Lester's recruit, Richard Fetzer. The two men were much alike: quiet, meticulous, easygoing, hard to scare, and evidently almost impossible to panic. Fetzer was also a little younger, but he had had his years in Nam. His eyes showed the changes that duty could make in a man. A wife who had recently run off with another man had also marked him as ready for this kind of gamble.

They were all without women, Keel realized.

The telephone rang, startling him badly. He stared at it for three more rings, wondering whether he should answer it. If he didn't, the service would. Who could it be? On impulse he picked it up.

"Smith-Peterson," he said awkwardly.

"Smith-Peterson?" a man's voice brayed.

"Yes."

"Aerial survey, right?"

"That's right."

"Listen, my name is Davis and I'm with Palmer-Winstead Pipe. We're laying out a new natural gas pipeline route through northern Arkansas and on over in this direction. We need a hell of a batch of aerial photographs. You guys do that kind of work?"

Keel thought fast. "Ordinarily we do, Mr. Davis, but I'm afraid all our pilots are working on other projects right at the moment."

"Well, what we want are two, three hundred pictures along the route and two alternates. We pay top dollar. I been asked to locate some bidders on the job. I got your name from information. I guess that means you're new around here. If you want to bid on the thing, I can send you the information."

"As I said, Mr. Davis, we're booked up right now."

"Well, we'd want to start in about a month. How about in a month?"

"I'm afraid we've got some jobs backed up."

There was a pause. "You don't want to bid, then?"

"I'm afraid we'd better not. But thanks for calling. Think of us again in the future, will you?"

The caller mumbled something and broke the connection. Keel replaced his receiver and sat staring at it. It occurred to him that they might really be able to make a go of the business if that was what they were after. This struck him as very funny.

Thursday, October 10

Swinging out of the dense Interstate traffic, Jack Abercrombie turned onto the ramp that channeled traffic directly toward Atlanta International Airport. The sky was heavily overcast, threatening rain, and as Abercrombie jockeyed through the cloverleaf he got a glance through the windshield toward the sky over the field itself. A Delta 707 had come out of the gunk to the west and was gliding down toward touchdown. At the same time, a 707 smoked off a runway toward the east, climbing steeply and entering a turn as the scud layer swallowed it up. The sky was near instrument minimums, but Atlanta was conducting business more or less as usual.

Of course Atlanta had to handle its traffic with a fair degree of efficiency, Abercrombie ruminated, as he turned nearer the sprawling parking area beyond a fence. The last figures he had seen showed Atlanta with more than 500,000 aircraft operations per year, and more than twenty million passengers. You didn't handle that kind of traffic out of your back pocket.

And this, of course, was all to the good. Abercrombie knew that the strike would have no chance of succeeding unless Atlanta was quite well organized and quite busy.

He was pleasantly tense as he looked for and found a parking slot in the massive paved area that lay north of the terminal building. The Atlanta *Constitution* had really been awfully nice about letting him look at its voluminous clip files, and the Chamber of Commerce information helped, too. He already had much of the information he needed on this trip. He could hold to his self-imposed time schedule.

Walking through the lot, he neared the Atlanta terminal, a wide, tall structure composed on this side of horizontal strips of glass and steel that made the structure look more like a resort hotel than an air terminal. The squat, darkglassed tower atop the building, of course, left no doubt about its real use. Abercrombie could not help wondering what the reaction in that tower would be in just about four weeks.

58

Entering the terminal, Abercrombie made his way to one of the great, echoing passenger areas that provided a panoramic view toward the field. He walked near the glass, changed his position, and found the spot that provided the best outlook.

From itself, as if by cell division, the terminal threw out long, spider-leg loading wings. Abercrombie could look out over the length of two of these, with others on either side. Motorized loading gates of the type that were driven right up to the door of the aircraft, to form instant tunnels, extended from the wings. Here and there was one vacant and retracted. Abercrombie could see more than twenty big jets on the ground for servicing or taxi. He could see five Deltas alone, and another was just trundling away.

Out beyond the clutter of parked and loading aircraft were the maze of taxiways and ramps. Most of Atlanta's traffic landed east-west, and Abercrombie could see one of these runways, 8/26, extending left and right in the near distance. Beyond it was the X intersection of two more runways, 3/21 and 15/33, and then—far out beyond—the two parallel runways, 9L/27R and 9R/27L.

A Piedmont flight clawed for altitude and vanished into the overcast. A Southern flight came in and one of the Delta jets got out of there. Abercrombie imagined the clipped chatter on all the frequencies. Flights were coming in and out, but there was probably a stack overhead. Nerves were fraying; pilots and controllers were fighting the clock, the weather, engines that gulped fuel alarmingly at lower altitudes, and the very complexity of the system. Atlanta was at the heart of a Terminal Control Area, the most complex radar control system yet devised for the handling of dense air traffic. You didn't get into this field without complex avionics gear and staging by air traffic controllers. Not legally. But the price you paid for such positive control was added complication of technique, finer tuning of men and machines, greater strain everywhere. Like the most expensive watch, Atlanta worked because it was finely balanced and incredibly intricate. But a fine watch, because of its very

59

precision, could be thrown off by the smallest mote of dust. . . .

Having completed his observations at this level, Abercrombie walked to another area of the terminal. He made some additional mental notations. He went to a third area, and then a fourth.

Although it sprawled over some 3,800 acres, Atlanta International was securely hemmed in. Interstates 85, 75, and a leg of 285 formed a huge triangle around it, and the boundaries were very close on all sides but the south. Residential areas crept in close on the east, as well. With all of Atlanta's metropolitan area sprawling out to the north of it, the field had nowhere to go for expansion but a limited area to the south, and there the open terrain was unfavorable for development. The airport was a finely tuned environment, closed in, vulnerable to any speck of dust that might penetrate.

Looking innocent and casual, Abercrombie poked around. He went to the baggage claim area and then to several of the ticketing counter areas and struck up brief, idle conversations. He chatted with an airport policeman and then, partly by design and partly by luck, with an air traffic controller about to go on duty upstairs. He also picked up some information about Delta's maintenance facility nearby.

Leaving the terminal, he went back to his car and, consulting a map to be sure, drove the circuit around the entire area, squeezing off quick photographs through the window of the car. He did not see anything that was too discouraging, and as he drove toward downtown Atlanta in swarming traffic, he dictated information and impressions into a little Sony cassette recorder.

Saturday, October 12

Tired yet pleased with himself, Mike Fair eased the yoke back slightly and let the Cherokee Six settle onto the runway at West Memphis. The mains touched firmly and he let the nosewheel contact the pavement as he dumped flaps and braked for the turnoff. The flight from Nebraska had been steady and uneventful, and the Six was a very pleasant airplane to fly.

Taxiing to the T-hangar area, Fair saw the man who had hired him, Peterson, signaling beside one of the hangar stalls that had its doors pulled open. Peterson's car, an old Ford, was parked just beyond a gate. Fair waved recognition, taxied down the row, swung the Six around so that it faced away from the hangar opening, and cut the engine. The propeller ran down; he flipped off all the switches, removed the key, gathered up his charts, and climbed out onto the wing.

"How did it go?" Peterson, who wore owlish sunglasses, called up.

"Fine!" Fair told him. "Nice airplane."

Peterson had a steel bar that could be hooked to the nose gear to push the plane in. "Want to help me get it inside?"

Fair nodded, put his things on the pavement, and walked a wingtip into the cramped space afforded by the T-hangar, so called because its rear was very narrow, just big enough to accommodate the tail section, while the front section flared out to provide space for the wingspan.

"That's good!" Peterson called.

Fair nodded and stopped pushing.

Peterson walked around the aircraft, stepped up onto the wing, and leaned inside to set the hand brake. He slammed the door and stepped down. "Nice and clean inside."

"Did you see the low time on the tach?"

"Right. That's good."

"She flies a little faster than the book," Fair said, anxious to impress his temporary employer. "The air speed trued out over 170."

Peterson was interested. "At seventy-five percent power?"

"A little less. Of course we were empty."

"How about fuel consumption?"

61

"The book says an 890-mile cruise at seventy-five percent, but she did better on this flight. I didn't figure it exactly, but—"

"You must have some papers for me," Peterson cut in.

Fair handed over the lease papers and other materials, explaining them, although, as he said, it probably wasn't necessary. At twenty-two, he was just getting a start in aviation. Jobs like this helped the logbook and the pocketbook about equally. He wanted to please.

"Okay," Peterson said when the conversation had begun to run out of topics. "We appreciate it, Mike. As I told you, we'll probably ask you to make another pickup for us in about a week."

"You know how to get in touch with me," Fair said.

"Right. Thanks again." And Peterson handed Fair a check from Smith-Peterson Aerial Survey Co. for the agreed-upon fee.

Sunday, October 13

The radio squawked, *"Cherokee seven-one Sierra, expedite your approach."*

Donovan, in the right-hand seat, thumbed the microphone. "Roger."

Keel added a touch of power as the Cherokee Six glided down over the jumble of wires and poles along the Interstate highway. Just ahead was the massive sprawl of Atlanta International. "Touchy, aren't they?"

Donovan grinned. "We're supposed to think we've got a 707 on our ass."

"We probably do have a 707 on our ass."

"He can wait."

"Get a picture toward the terminal now."

Donovan swung the small camera around toward the windshield and squeezed off two shots, then turned back the other way to get another. Keel brought the Six in over the runway numbers and touched down.

The radio ordered, *"Cherokee seven-one Sierra, turn left next intersection, contact ground twenty-one point nine."*

They were almost onto the intersection and rolling at 50 mph. "Bastards," Keel said, getting on the brakes hard.

Donovan acknowledged the order and changed frequencies as the plane trundled off the active runway. "We'll be giving the orders soon enough, Tom. Keep cool." He thumbed the mike. "Atlanta ground, Cherokee seven-one Sierra off the active, taxi transient parking."

They were directed among the lumbering big jets to the general aviation area, where a nice man met them to collect the user fee levied against every small plane for every landing, as a means of getting revenue and discouraging general aviation aircraft from messing up playtime for the big boys. Having paid and dealt with the gasoline man, they went into a dusty hangar and had Cokes and talked to the Flight Service Station on the telephone.

After stretching their legs awhile longer, they walked back to the Cherokee, preflighted, and fired it up again. Ground control made them taxi all over the place and wait awhile. Finally they got off. Keel was busy flying, but Donovan was just as busy shooting more pictures.

"It's good," Donovan muttered as they gained altitude. "It's just as good as I said, right?"

"It's perfect," Keel said. A cold sweat of anticipation soaked his clothing. "There's no way they can stop us."

Tuesday, October 15

The driveway was so closely shrubbed on both sides that branches made howling noises along the sides of Bill MacReady's old Ford panel truck. Backing beyond the big old house, MacReady got the panel into the rear driveway area that fronted a crumbling garage which evidently had some sort of apartment built atop it. Trees hung down over the area and there were bushes and flowers everywhere in wild

63

profusion. MacReady waited. The rickety screen door at the back of the old house opened and a skinny red-haired man came out. He made a motion with his finger across his throat and MacReady obediently cut the motor.

The redhead jangled over. He wore pale slacks, very wrinkled, and an old sweatshirt that had had the sleeves cut out. "MacReady?"

"Richard Fetzer?" MacReady countered.

The redhead grinned. "If I ain't, and you ain't, then we're in big trouble."

"Well," MacReady said, getting out, "it wouldn't be the first time."

Fetzer glanced at the panel truck. "Hope this thing can hold everything."

"It can." MacReady looked around the shrub-choked area, at the old trees, up the side of the old house. Gutters were rusted out and falling down and the paint was scaling from the walls. "This your place?"

"My folks'," Fetzer said.

"They in there?"

"My mother is. My father is dead."

"Should I be here if your old lady—"

"Relax." Fetzer's eyes were pale and calm. "She's seventy and she's deaf and almost blind."

MacReady chuckled. "And you need the money so she can have an operation. Yeah. I've seen that movie."

"No." Fetzer's eyes changed, became distantly hostile. "But nursing homes cost a lot too."

"Guess we better load up," MacReady said cheerfully. "I got a long drive ahead of me."

They walked to the sagging doors of the garage. "I'm not sure I'd want to go long distance in that panel," Fetzer said.

"That old tub will go anywhere," MacReady said. "The engine is like new and so is the transmission. My only problem is holding it down to about 50 so no one stops me and wants to search the back."

Fetzer wrestled with one of the doors. "I guess you know what you're doing."

64

"You better believe it. I've already made two long trips in that mother, and I've got more ahead of me. I'll bet my life on that old panel."

The door slid open. The garage was filled with all kinds of junk and odds and ends. To one side were six new fifty-five-gallon steel drums. One had a small carton on top of it.

"Six?" MacReady said. "I thought there were three!"

"We have to duplicate," Fetzer explained.

"What for?"

"With gasoline the way it is, we can't be sure of the supply at the last minute. We have to fill the planes, then siphon off into three of these drums, then pump it back into the other three drums at the last minute, after they're installed."

MacReady scratched his head. "I guess the panel will hold all six."

"They're empty. They're not heavy."

"I know. I've just got some of the other stuff in there already, is all."

Fetzer turned one of the drums on its edge. "Let's see how they fit."

"What's in the carton?"

"Hose, fittings, and tools."

MacReady put the carton under his arm. It was heavier than it looked. He carried it to the back of the panel truck, opened the doors, and slid it inside. He then helped Fetzer lift the drum in. They went back and forth to get the other drums. They all went in, snugly.

"I guess that does it," MacReady said, slamming the back doors.

"Is the dynamite in there too?"

"Yeah. Sure."

"Phil had it all right, then."

"Yeah. He said he told the dummy at the supply house that he needed it to blast stumps on his farm."

"I haven't seen Phil for a few days."

"No wonder, mother. He's up to here in charts, maps, all kinds of stuff. I'm glad I don't have to fiddle around with *that* part of it."

"You go right to Memphis from here?"

"Yeah. Field called Arlington. It's about twenty miles northeast of Memphis, actually. Then I got to haul up to Columbus to see my parole officer."

Fetzer frowned. "How do you explain all these trips to him?"

"He doesn't know, man. I'm still working at Cleveland, right? Right. That's all he knows."

"How do you get this time off?"

"I'm part time. How's that for a lick?"

"Be careful driving up to Memphis."

"Naturally. Listen. When do you come up?"

"Two weeks."

"That's right on the brink of the big event, huh?"

"Close," Fetzer said, tightening his lips.

MacReady wondered why Fetzer seemed so uptight. It was not important enough to inquire about. The guys in charge had their reasons for the people they'd picked, even an obvious loser like this one.

He shrugged. "See you later, pal." He got into the truck, started it, and drove expertly through the narrow driveway passage to the street. He moved out cautiously, judging by the slow sound of the engine, and Fetzer had a last glimpse of the panel truck as it trundled down the old street between rows of parked cars.

Fetzer stood in the back driveway for a moment, settling down.

He had wondered why Phil Lester had been unusually taciturn when MacReady was mentioned. Now he understood. MacReady was not like the others. He was young and crude, and Fetzer didn't like him the least little bit.

It was a sharp disappointment. Everything earlier had seemed so perfect. Meeting MacReady cast a pall over his hopes. MacReady was not the kind of man he particularly wanted to risk his life with.

Shrugging it off, he turned and went into the old house. The odors of dust, decay, and leaking natural gas came at him dankly as he entered the dingy old kitchen with its high ceilings and rotting wooden cabinets.

As he went from the kitchen into a narrow hallway with peeling old wallpaper, a loud unmodulated voice came from the front sitting room. "Sonny? Is that you? Where is everybody? What time is it?" It was the voice of his mother. Since her mind had begun to go, she had many days like this when her voice betrayed the terrible vacancy that had begun, after the long illness, to creep across her brain.

"I'm here, Mother," Fetzer called gently.

"Where are you? I don't understand. Where is my bird? Is this Sunday? Sunday. Sunday. Go to church. Daddy? Is that you, Daddy?"

Fetzer opened the heavy doors that led to the sitting room. As he did so, a new and sharply unpleasant odor assailed him. His mother had had another of her accidents. He went in to her. She was in her rocker and she did not know him.

Monday, October 21

Mike Fair flew commercial to Omaha and drove a one-way rental car from there to the aircraft leasing company's home field. It was a nice day for flying again. They were glad to see him; they had the Six on the line and the papers ready for his signatures.

"I guess that does it for a while," the man said as he walked with Fair out to the aircraft.

Fair was surprised. "They're not going to lease a third plane?"

"Say!" The man smiled. "I guess they didn't tell you."

"Tell me?"

"Smith was up here himself last Friday to pick up the second plane. They want three, all right, but this one you're taking back today *is* the third one."

"That is really strange," Fair said. "I wonder why Peterson didn't tell me yesterday when we talked?"

The man grinned. "Maybe it was spur-of-the-moment, you know?"

"I haven't met Smith yet."

"Well, I'll tell you what. He's a damned fine pilot. We checked him out in the aircraft and he took to it instantly. Nice guy, too. But wait till you get a look at the hairpiece the poor guy wears."

"Hairpiece?" Mike Fair echoed blankly.

"I don't know if he's totally bald underneath or what, boy, but I've seldom if ever seen such a lousy wig. It's too long, like he's trying to be young again or something. And God, it doesn't even fit. I really felt kind of sorry for the guy, if you want the truth. I guess he can't afford any better, trying to get this new company going."

"I'm kind of surprised to hear he picked up a plane the other day."

The man nodded. "You win some, you lose some. Maybe they'll give you some time on the job, or ferrying 'em back to us."

"I hope so," Fair said.

"Good luck!"

Fair scrambled into the Cherokee and got his mind onto the job at hand.

Wednesday, October 30

Darkness was coming on, and the air had an autumn bite to it. At wooded Lake Thunderbird, twelve miles east of Norman, Oklahoma, they had a charcoal fire going in the campsite stove, and all the paraphernalia stacked around MacReady's panel truck and Keel's old sedan was typical camping gear. The area was deserted except for them, the other concrete picnic tables white ghosts in the evening under the blackjacks. Out on the lake, which was visible as a cool blue except for the stain of crimson sunset through the trees, a lone powerboat sent back its throbbing message from a great distance.

They were all together for the first time, and the last.

Until the strike itself.

MacReady walked around the camp stove, slapping his arms against his sides. He wore only a tee shirt over his faded jeans and hightop shoes. "It's *cold!* What kind of place is this to meet anyway?"

Donovan, seated on the edge of the picnic table beside Keel, gave the younger man a cool stare. "A safe place. I explained that."

"And not even a beer to stir the old tired blood!"

"I explained that, too, Bill," Donovan added patiently. "I think there's a law against beer in this park, and we can't take any chances."

"Those kids we saw a while ago had beer."

"They might not have quite so much to lose by getting arrested, either."

"Well, I don't see why we had to come to Oklahoma anyway. Just because it's convenient for *you*—"

"Bill," Donovan cut in, "don't be quite such a royal pain in the rear. All right?"

"Yassuh, boss, yassuh!"

Donovan looked at Keel, beside him, then at Fetzer and Phil Lester, who stood nearby. "Bill's right about one thing, anyway. It's going to get colder as the sun goes out of sight. So let's get our business done and we can get out of here."

They all nodded, and even MacReady hunkered down and kept quiet.

"I'm hung up on the job until after this Friday," Donovan began. "Tom Keel is in the same situation. Bill MacReady, here, is clear now, thanks to getting laid off. You two" —he glanced at Fetzer and Lester—"will be going back for the rest of the week?"

Phil Lester nodded. "I told 'em my momma died, so they'll have me on extra Saturday. Then I'll call in sick and join you all."

"Fetzer?"

"I'm all right," Fetzer said. "Vacation."

"So," Donovan went on, "we'll all be clear and available after Sunday at the latest. Make sure you fly under phony names, and on separate flights. Bill, you'll be driving with the last of the equipment. You know where you're staying near Atlanta."

"Right," MacReady said.

"Phil?"

"Well, you know I got to come to Memphis first."

"Correct. We meet Monday at Arlington. Fetzer?"

"I'll be at that rooming house in Marietta," Fetzer said.

"Good. Abby, Tom, and I will get the planes flown in on Tuesday, November 5. Right now they're hangared at West Memphis and Arlington. Gas has been siphoned out into the fifty-five-gallon drums in the T-hangars at Arlington and the planes are refueled. The extra drums are there. Phil, can you install the fittings and connections in all three planes Monday night?"

"No sweat," Phil Lester said gently.

"Good. We'll pump the extra gas into the drums once we've installed them behind the front seats in each Cherokee. Then we'll fly them to the Atlanta area, practice our circuits on the way, land at the prearranged fields, get the tanks topped off again, and be ready on that angle. I've got the guns, the ammo, the dynamite, blasting caps, and everything else already hidden in the back of the baggage compartment of seven-one Sierra; we'll split those up before we ferry the planes to the Atlanta area."

Donovan paused as a car went by on the distant highway, its tire sounds whining in the growing dark. "Bill MacReady will get with Lester and Fetzer to make sure you both understand how to handle the dynamite. There's nothing to it; he can show you in five minutes. You'll be belted in back there, but it might be colder than blue blazes with the cargo door off; still, even with numb fingers you shouldn't have much trouble, because you'll have those handwarmers to do double duty—warm your fingers and light fuses if cigarettes don't work."

"How about the guns?" Lester asked.

"Tom or I can check everybody out on the guns. Nothing complicated there."

"Not unless we got to shoot 'em."

"If you have to shoot them," Donovan added, "we're probably going to be in plenty of trouble already."

No one said anything. The sun was gone and it was getting colder. The campfire provided a dull crimson light that flickered over their faces.

Donovan went on, "Tom has some details. Everybody ought to make some simplified notes. Keep the notes *very* simple; if somebody falls down a flight of stairs and ends up being searched for identification, we don't want the authorities with a nice, detailed blueprint that even an idiot could figure out."

Notebooks and pencils or ballpoints came out. The tension had risen, and even MacReady failed to wisecrack.

"Tom?" Donovan said.

Keel didn't need notes. "When we fly the Cherokees into the Atlanta area, two will go into Fulton County and one into DeKalb-Peachtree. We'll land the two at Fulton County a few hours apart, and park them apart. We'll top the tanks again and tie the planes down. The drums with the extra fuel in the back will be covered with tarps so no one will see them.

"The day before the strike, we'll fly the few miles to our separation fields. Right now we assume they will be Gunn, which is eight miles east of Atlanta; South Expressway, ten miles south; and Berry Hill, seventeen miles southeast of Atlanta. Between now and then we'll check these fields out, and if there's any problem we'll pick another nearby small airport. These are all shown as currently active on the terminal area chart, and all are nicely close in and not too big, as you'll see when you check your own charts.

"I've worked on area radio frequencies to figure out what frequencies we might be able to use discreetly during the strike," Keel went on methodically. "Our rendezvous frequency will be 122.9. We may need to change frequencies if we run into a situation where our messages have to go back and forth hot and heavy, and we want to keep the authorities channel-skipping, trying to find us. So here are our alternates. Number one—and that's how we'll call it if everybody is to switch—is 118.4. Channel two is 125.5. Channel three is 118.7."

"Wait a minute, wait a minute," Abercrombie said, scribbling.

"Sorry," Keel said. "Did you get three, 118.7?"

"Yes."

"Number four is 123.9. Number five is 119.9."

"I'm not sure I understand this frequency business."

"All right." Keel hesitated and drew a slow breath. "Our tentative date for the operation is a week from Friday, November 8. We take off from the separation fields about four o'clock in the afternoon and rendezvous at the Rex VOR at two thousand feet m.s.l. That's within radar coverage for Atlanta but just outside the Terminal Control Area, ten statute miles due east of the airport. We make whatever radio contact we need on the rendezvous frequency. At that point, the lead plane may say, 'Go to channel one,' which tells the other two planes where we'll talk next."

Abercrombie scratched his head. "I still don't quite see the need for *all* the frequencies."

"Maybe we won't use them all," Keel replied. "But if we do run into a situation that requires a lot of communications among ourselves, we don't want people on the ground easily finding us on their dial and monitoring everything we say. I'd rather have too many alternate frequencies than not enough."

Abercrombie shrugged. "I'll memorize the blasted things."

"When we go in," Keel resumed, "we'll all monitor the tower frequency. But, again, if we need a plane-to-plane message, the leader will call out a channel number and everybody will immediately switch."

"What's the tower?" Abercrombie asked. "Never mind. I can look it up."

"It's 119.1," Keel replied promptly.

"Rog."

"Donovan is the flight leader," Keel went on tautly. "His Cherokee is designated 'Ringleader' in radio contact.

We'll use code names for the other two planes too. I thought we could call them 'Falcon,' and 'Snoopy.' "

"Snoopy!" MacReady snorted.

"Give us a better name," Keel said icily.

MacReady looked at him in the flickering firelight and slowly spread his hands. "I *like* Snoopy. I do."

"I'll have Falcon," Keel added. "Abby, you'll pilot Snoopy."

Phil Lester asked, "How about us shotguns? How do we split up with you three fly-boys?"

Keel shot Donovan a quick look. They had talked about the forming of the teams over a six-hour period. The argument had become bitter. The fly in the ointment, of course, was MacReady. It had not been easy and Keel still did not entirely like it.

He said now, "The teams are Donovan and Fetzer, Abercrombie and Lester, myself and MacReady."

Abercrombie, despite the poor light, showed visible relief. He turned and mockingly extended a handshake toward Phil Lester. The slender mechanic grinned and held out his own right hand.

The anger bitter in his throat, Keel added, "Donovan is Ringleader. That means he initiates orders. The others obey, and only feed information. Once this operation is under way, we can't have arguments."

Fetzer said, "I guess each team gets together separately and works out its escape route."

"Precisely. You all understand the plans when we leave the immediate area. Beyond that, I don't *want* to know where the other two planes are headed; that's their business. My partner and I are taking care of our own hides at that point."

No one replied. For an instant it was very still. Unspoken was the crux of earlier discussions on this point: if one team was captured, the men could not tell their captors where the others had gone, because they simply would not know.

It was MacReady who broke the silence. "You haven't mentioned the guns."

"I told you where they are now."

"You know what I mean."

Keel waited, making MacReady say it.

MacReady obliged. "We only got two of those AK-47s. There are three planes. What does the odd man do, and who *is* the odd man?"

Donovan stepped in smoothly. "I have a weapon for my man, because rank has its privileges. Since I know Phil Lester was a good hand with weapons in Nam before he got mechanic duty, I've decided he'll have the other automatic weapon."

"You mean," MacReady said, "Tom and me go up with no gun?"

"Right," Donovan said.

"That's not fair! I want a gun!"

"You don't have a gun, friend. Tom, here, has already agreed, incidentally."

MacReady glowered at Keel. "You agreed? Are you out of your tree? You and me are going up there with no *gun?*"

Keel said, "Nobody will be able to tell we don't have one. We'll have dynamite."

"Yeah, but still—"

Donovan cut in, "That's the way it's going to be. Not a thing to worry about."

"Not for *you,*" MacReady said. "You'll have one of the guns."

"It's okay," Keel said. "We'll manage."

The truth was that he did not *want* MacReady in the airplane with an automatic weapon. He and Donovan had been in instant agreement on this. Donovan had admitted, for the first time, that the man's personality seemed to have disintegrated slightly in prison. Donovan, too, was worried about him, but thought he would hold together if he was not given the temptation of a gun in his hands.

"I don't like it a damned bit," MacReady said now.

"The money will count out just the same," Abercrombie suggested.

"Yeah, but it's the *idea* of the thing."

Donovan smiled. "Look, old chum, we all have to make the best of things. All right?"

MacReady glared at him, but as usual Donovan's easy manner won out. "Okay. But I still think it's a bad deal."

"There are a few other details," Keel said, and launched into them. Within twenty minutes they had touched all the major bases. MacReady agreed to drive Abercrombie and Phil Lester back into Norman in his panel, which would allow that team a few minutes to begin initial discussion of escape routings. Keel said he would drive Donovan and Fetzer for the same reason.

He told MacReady, "You and I will huddle Saturday night."

"Right. I got some ideas."

Keel made it a point to tell him, "I do too."

They gathered up their gear, snuffed out the fire, and got into the vehicles. Full night was upon the lake area. As Keel drove out of the campsite, the car's headlights cast a yellowish glare onto pitted red earth studded with small boulders. It crossed his mind that the last thing he wanted was to get stuck, but the ground was hard and dry and the car pulled out strongly onto the pavement.

"Well, gents," Donovan said, "we're on the last leg." He was in the front seat with Keel, while Fetzer was in the back.

"Did you think it went all right?" Keel asked.

"Very well. *Very* well."

"There certainly weren't any major problems."

"I told you there wouldn't be."

They were talking about MacReady.

"If the rest goes as well," Keel said, "we're home free."

"The rest *will* go as well."

From the back, Fetzer asked, "Do we want to talk about escape routings now?"

"I don't really think so," Donovan said. "We can get together a little later."

"I thought you probably really wanted to get your two heads together," Fetzer said.

"We've pretty well finished planning," Keel said, glancing at Donovan.

"Sure," Fetzer replied. "But you're a little worried about MacReady, correct?"

"You noticed." Donovan sighed.

"I'm glad you got it around so he won't have a gun, I'll tell you that."

Neither Keel nor Donovan replied. They reached the highway and Keel waited for an oncoming car, then pulled out behind it, heading west toward Norman.

Fetzer persisted, "It's none of my business, but are you nervous about flying with him, Tom?"

Keel considered it, then opted for honesty. "A little."

"He'll be fine," Donovan said.

"I hope so."

"What I worry about," Fetzer said, "is whether he'll be careful enough afterward."

"He will be," Donovan said, and then he turned to look back. "Now look. This is no time for any of us to worry about any other member of the team. You know that."

"I know," Fetzer said seriously. "You guys are straight. I like both of you. I trust you. It's a good plan. I'm ready for all of it. But I know I can talk with you—let it out. I know MacReady worries you guys, too."

"Is it that obvious?" Keel asked.

"No. But I know, man."

"He'll be all right," Donovan repeated. "And I'll tell you why. He already has been to prison. Even a slight implication in any of this, and he's back behind the walls automatically. He's the most vulnerable of all of us and he knows it. He's reckless. He's loud. He's a boor. But he'll hang in there. He'll play it right because he has to, to protect his own skin. Whatever you may think about MacReady, he is *not* suicidal."

Saturday, November 2

The draperies of the motel room were closed tightly, the door bolted. Standing in front of the bed, Keel pointed at the large aeronautical chart spread out on it. MacReady frowned down at the unfamiliar symbols and legends.

"Here," Keel said, pointing at the marker in the south-central portion of the national map, "is Atlanta. You can see by the large circle how much range the Cherokee will give us. Theoretically, we can go in any direction."

MacReady continued to frown at the map. "Well, I can't see going up this way." He pointed to the northeast; the Cherokee could carry them into the populous areas of Ohio and Pennsylvania, or into the East Coast megalopolis.

Keel felt a trace of encouragement: MacReady was applying himself seriously to the problem. "You're right. I agree. And if you notice, our escape area is somewhat limited to the east and south, also. There aren't that many areas of Florida where we could be sure of landing unobserved."

"Not unless we go into the swamp, and I want no part of that, boy."

"Fine," Keel said, trying to hide his irritation. "That pretty much means we're already in agreement. We go west, in some general way."

"You got something in mind?"

Keel pointed to the map. "Here."

"That's in the mothering *ocean.*"

"No, it's offshore. Here. It's an island."

MacReady's face furrowed. *"Then* what do we do? Swim?"

Keel explained in minute detail, watching MacReady's face as he did so. MacReady was stubborn and argumentative. They went over all of it again. Again Keel was struck by the intensity of his dislike for this man who had become his closest partner in a gamble with death. He wondered if he ever would have begun if he had known he would wind up with a partner like this.

MacReady, however, surprised him. "You've already made all the arrangements?"

"Yes."

"Then what are we arguing about?"

"You have to agree. We're in this together."

"Look," MacReady said, placing a heavy hand on Keel's shoulder. "If I didn't think you people had a lot on the ball, I would never have got *into* the deal. If this is good enough for you, why, then, I'll go right with you."

Keel hid his surprise. "Fine, then. And none of the others will know."

"Right."

"Once we're ashore, you and I will split up, too."

"I get you."

"I have information on the area that I can explain in detail later. We'll be able to get to town with no trouble, because I'm getting my car down there tomorrow, parking it where it will be safe, and getting back to Memphis by commercial air. You need to be thinking about whether you'll want bus or air out of that area, and how you'll set it up. I suggest that we both bring along a suitcase of clothes, not only for appearance's sake if someone sees us on the road, but because we might be on the move for a few days right afterward."

"Right, right," MacReady muttered, still studying the map. "I'll have to get back to Cleveland to my parole officer. A half-million dollars hid in my flat, and I'll have to go to my parole officer."

"Just make sure you remember the system we discussed for passing the money."

"Don't worry, boy. If I get that far, I'm not about to blow it by getting caught trying to spend marked bills."

Beyond all the obvious worries about the strike itself, the period following it, disposing of the money, was the part that continued to preoccupy Keel the most. The plan to launder the cash, or exchange it at a discount in Mexico, had been abandoned. Each man would take his own chances.

Of course it was possible that the money would be clean, thanks to the haste with which it would have to be collected. But they could not count on this. They had agreed to spend the money individually, a little at a time. By going

78

to a series of stores and merchants in a given town, quickly making small purchases with large bills and pocketing the clean change, each man could clear several hundred dollars per day. They had exhaustively discussed ways to make sure they provided no pattern in their spending locales, types of stores, or amounts exchanged.

It would take a very long time to spend $500,000, but it was the kind of suspense Keel could live with.

For all of them but MacReady, the problem would be somewhat eased by the fact that they would be taking on new identities. Keel already had his new birth certificate from the state of Louisiana tucked inside the lining of his suitcase. He would be Thomas Vanning after the strike. The real Thomas Vanning had died in Vietnam, but state offices of vital records did not check such matters closely; a visit to the state office, a request for a duplicate of a lost birth certificate in Vanning's name, and a crudely forged DD Form 214 had been all that were necessary.

So, for all of them but MacReady, there would be new lives and new identities. None would ever work in his own area of expertise again. Keel did not know what the others planned, but he expected to go to the Pacific Northwest and then possibly on to Alaska. A man could make trips now and then back to the contiguous states, chosen at random, to exchange money.

MacReady had a more serious problem. He could not immediately drop from view. The authorities would sooner or later—and probably sooner—check parolees and known offenders for just such a telltale disappearance. He had to remain in Cleveland for at least six months after the strike, dutifully reporting and being exceptionally careful about passing even the smallest amounts in scattered faraway places.

So, here too, if there was a weak link, it was MacReady. But he had been cheerful about it. "A man can wait a long time for that much money!"

And perhaps he would be as good as his word. Keel tried to tell himself he was borrowing trouble when he worried about it. It was the chance they all had to share.

But it did continue to bother him. Strangely, in terms of the worst tension, he was already past the strike. It was the weeks, months, and years beyond that would tell the tale.

He thought briefly of his brother and his brother's wife. Contacting them about a month after the strike would be one of the high points. He wondered what their faces would look like when he casually said he wanted to invest—and handed them the money, just as much as he had been able to clear up until that time. They would not know of his new identity, of course; they would not know any of it. It would be a windfall, a shock—the first good shock in a life rotted by the bad kind. *That* moment in itself would make it all worthwhile, even if events conspired to make it impossible ever to see them again. . . .

It was a thought to cling to.

Monday, November 4

"We'll practice the formations," Donovan said crisply. "Circles, ovals, a figure 8, a box, and a triangle. We'll work out the radio signals to go from one to the other, too. Then we'll tool on down to Atlanta and put the birds on the ground."

"We should do it right down on the deck," Keel said. "Two hundred feet off the ground."

"Correct."

The two men looked at each other.

"We're right on the brink now," Donovan said.

"Yes."

"We've come a long way since this was just a gleam in your eye."

"It's going to work."

"Of course it is. Of course, also, some of us will eventually get caught."

"We might not," Keel said.

"I'm afraid it's inevitable. There are too many of us."

"That should work in our favor. One man might be

traced. We're just six of dozens who drop out of sight every week. And the pattern of our random spending will confuse hell out of them."

Donovan thought about it. "I hope so."

"We don't have to get caught. None of us. People have gotten away with skyjackings before."

"Not many."

"Not many ever had this good a plan."

Donovan chuckled. "I hope so. I sincerely hope so."

"What if we *do* get caught?" Keel said, changing directions.

"I don't know," Donovan said. "I won't talk, certainly."

"I know that. But if you're caught, how will you feel?"

"Badly!"

They laughed, gallows humor.

"Actually," Donovan added, "this is going to be the climax of our lives, do you know that?"

"I know," Keel said.

"Do you?" Donovan studied his face.

They understood each other perfectly.

Friday, November 8

Rain dripped from a scummy cloud layer only a few hundred feet overhead. The airport was dingy and vacant-looking as only an airport can be on a socked-in day. Above the terminal, the rotating beacon flashed green and white, green and white. The gas trucks stood silent by the line shack, and the planes parked along the ramp looked bleak, like crippled birds hiding from some unseen, but sensed, disaster.

At the far end of the middle row of parked aircraft, Abercrombie and Lester sat in their Cherokee Six. The rain sifted steadily on the thin aluminum roof and streamed down the rounded windshield plastic. Abercrombie sat behind the left-hand control yoke, staring somberly at the wet ramp in front of the plane. The rear seats had been removed, and it was in this area that Lester worked around like a slow-moving crab, wiping at panels, the center-bolted 55-gallon drum, and other smooth surfaces.

Both men wore thin driving gloves.

"If you haven't gotten all fingerprints off by now," Abercrombie said, "you never will."

"Old friend," Lester drawled, "I've wiped everything in every aircraft two times already, but chances of you or me leavin' a stray print in this bird are the greatest. So I got nothin' better to do an' I'll just wipe her down one more time."

"Just so you're sure that cargo door can be removed fast enough."

"I showed you, didn't I? I even got MacReady where he could do it fast, didn't I?"

Abercrombie glanced at the heavy coats and gear stored on the floor in front of the right-hand seat. "It might get really cold up there with that door off."

"Cool you down," Lester said.

"We're not going anywhere today anyway, that's for sure. This weather is here for the weekend."

"You're nervous."

"Aren't you?" Abercrombie snapped back.

"Yep," Lester admitted cheerfully, and kept wiping things.

"I wish we were at the other field."

"Boy, you fret about *anything!* Why do you wish we were over yonder?"

"At least two crews are over there. We're stuck by ourselves."

"Well, old friend, at least we get to call 'em in just another few minutes."

Abercrombie grunted but did not formulate a reply in words. He knew what the verdict had to be when he walked the two hundred feet to the outdoor pay telephone booth and dialed a similar booth at the other airport. The warm front was stagnating right across the area; the rain and wretched visibility would continue for at least another twenty-four hours. They had no choice but to postpone the operation until Monday earliest.

They had discussed weather scrubs. They could afford up to five days of delay. Beyond that point they would have to fly out of the area and set a new target date. Each man knew where he was supposed to go in the event of an overnight postponement, or a delay over the weekend. This contingency—like all others—had been foreseen and provided for.

It did not make Abercrombie feel much better. He was beginning to wonder very seriously how he had ever gotten himself into this thing. This, he recognized, was emotional letdown; he had been psyched to the highest pitch for the operation to take place *today,* and now he had to readjust his emotional clocks. It was not easy.

Swallowing, he simultaneously wished for a cigarette and felt the scratchiness deep in his throat. The two were related in a way he did not like to think about. He found himself speculating for perhaps the hundredth time about the deep-down reasons why the other men had been willing to commit to this scheme. For him it was simpler.

He glanced at his watch. "I think I'll go on over to the booth."

"It's a little early yet."

Abercrombie patted the tubing and valves coming out of the lashed-down steel drum and snaking into the Cherokee's floor to connect to the usual fuel system tubes. "I need a smoke anyway."

Lester didn't comment further. Abercrombie slid across the seat and popped the door open, stepping out onto the broad white wing. The rain pelted gently against his face. He swung to the wet pavement and walked toward the telephone booth against the wire fence, reaching for his pack of cigarettes as he went. Snapping the Zippo, he fired up the Camel and inhaled deeply, sending some fresh tar and nicotine down to the flourishing cancerous lesions nestled in his throat.

In his hotel room, Tom Keel restlessly went to the telephone and dialed the number for Pilots Automatic Weather Telephone Service. Tight with uncertainty, he waited while the hookup was completed. There was a sharp clicking sound and then the recording came on the line.

"Aviation forecast valid until 1800 Eastern," the man's hollow voice began. "Synopsis. Low-pressure trough extending through the Atlanta area and on a line from Charleston to Augusta to Birmingham to Memphis. Front moving very slowly northward and into the Chattanooga area by nightfall. Rain, scattered ground fog, visibilities less than two miles, and occasional impacted thunderstorms predicted throughout the area prior to passage of the trough line. Clearing from south to north, slowly, beginning at about 1600 Eastern in the Atlanta area. Flight precautions—"

Keel broke the connection.

There was no possibility of making the strike today. But the miserable weather was finally being nudged northward, and by morning the skies were likely to be clearing swiftly. By tomorrow afternoon—Tuesday, November 12—conditions would be close to ideal.

Keel knew he did not need to contact any of the others. They knew the situation and could call the same number for updates. They would remain scattered today, in virtual hiding. *But tomorrow was the day.*

After all the preparation, Keel was more than ready. The waiting was shredding his nerves by degrees. Pacing now, he mentally reviewed the plans and the low-altitude maneuvers they had practiced on the way in from Memphis. There were no holes and no ragged edges.

His mind flickered over the final actions they had taken in the Memphis area. The T-hangars and all tools had been wiped scrupulously for fingerprints. Nothing of help to the authorities had been left behind. The office and its contents were also clean, double- and triple-checked. If the day came when someone backtracked them to the building manager or to the kid who had flown two of the Sixes in from Nebraska for them, the descriptions would include hairpieces, Donovan's genuine beard which was now gone again, dark glasses, uncharacteristic clothing. If missing persons lists were compiled, they would not narrow the field enough to be greatly helpful. The FAA might print out a list of current pilots, but the list would look like the New York telephone directory. Even if someone like Phil Lester opted for returning to his old life and identity—an option left to each man for his own decision—there was no way to track him down and identify him from clues carelessly left behind.

Even the remote possibility of an aircraft failure had been hedged as far as humanly possible. The Cherokees were all low-time aircraft. Lester and Richard Fetzer had meticulously examined the engines, changed the oil and filters redundantly, and even cut the old filters apart, examining them for the slightest telltale sign of metal fragments. The planes were perfect.

Everything that could be foreseen had been handled.

Still Keel paced, his mind restlessly probing for something—anything—they might have overlooked.

By late afternoon, he had to get out for a while. Going down to his rental Pinto in the hotel garage, he drove carefully through downtown traffic, heading south. The rain had abated and the overcast appeared to be starting to break slightly. The pavement was wet, and passing cars threw mud and spray onto the windshield.

He drove to Atlanta International.

The sky seemed lower here, over the bleak-looking blue and white terminal building. The parking areas were jammed, however, and there were aircraft on the ground. Keel saw a DC–9 break out of the clouds and continue its majestic descent for an ILS landing.

He did not park or try to enter the terminal. He did not particularly want to establish human contact with the thousands of passengers milling about in its cavernous interior. Tomorrow it would be similar, and he would hold the lives of everyone here in his hands. It would not be helpful to remember the faces of children he might see inside today.

He slowly drove on through the parking area, heading

back for the feeder road. He had to eat something. He had to get some sleep tonight. Tomorrow was it, without question, and it would require all his skill, calm, patience, courage, and stamina.

Tomorrow.

STRIKE

The sky over Atlanta was glass-clear, and Atlanta International was busy. Delta Flight 223, a Boeing 720 from New York City, had just landed on runway 8 and was taxiing on runway 3 toward the terminal, where thirteen other airliners were loading or unloading passengers and freight at the embarkation fingers. A Delta training flight was holding on runway 9L for takeoff. Southern 870, a Martin 404 from Valdosta, touched down on 9R with distant puffs of smoke from its tires. Piedmont 241, a Fairchild FH–27 from Hickory, North Carolina, was on three-mile final, to be followed by Northwest 714, a DC–10 from Minneapolis, and Eastern 904, a 727 in a little early from Mexico City. There were another dozen big jets due within the next fifteen minutes.

In the bluish brightness of the glass-enclosed tower, controller Paul Albright felt the pressure. But it was a normal part of the job and meant nothing. One of four controllers behind the formica-topped console table that bristled with switches, telephones, microphones, and other electronic gear, he easily held the entire tactical situation in his mind. He was thirty-one, had been at the job for five years, and felt as if it had been a lifetime.

One of the controllers on Albright's right, working ground control, pressed a microphone control button. "Delta 223," he said crisply, "continue taxi." Below the tower, obediently, the Boeing 720 trundled off runway 3 and onto the broad concrete apron.

87

Albright touched a button of his own, which transmitted on one of the frequencies used for aircraft still in the air, or on an active runway. "Southern 870, turn left next exit, contact ground 121.9."

One of the small loudspeakers in the raised deck in front of him crackled back, *"Southern 870 roger."*

"Delta training flight continue to hold."

"Delta trainer continue to hold."

Albright turned to the ground controller on his right. "Let 870 cross nine-left. I'm holding the Delta." He leaned back momentarily in his chair. "We've got it sorted out now. We'll get the Delta off and then we're back to landings on nine-right, takeoffs on eight." He saw Southern's Martin 404 clear the runway and heard the pilot's voice crackle over the ground controller's loudspeaker almost simultaneously. Concentrating the sound out, he touched his transmit button. "Piedmont 241, cleared to land, runway nine-right."

"Piedmont 241 cleared to land."

Albright turned to Bill Sloan, the other air traffic controller, on his left. "You've got it." He leaned back again, conscious of the ache in his back and the dull headache, and reached for a cigarette. Lighting it, he reached for, and sipped from, his cup of coffee. It was cold.

A slight glitch in flight sequencing had required the tower to vary momentarily from its usual procedure of using the farthest-separated parallel runways together, one for takeoffs and the other for landings. But this was being straightened out now, and the planes in the pattern were properly lined up for 9R, the preferred runway. Aircraft on the ground, ready for departure, were now being sent to line up, like obedient turtles, for takeoff from runway 8. It was good to have things proceeding with perfect normalcy right now, Albright reflected, because airlines insisted on scheduling arrivals and departures with little or no regard for total traffic problems; in the next thirty minutes, Atlanta was slated to handle thirteen departures and seventeen arrivals.

Hey, airlines! That's one a minute!

What's wrong with that, boys? You slipping? You think that's traffic? You can handle it, right?

Riiiiiiight!

Albright started to get up for fresh coffee.

The telephone on his right buzzed and lit up. It was the direct line from Atlanta Approach Control, the radar facility that had positive control of all aircraft in the vicinity.

Albright picked it up. "Tower. Albright."

"Paul? Listen. This is Eberhart at approach. We've got three targets inbound from the Rex VOR. No contact by radio. Do you know anything about them?"

Involuntarily Albright looked out through the glass wall toward his left, eastward toward the place on the horizon where the Rex Omnirange station was located ten miles away. "I don't have a thing."

"They've penetrated the TCA. Hang on." The telephone at the other end was put down, and Albright could hear the radar man's voice echo as he spoke over the radio: "Aircraft inbound from the Rex VOR. You are entering the Atlanta Terminal Control Area. State your intentions."

Albright waited. Every so often, a light aircraft forgot all sanity and a book full of regulations and flew blithely into the sacrosanct TCA. He landed to learn that the FAA took a very dim view of such proceedings, and usually was given a lengthy period of time on the ground, without his license, to ponder his transgressions.

Three aircraft, however, was highly unusual.

Eberhart came back on the telephone connection. "No word, Paul."

"Let me try," Albright said. "I'll let you know."

Hanging up, he thumbed the air frequency. "Aircraft inbound to Atlanta International from the Rex VOR, state your intentions."

He listened. There was a hissing silence. It crossed his mind that there were probably several commercial airliner pilots also listening with more than passing interest; uncontrolled aircraft in here meant chaos, and the potential for the ultimate disaster—midair collision.

89

Out on runway 9R, Piedmont 241 touched down. Albright caught a glint of sun off the Northwest Airlines DC–10 that was supposed to be next; it was several miles out, approaching nicely.

The other controllers, with that part of their minds that was always alert to the slightest unusual happening, were aware of Albright's last call. They were watching him. From the half-deck below, the shift supervisor, Rollie Stoner, came up the metal staircase to stand behind Albright's chair.

"What's going on?" Stoner asked.

"I don't know. We've got three inbound from Rex VOR, no radio contact, but—hold on." He thumbed a button. "Piedmont 241 turn left next intersection, plan to hold short of runway nine-left, contact ground 121.9." He looked back at Stoner, a slightly aging, chubby man with porkchop sideburns. "Might be cropdusters, but—"

One of the ground controllers moved violently in his chair. *"Jesus!"*

Albright swung around to stare through the glass. Just as he did so, a low-winged, single-engine white aircraft came into view. It was *very* low, flying east-to-west, directly over the center of the field.

"What's he *doing?*" somebody gasped.

"God almighty, that—!"

The plane—a Cherokee Six—neared the western end of the airport. It banked sharply to the right, swinging with frightening speed in an arc that would bring it very near the tower itself. At the same moment, Albright's numbed senses registered a second Cherokee off to the left, coming from the east on a similar course.

For an instant everyone was talking at once, and then discipline reasserted itself and there was just as suddenly a stunned silence. Albright acted on training and crisis-quickened reflexes. He jabbed the transmit button.

"Northwest 714, execute missed approach. Repeat. Do not land. Execute missed approach. Eastern 904, execute three-sixty to the left, now. All other aircraft maintain present headings and stand by."

The windows of the tower vibrated wildly as the first

Cherokee roared just overhead, vanishing momentarily in a turn. But now a *third* Cherokee was in sight, flashing across the center of the field where two of the runways formed an enormous X.

Rollie Stoner leaned over Albright's shoulder and barked an additional order over the air: "All aircraft in the Atlanta area maintain temporary silence on Atlanta tower frequency. Contact Atlanta Approach. Out."

"What the hell *is* this?" Bill Sloan asked.

"I don't know," Albright admitted, "but—"

The loudspeaker rattled and came to life. *"Atlanta tower, this is the lead Cherokee over your field. We are bandits. Repeat, we are bandits. We have explosives and automatic weapons. Order all aircraft to hold. No aircraft will land, take off, or taxi. No passengers will disembark. Acknowledge now."*

For an instant there was nothing but a paralyzed silence and inaction inside the tower. Albright happened to glance at the digital clock in the panel assembly. It was 4:52.

4:53 P.M.

Rollie Stoner shoved in between Albright's and Sloan's chairs. "I'll take it," he said. He pressed the transmit button, squinting out into the sun at the lead Cherokee as it completed a broad circuit of the field and swooped past a second time. "Cherokee 71-Sierra, you are cleared for immediate landing on runway 8. Other two Cherokees, stand by. Federal regulations—"

As Stoner spoke, his face glistening with nervous sweat, the second Cherokee had swept in over the center of the field on its second pass. Something toppled out of it toward the ground, a small, turning object. There was a puff of smoke and dirt and then a small thunderclap impact that rattled the windows of the tower.

"They've got bombs!" somebody yelled.

Stoner, his face blank, stopped transmitting.

The loudspeaker blared again. *"Atlanta, that was a*

sample. Hold all aircraft. Now. The next dynamite package will be on this Southern jet taxiing on taxiway Charlie."

Albright stared at the smoking crater in the grass near the center of the airport. Another of the Cherokees zoomed just overhead. He turned and looked at Stoner, who stood glassy-eyed, licking his lips.

It was, Albright saw suddenly, beyond Rollie Stoner. The man had frozen despite all his years of training and experience.

But something had to be done instantly.

Albright leaned in and pressed down all the transmit buttons simultaneously, talking to all aircraft, whether in the air or on the ground, at once.

"All aircraft in the Atlanta area, attention. This is Atlanta tower to all aircraft in the Atlanta area. Emergency in progress. Taxi off runways and hold. All others on the ground, hold your present position. Do not return to the terminal. Do not attempt to land. Orbiting aircraft contact approach, 126.9 or 118.1, for sequencing out of the area. Observe radio silence this frequency. Out."

Another of the Cherokees passed directly overhead at low altitude, the rich roar of its engine shatteringly powerful.

The radio spoke again.

"Atlanta tower, this is the lead Cherokee. All aircraft will continue to hold. Failure to obey will result in that aircraft's destruction. You will stop all vehicle traffic on the field. Block all traffic into and out of the airport area now. You have five minutes, or we will demonstrate our automatic weapons for you on one of the aircraft on the field. Acknowledge now."

Albright waited a moment. No one else moved. It had become his baby. His sweaty hand slipped off the transmit button and he had to try a second time.

"Cherokee leader, this is Atlanta tower." How calm his voice sounded! "Message acknowledged. Aircraft will hold. We will attempt to hold all vehicle traffic on the field. We will send word about stopping traffic." Albright paused, his hand still on the button to hold it open. Then he added with a sense of futility, "State your intentions."

The radio crackled back, a voice that had already begun to sound familiar, slightly southern, pitched high over wind roar and engine noise: *"Atlanta tower, obey orders and stand by. Get your airport manager to the tower. Now."*

4:57 P.M.

The big desk in Ted Kuhlman's office was covered with reports, invoices, and canceled orders. Trying to wrestle some sense out of the chaotic aviation fuel situation, Kuhlman had resorted to something even more confusing to him personally—the desktop calculator that ordinarily belonged to Barbara, his secretary.

Stabbing at buttons on the panel of the calculator, Kuhlman had to squint because smoke from the cigarette dangling in his lips was making his eyes water like crazy. He added the long list of fuel figures, subtracted present inventory, multiplied by current use rates, and got a bewildering panoply of flashing numerals on the readout screen just for an instant before two red lights flashed and the calculator cleared itself back to zero.

"God damn it," Kuhlman said. He pushed the intercom box button. "Barbara?"

"Yes, sir?" she replied.

"Can you come in here, please?"

"Yes, sir."

Kuhlman stared at the irritating electronic machine and at the mess all over his desk. What he really should do, he told himself, was pack it in and go home. If he left right now, he could get there in time for Walter Cronkite and a martini. Correction: two martinis. Every newscast was a two-martini occasion these days.

The problem was that the fuel utilization report, and accompanying projections, had to be in Washington by the fifteenth. His assistant manager, Frank Andrews, was catch-

ing up on a week of overdue vacation time th
fuel management officer had screwed things up.
did—(too often, according to his doctor, who
Kuhlman was taking things into his own hand
was, the calculator would not cooperate.

The door to his large paneled office opened and
came in with her note pad. A tall brunette,
thirty—half Kuhlman's age—and very pretty
along.

"My, my," she murmured, looking at
"What have we here?"

"You know very well what we have her
said. "The calculator won't work right."

"What seems to be the trouble?"

"Well, look. I punch in the numbers like th
onstrated, slowly—"and then I ask it for an a
God damned stupid thing—" The mach
cleared itself and went blank again.

Barbara moved around the desk, enter
space, and leaned close to examine the mach
punch the 'operation' button between operat
chine will know what it's supposed to do."

Kuhlman breathed her perfume, liking its
demanded, "is the operation button?"

"Here. Plus, minus, multiply, divide—the
along here."

Kuhlman stared at them. "Oh. Those."

"Did you read the instructions?" Barbara a

"Instructions?" Kuhlman felt guilty. Then
that the best way to react was by counteratta
have time for any God damned instructions!
that!"

"Why don't you just let me do it for you, T

"Because you and Jill have all that stuff to ge
Chamber of Commerce, plus the correspondence
tacting people for the luncheon next week, plus
dar—"

"Working on your calendar won't do muc

94

office—emergency in progress. Get the FBI to call me on the straight line into the tower. Have Sally and Jean call all the on-duty ticket agents, tell them we've got an emergency in progress, all flights holding, give nobody any information. We can't have a God damned panic on our hands. Anybody wants to know anything, have Sally hold them in the office here. As soon as you're clear, get your tail up to the tower and join me."

"What's happened?" Barbara called after him.

He looked back. "Babe," he said softly, "I don't know exactly. And I wish I weren't on my way to find out."

5:01 P.M.

In the Atlanta Approach Control facility it was bedlam. Extra controllers had already been dragged in from God alone knew where. All radarscopes were in use, and all telephones. Every time a telephone was put down, it rang again instantly.

"National 448," a controller intoned smoothly. "Atlanta International is closed temporarily, emergency in progress. You can hold present position or divert."

"Affirmative, American 226," another controller chimed in on a different sector frequency. "We have no further information. Suggest you hold pending developments."

Gregory, one of the younger controllers, listened to the cacophony as he stared at the big screen. There were more than a hundred targets in the area, from a Boeing 747 to a poor little Cessna 150 just squawking his transponder to be polite. The Terminal Control Area proper, the area immediately around Atlanta, had been cleared; the larger control area teemed with targets—and problems.

Some of the incoming flights would divert shortly, Gregory knew; fuel would make this mandatory. Others could hold for a long time. But all across the continent more planes were piling in toward Atlanta, and Atlanta was paralyzed. And still no one knew *exactly* what was going on.

Things were going to get worse before they got better. Even the slightest snafu meant hours of untangling aircraft from one another's flight paths.

It was Gregory's job at the moment to man the direct line to Atlanta tower. He was to find out what was happening. He looked now at the telephone. It was the only one that had not rung.

5:03 P.M.

"Okay," Ted Kuhlman said, wrapping his paw around the hand microphone. "I'll talk to the bastards." The sun was low on the western horizon, beyond the haze and clutter of the Interstate, and in the tower it was curiously silent, although each controller remained at his desk position, mute and grim faced.

Kuhlman pressed the red stud on the side of the mike. "Cherokee leader, this is Atlanta tower, the airport manager speaking. Go ahead with your message."

The voice came back briskly over the speakers, very loud at such close range. Inadvertently Kuhlman squinted out at what he took to be the lead plane, now banking sharply to the west against the crimson sun-glare.

"Atlanta tower, is this the airport manager? Kuhlman?"

Kuhlman was startled, and wondered for an insane instant whether they knew him personally. Then he realized they had just done some homework.

He pressed the button. "Affirmative, Cherokee leader."

"Here are our orders for you," the voice came back. *"One. No aircraft moves from its present position. Two. No aircraft lands or tries to take off. Three. No aircraft disembarks passengers. Four. No vehicle traffic moves anywhere on the field. Five. No traffic enters or leaves the airport parking area. Six. All runway and taxiway lights will be turned on now. Seven. No police or military vehicles will appear on surrounding roads. Eight. No gunships of any kind will appear in the area. Nine. No other attempt will be made to*

98

interfere with us. Any failure to follow these instructions will result in destruction of an aircraft on the field of our choice. We mean business. Don't sacrifice lives by trying us out. We are also prepared to attack the terminal itself. Do you understand the conditions?"

Kuhlman tasted blood where he had angrily bitten his tongue. He thumbed the microphone. "Stand by."

"Give us the lights now, Atlanta."

The faces of the other men in the tower were blank, waiting. Kuhlman knew there was no one else to decide. His mind raced over calculations, none of which looked any good. "Give them full lights."

Stoner, the shift supervisor, disappeared to the lower level. In another instant there was a sound of switches being thrown. Out on the field, all the white, yellow, and blue lights sprang into life, pale in the remaining daylight.

The loudspeaker spoke. *"Thank you, Atlanta. Now get that parking area sealed off. Over."*

"We can't close everything off," Kuhlman grated into the mike. "It's going to take time. Over."

"You've got five minutes, Atlanta."

Kuhlman turned to the nearest controller. "Call security for me. Extension six-eight. Tell them to get the parking gates closed. I don't give a God damn how much people complain. Tell them I want it done pronto."

The controller walked to a wall telephone and dialed, speaking into it urgently.

Kuhlman watched one of the Cherokees thunder past at close range. He was still having a hard time believing it. It was so unheard of that none of his vast experience helped him cope. He could not put any of it together.

He held the microphone close again with the practice of old times. "Cherokee leader, this is Kuhlman. We will try to comply with your orders. What do you want from us? Repeat, what do you want? What are your other demands? You are endangering the lives of thousands of innocent people. Over."

"Atlanta, this is Cherokee leader. You have a nice collection of planes out here. Order them all to taxi to taxiway

Delta and line up near the center-section. We want a nice, neat line of them. Then stand by to copy further instructions."

Sweat stung Kuhlman's eyes. "Clarify, Cherokee leader. You want the planes presently in taxi positions lined up on taxiway Delta? Aircraft loading on the ramp are to remain where they are?"

"*Affirmative. We count eleven aircraft in taxi position. Get them onto Delta. We are monitoring your ground frequency to verify instructions.*"

Kuhlman wiped his arm across his face. The controllers watched him for orders. He knew he was making the big airliners a more centralized target if he obeyed by having them cluster on the single long taxiway at the center of the field. But if he did not—

He decided. He signaled to the ground controller nearest him. "Go ahead. Get them all taxied out there, like the man says."

The controllers turned, studying the situation. "Take Piedmont first," one of them suggested. Another man reached for his mike controls.

As he began to speak, a sound on the staircase turned Kuhlman's attention. Jack Wentworth, the chief of airport security, huffed up the steps to stare wild-eyed at the confusion. "What's happening? All the flight boards in the lobby have 'Delay' all over them, and passengers are starting to get excited. What are those little planes doing out there?" Wentworth's small black eyes were alight in his pasty round face.

"Get your people together," Kuhlman began. "First—"

Atlanta tower," the loudspeaker grated, "*while the birds taxi, we will give you your final instructions for this time.*"

"Hold it," Kuhlman said, and wheeled back to the board. He picked up the microphone again. "Go ahead."

"*Atlanta, you will contact the following airlines: Delta. Southern. Northwest. Each has one or more planes on the field at the present time. Each airline will deliver one million dollars to the field, in a suitcase, within one hour. The*

100

cash will be delivered in police cars clearly marked with flashing red lights. When the three million dollars has been delivered, you will notify us for further instructions."

Kuhlman frowned into the sudden silence. Then he thumbed the mike angrily, "Cherokee leader, nobody can come up with that kind of money in an hour! Clarify! Over!"

"One hour," the voice came back. "If the money is not here in one hour, we will destroy one aircraft. We will destroy an additional aircraft every fifteen minutes until our demand has been met."

The loudspeaker fell silent. One of the small planes thundered close overhead, slightly shaking the tower structure. Kuhlman looked at the men around him. Their eyes showed a bafflement and shock as deep as his own.

"Jesus," someone whispered reverently.

"They can't get away with this!" someone else said.

No one answered that, and Kuhlman knew they were thinking as he was in response. Of course the Cherokees couldn't get away with it. The whole operation was absurd —a fairy tale.

But *how* were they going to stop it?

5:10 P.M.

Tom Keel slammed the Cherokee into a tight bank, holding the pattern and his scant altitude. The turn put him directly into the setting sun, and he could not see Donovan's Cherokee somewhere ahead of him. The fleeting possibility of a midair collision shot through his mind, but he had to reject it in the same moment; their practice had been careful, they knew their throttle and pitch settings, and he had had good spacing behind Donovan at the tower turn. There was enough to worry about without falling into panic because the sun momentarily made the windshield a golden blur.

Not that he was unable to see in other directions. The ground screamed under the nose at the kind of frightening proximity that Keel might not have been able to endure for

101

long if it had not been for the training in Vietnam. He could see the big jets turtling along toward taxiway Delta, and then there was the flash of a runway beneath the nose, and yellowed grass, and he was almost into the next turn, because he saw the smoky Interstate, now clogging with traffic, up ahead. At the same moment he caught sight of Donovan's Cherokee out the right side; it had made its turn and streaked back toward the tower.

The noise of the engine and wind rushing through the open cargo door was fantastic and unrelenting. Keel tried to keep it screened out as much as possible. They had been over the field only a few minutes, and the scantest glance at the panel clock showed they had fifty-five minutes to go before the first deadline. It was going to get much tougher. He had to stay on top of the airplane every moment and yet try to conserve as much of himself as possible.

He hauled the Cherokee into another right turn, feeling the pressure of an extra G pull at his face and gut. Coming out, he relaxed pressure on the control yoke ever so slightly to maintain altitude, and took a fresh bead on the tower. He could see the figures in the tower. It was very doubtful that they could even attempt to make out his features, but he no longer left quite so foolish about Donovan's final precautionary measure.

Behind him, strapped in the rear seat, MacReady yelled hoarsely, "Look! They're really doing it! They're doing just what we told 'em!"

Keel nodded but did not try to yell back. He adjusted course very slightly—no more than a relaxation of a finger pressure—and watched the tower zoom up bigger and bigger and closer and closer in the windshield, and then he eased back a bit and touched right aileron and rudder and went by on the right side. No closer than that, he told himself. That was close enough.

Coming around, he got a glimpse of Abercrombie's Cherokee well behind him, going into its turn at the west end, near the Interstate. It looked very pretty, and Keel was struck by the fact that already the crazy circuits had begun to be almost a routine. The wind roared, the engine crashed into his ears, and the full-on radio volume spattered static at him in a continuous wave. But it was working.

He flashed over the Delta maintenance facility, with the darkening eastern sky ahead and the millions of little house roofs closer in, and this was the time he could allow himself the briefest instrument scan. Everything was normal, well inside the green. He got his attention back on the course then. Around and around. He wondered what they were doing on the ground.

5:13 P.M.

Ward, the man who usually sat comfortably in the No. 1 tollbooth and made sure the cars were all paying properly, stood on the pavement and watched nervously as the two airport security officers hauled the white sawhorse out in front of the exit lane. There was already one in place on the far side, and somebody had gone farther out, toward the highway, to put up more of the same.

A woman in a white station wagon drove up to the gate, stopping near the sawhorse. She was attractive, a blonde. She stuck her head out the window.

Ward walked over.

"Will you move that, please?" She smiled. "I'm in kind of a hurry."

"I'm sorry, ma'am," Ward told her. "We have to have this blocked for right now. Security problem."

"Well, can I go around the other way?"

"No, ma'am, I'm afraid not."

You mean I'm just supposed to *sit* here?"

"Well, for right now, yes, ma'am. I'm sorry."

"Look," she said. "I have two little children at home. I just put my husband on a plane and I have to get right home. What's going on? Why can't I leave?"

"I'm sorry, ma'am. We'll open up just as soon as we can."

She stared at Ward. "I just have to *sit* here?"

"I'm afraid so."

103

She leaned back and clenched her fists on the steering wheel. "Shit," she said. Then she realized she had said it aloud, and moved quickly to straighten up her image. "Darn!" she said, as if that were what she had meant in the first place.

Two more cars had nudged up behind her wagon. Ward walked tiredly back to give them the bad news too.

5:15 P.M.

Ted Kuhlman stood in the lower level of the tower with Barbara McIntyre, security man Jack Wentworth, and a uniformed Atlanta policeman who had already arrived on the scene. The fluorescent tubing in the low ceiling glittered on the policeman's badge and buttons. He was young and pale, with a film of sweat on his face that gleamed too.

"You get downstairs," Kuhlman told Barbara, "and get through to those three airlines. Give them the score without holding anything back, and tell them what the demand is. I'll get down there to be available to talk to them further just as soon as I can—five or ten minutes."

Barbara nodded. "If they have more questions—?"

"I'll get back to them just as fast as I can."

"Right." She started to turn away.

"Wait," the policeman said. "You don't expect anybody to *give in* to this kind of terror tactic, do you?"

"I haven't gotten that far," Kuhlman snapped. "Right now I'm relaying demands. I haven't had time to get anything straight in my mind yet."

"They won't pay the money," the policeman said.

"Maybe," Kuhlman said. "Airline policy, officer, is to give the hijackers whatever they want, and not to risk passengers and crew."

"This isn't exactly a hijacking! This is more a—a—"

"Whatever you call it, I've got probably more than a thousand people stuck out there on taxiway Delta inside airplanes, and another five thousand or so in this terminal.

104

Not to mention the hundreds of millions of dollars in equipment. I'm relaying the demands. *Go*, Barbara!"

She turned and hurried out.

"If you ask me," the policeman said, "what we ought to do is shoot those buzzards out of the sky."

"With what?" Kuhlman snapped. "Your service revolver?"

"We could bring in machine guns."

"If you don't shoot them down simultaneously, the ones still in the air take out an airplane or two and part of the terminal. No, thanks."

"We could bring in the riot squad—"

The telephone on the worktable next to them rang sharply. Wentworth picked it up and snapped his name. "Yes sir. That's right. No. he's standing right here." He handed the telephone to Kuhlman. "FBI downtown."

"Why aren't they here yet?" Kuhlman asked. "Hello?"

"We're not there yet," the heavy voice grated, "because it takes a few minutes to get a team together and haul them out there. But they're on the way now."

"They can't drive in," Kuhlman said. "We—"

"I understand, I understand. They'll drive in close and then come the rest of the way on foot, scattered. As dark as it's getting, your fellers in the plane won't see them. My name is Crutchfield, by the way."

"Well, this is Kuhlman. Sorry if I yelled at you."

"It sounds like you've got something to yell about."

"You know most of what's going on?"

"The other call gave me enough. Three planes over the field, right? Armed, and carrying dynamite or something similar. What are they doing right now? What's the demand?"

"They're still orbiting at damned low altitude, and they want a million dollars each from Delta, Southern, and Northwest."

"How delivered?" Crutchfield didn't even sound surprised.

"Three suitcases."

105

"And from there?"

"They'll tell us when we notify them the money is here."

"How long do we have?"

"An hour. More like fifty minutes—forty-five minutes—now."

There was a low whistle. "You've notified the airlines?"

"They're being called now."

"All right. I'd like somebody to open a line between your office and mine, Mr. Kuhlman, and keep it open for information. I'll notify Washington. Then I'll contact the affected airlines, too. As soon as my team gets there, we'll have two-way radio communication."

Crutchfield's calm pressed Kuhlman to the wall. He let some of his own tension out. "The airlines will pay, won't they? I mean, you aren't going to try to screw things up, are you?"

"We won't get anybody hurt if we can help it, sir. Right now we have lots of time and lots of options, right?"

"We've got forty-five minutes, I told you! Good Christ, man. We don't even know if the airlines can get that much money together in time! Is there that much cash money in Atlanta banks on this kind of notice?"

"I don't know," Crutchfield said, and he sounded amused. "Do you suppose they'd take a check?"

5:18 P.M.

Haynes Talliaferro, a journeyman reporter for the Associated Press in downtown Atlanta, was watching a cost-of-living story coming in on the national trunk when the telephone rang. He was closest and he answered it. It was a friend at the police station.

"Hi, Benny, old boy," Talliaferro said. "What's up?"

Benny talked low and fast, as if he weren't supposed to be telling tales out of school.

"You're kidding," Talliaferro said huskily. "You're kidding me, Benny," he repeated after a moment. Then, "Good *God!* Benny, thanks, buddy. Thanks!"

Talliaferro broke the connection, sweatily looked up the number of the FBI, and dialed it.

The agent told him, "We aren't releasing anything on it."

"Then it's true?" Talliaferro said.

"No comment."

"It's true, then!"

"Sir, when we have something to say on the situation, you'll be notified."

The young reporter hung up and rushed across the room to his typewriter.

"Jake?" he yelled delightedly. "You better get this one from me in takes, boy!"

Talliaferro was beside himself with glee. He had never gotten to write a flash lead before. He typed:

FLASH   FLASH

Three small civilian aircraft over Atlanta International Airport at this time, armed, with guns. Airport paralyzed. Pirates want unknown hijack ransom from airlines or blow up a plane.

MORE   MORE

Jake, the bureau chief, nightside, was an old hand. He moseyed over to see what Talliaferro was typing. Jake took one look and tore the sheet of paper out of the typewriter. He glared at Talliaferro.

"You're sure about this?"

"Yep!"

"You checked?"

"Hell, yes!"

"I'm going to check again."

Traffic in and around Atlanta was near its peak. The sun was well into the west, almost on the horizon, making dark canyons of downtown streets. Out on the Interstates and expressways, cars were bumper-to-bumper; a light haze of exhaust fumes made headlights bluish, and tempers were getting frayed.

A great many drivers had their radios on.

Several stations broke into recorded music, or more routine news, within seconds of each other.

Reactions varied.

A great many listeners experienced shock and said, "They'll do anything!" without defining who "they" might be.

Others felt anger, or disgust, or something akin to fear, while others felt a pang of concern and thankfulness, saying, "I'm glad *I'm* not out there right now!"

Some others reacted quite differently, saying, in effect, "I want to see this for myself," so that almost immediately traffic toward the airport began to thicken.

5:24 P.M.

His coat and tie off and shirtsleeves rolled to the elbows, Ted Kuhlman strode across the large reception area outside his office. It had magically become sheer chaos, a nerve center for a battle that no one yet knew how to define.

"All right, God damn it," he said. "Let's get organized around here!"

As usual, no one paid much attention to him. Ordinarily it didn't matter, because the loud voice was just part of the image. Old-timers in aviation were expected to yell and cuss occasionally. This time, however, the people in the room paid little attention because of the thick cloak of tension all around them.

At the main reception desk, both telephones were alight with blinkers showing calls on hold. Barbara was talking on one line, standing beside the desk, and another secretary named Saundra was behind the desk and talking on another. Jack Wentworth, the security man, had left the room to brief the airport guards on duty, but Fezzard from plant maintenance, Nash from food services, and Epsteen, who directed baggage services, had been summoned and were here. So was the airport public relations and publicity man, Mack Palmdale. And Rollie Stoner had come down from his post as shift supervisor in the tower.

Kuhlman paced and talked to them over the chatter of the two women fighting the telephones. "We're going to have crowds backing up and a lot of people asking a lot of questions and probably getting short-tempered. We'd better try to keep employees overtime in the restaurants and snack bars. Fez, that's your department; get around to everybody as fast as you can and explain that we'll have an extra crush because nobody is getting out."

Nash, a burly man, said, "I can help him."

"Sure," Kuhlman said. "But your whole schedule for servicing all the airlines is screwed up as of right now. Handle that first. In the same way, baggage is going to be hopelessly screwed up. Deal with that the best way you can.

"The point, though, is not how our housekeeping gets messed up. We can get it straightened out. The point is, we've got an honest-to-God emergency here. The people in this airport are going to start asking a lot of hard questions—"

"They've already started," Palmdale said. He was a small, youthfully elegant man with a good mind. "As soon as your orders got to all the passenger loading areas to get all the people off airplanes at the loading ramps, the questions started hot and heavy."

"Not only that," Fezzard added. "On the way here I noticed that we've got a real jam-up on the B Concourse. Everybody was streaming off that Delta 747 and they overflowed the passenger lobby area. Then we unloaded a couple of 707s and a couple more 727s and God knows what all, and that concourse looks like Bourbon Street on New Year's Eve."

"We'll have to get an announcement on the public address system as fast as we can," Kuhlman said.

"They're bombarding all the ticket desks with questions right now."

"Right," Kuhlman growled, feeling the pressure build. "I'll have to get a batch call to all the airline desks both here and downtown right away, make sure they know what the score is. We want people informed so they won't bitch, but we can't let them think they're in real danger or we might have a panic. The last thing we need is a stampede for the exits."

"How long is this going on?" Palmdale asked.

"I don't know, exactly. We have—"

"Boss?" Barbara called.

He turned to see that she was holding out a telephone to him.

"Delta," she told him.

Kuhlman went to the phone. "Hello!"

"Ted, this is Ebbets at Delta downtown. How are you? Is everything the same there?"

"It's the same, sir. Which is to say, not too good. You've got the demand they sent through our tower?"

"Yes." Ebbets, a top-ranking vice-president for Delta, sounded quite controlled. "You know our policy, Ted. We have the money available and a man is already with the banker. We're rushing it through."

Kuhlman closed his eyes. He was getting a headache. "It gripes my ass, sir, but I don't quite know what to do but give it to them."

"We've already had a quick meeting of the minds down here, all of us who could get together quickly. It gripes us too, Ted. But we're not risking passenger or crew lives. Not to mention aircraft. If it comes to a showdown, our cash will be in your office to hand over to these people."

"How long will it take to get the suitcase out here?"

"You'll have it within thirty minutes. I understand the police car is already standing by to bring us out."

Kuhlman felt a tingle of surprise. "You're coming yourself?"

110

"It isn't every day a man gets to flush a million dollars, Ted. I'll see you in a little while."

Kuhlman hung up. Saundra shot him a pleading glance. "Will you talk to United Press International?"

"No, damn it," Kuhlman said, "and I won't talk to AP or CBS or NBC or anybody else, either!" He swung around on Palmdale. "You've got to get some of your office staff back in here—"

"I don't *have* an office staff," Palmdale said pitiably.

"Then *get* one! You've got to get out a release on what's going on, and right now. You've got to handle all these news people. Saundra, all media calls go to Mack's office. Also, Mack, I want you to rough out a statement I can get on the PA system with to tell everybody here what's going on. But try to make it reassuring without pulling punches. Get on it. Find somebody to help you."

"What," Palmdale asked, "will I tell them?"

"The people you ask to help you?"

"No! I can find some help. I mean—what will I say in the text for you to read? Or what do I tell the media people?"

"The truth."

"The truth?" Palmdale looked stunned.

"Right. The truth. The truth. Just don't make it sound worse than it is, right? We aren't trying to start a riot here. Just make it straight, but calm. Get on it!"

Palmdale looked around the room. "I'll need a stenographer . . . and somebody to help answer the telephone—" He was slightly dazed.

"Boss?" Barbara said from the desk again. She had another phone. "The police."

Kuhlman turned to Fezzard and the others, who still stood there. "Go ahead and get on with what you have to do. Remember, the one thing we *can't* have is a panic."

"What about people who are irate?" Epsteen asked.

"If that's all we had to worry about—" Kuhlman began, then broke off. He gave Epsteen a leer. "Have them line up at luggage information center. Give them a form to fill out or something. Just keep them busy any way you can. Go!"

111

He turned and grabbed the telephone from his secretary. "Hello!"

It was the chief of police. He was in the mayor's office. The mayor was on an extension. They wanted to know the "current status." The mayor was concerned. Kuhlman said he was, too. The chief said he had as many cars as possible on the expressways around the airport, and was working on a plan to get as many men as possible onto the grounds without being observed. He started saying things about hand-held machine guns and antipersonnel devices.

"Wait a minute, wait a minute!" Kuhlman said. *"None of that stuff!"*

"We're trying to beef up the area, Mr. Kuhlman—"

"And those planes. If they see any of your beefing up, who pays the funeral expenses if they cut loose on one of the airliners?"

"We're not doing a thing without full agreement of all parties concerned, sir." This was the mayor and he sounded stiff-lipped. "But you're not alone in this. You have full support."

"If you want to support me," Kuhlman shot back angrily, "keep all the patrolmen and cars and machine guns and bazookas and everything else clear the hell *away* from this area! We can't afford any provocation."

"Provocation? This is a matter of preparedness—law enforcement—"

"My ass. We've talked to the airlines involved, at least those who have to cough up money. They're going to cooperate. We can get out of this thing without any more trouble if we go along. There's nothing else we can do."

There was a brief silence. Then the mayor came on. "Naturally, Ted, the city of Atlanta will act responsibly. You can be sure no action will be taken without full coordination of all involved agencies. We only want you to know the steps that must be taken, and are being taken."

"Get somebody out *here* to coordinate it, then," Kuhlman said. "You can't do it downtown. In the meantime, don't do *anything!*" He hung up.

112

Barbara held out another telephone.

"No," he said, and took her wrist instead. "Come in my office a minute."

"But this is—"

"Come *on!*"

Startled, she put the telephone down with a clatter and followed him.

He slammed the office door closed behind her. "Do you know what's going to happen?" he demanded. "I'll tell you what. The city and the federal people and my own security guards and everybody else are going to go ape and blow this whole thing wide open. Everybody's got his own little counterattack already set in motion. And *nobody is in charge.* It's already starting. That was the mayor with *his* little plan."

Barbara was pale, with bright spots of nervous color in her cheeks that looked far too vivid, but she tried to keep her voice steady and almost succeeded. "You're excited. Nothing bad has happened yet, and if the airlines bring the money—"

"They'll bring it," Kuhlman snapped back. "But all the law people are starting to run around like maniacs. It's going to be like Los Angeles, where they shot the tires out, or Miami when the sharpshooters cut loose at the men in the door. Passengers and crew get killed that way. But here we don't have just one airplane, even. I've got *all* these planes —all the lives of the people inside here—"

"We'll just have to meet the demands," Barbara said.

"*If* we can keep all the law agencies in line, yes! But how do we do that?"

"Are you sure there isn't some way to stop this thing safely, without giving up the money? I mean, if someone has a really workable idea—"

"Name me one," he shot back at her.

"Well . . ." She hesitated, frowning. "If the police could shoot from the ground—"

"And hit three planes simultaneously? Because if you hit only one, or even two, the remaining one can drop something right on top of this terminal. Did you ever consider how some areas of this terminal might hold up to a nice little aerial bombing?"

"If two planes were crippled," Barbara said, "the third would probably try to run for it."

"While the other two were busy crashing on the terminal, or on taxiway Delta," Kuhlman said. "Right."

"Military fighters, then," she countered. "They could come in."

"Those things work all right several miles straight up. How good would they be a hundred feet off the ground? And if they did cut loose with a rocket or something, how would *that* look inside the main lobby area?"

Barbara sighed and looked away. "There must be some method."

"There isn't. The only thing to do is give them their money and get them the hell out of here. *Then* try to catch them."

"You're probably right. If so, the thing to do is make sure that you do it precisely that way."

"*Me?*" he demanded. "How do *I* do that? I'm just the airport manager!"

"Somebody has to be in charge."

"Not me, babe. That's not *my* bag. I fill out reports and give Chamber of Commerce tours."

"Not in this case," she said, cooler now, implacable. "Someone has to be in charge. It's *your* airport, Ted. If someone is to have an ultimate responsibility, you're the one."

"I don't want that kind of charge. You know the public. A good number of them will say, 'To hell with the consequences; give us our law and order; shoot them down.' What if I do push myself right into control of the whole situation, and then these bandits get clean away? Then it's *my* ass."

Her eyes were remarkably clear as she stared at him. "If you *don't* risk your *ass*, as you so neatly put it, then didn't you just get through telling me that it's going to be the passengers' asses? Or the people in the lobby's asses? It looks to me like you're in charge whether you like it or not."

Kuhlman stared back at her. The enormity of his dilemma had just begun to make itself clear in his mind.

She smiled thinly. "So you're damned if you do, damned if you don't."

"Maybe," he said huskily, "it won't come to that."

She would not reply to that. She was so tough, mentally . . . so tough.

He paced a moment, then shelved the painful sense of impending ultimate choice. "Get to all the ticket agents," he ordered. "Fill them in. Raiders still over the field, ransom demanded, money on the way, no danger if everyone stays calm, et cetera, et cetera."

"You're going to make a PA announcement soon?"

"Yes, but get going anyway. The announcement might take a little while. What time is it? Christ!"

She fled, leaving the office door ajar. Kuhlman thought for a moment about the mess, and then again he found he could not quite face it squarely. He trudged into the other office.

There were several bulky men there. They were football types, with short haircuts and dark suits, most of them, and some had attaché cases and others—startlingly—had cases like those used for guitars and other musical instruments.

"What's this all about?" he asked as he saw two of the men raise the cases to a worktable and begin unsnapping fasteners.

One of the men, slightly older, detached himself from the group and came over. "Mr. Kuhlman? FBI. I'm Rickman, agent-in-charge of this detail."

Behind him, the men had continued opening cases, and Kuhlman felt new shreds of his control over the situation begin to peel away. From the cases, the agents were removing, in sections, sniper rifles and more complex weapons that looked like machine pistols.

"You're lucky it's near the fifteenth. At some other times in the month, you'd have to go to half the banks in Atlanta to come up with this kind of cash."

James Filson watched almost unbelievingly as the banker stacked the packages of money into the Samsonite suitcase. "I'm not sure I ever really believed there was this much cash around anyway."

The banker smiled without humor. "Thank the Federal Reserve system."

One of the two FBI agents standing in the vault with them said, "This is the complete list of serial numbers?" He was holding a sheaf of onionskin pages.

"No," the banker said. "There are eight lots here. Three are coded, and you have those on the first page, sequentially. The rest are only randomly recorded. That's why you have all the individual numbers."

"If we had time to go to New Orleans, we could use prepared money."

The possibility of any further delay gave Filson a stomach twinge. "We've discussed that. We won't delay."

The FBI agent's eyes were like opaque glass. "I know, sir. Just thinking out loud."

"You'll just have to stop them when they start their escape. Or track them down."

The FBI agent did not respond. He riffled the thin pages. Then he turned and handed them to his aide. "Get these over to Center. Go ahead and transmit the numbers, contingency basis."

The other man nodded and left the vault.

"What did that mean?" Filson asked.

"If we stop them on their way out of the area, there's no problem. But in the meantime, we'll start circulating number lists nationally. That's in case they do get out of here with it."

"You'll try to catch them when they spend the money?"

"Among other things."

116

It occurred to Filson that he might ask what the "other things" included. He knew what kind of answer one usually got from law enforcement officers about their procedures. If they wanted to be extremely polite, they were only evasive.

Filson continued to watch his company's million dollars go into the suitcase.

At the same time, on the southwest side of Oklahoma City, one of the "other things" was being started. Aircraft registration numbers of the three Cherokees had been copied by Atlanta tower and transmitted to both the FBI and the FAA. Information on aircraft registrations, pilot certification, and related matters were stored in the big computers used by the sprawling FAA facility near Oklahoma City's Will Rogers Airport. The Cherokee numbers were now on a photofax here. A special crew had been called in to find these particular numbers in the printouts which the computers, at this moment, were beginning to churn out.

Other preparations were being made in Washington. Agents were being reassigned and charts studied. Telephone wires were hot. A special small jet was on order to carry four top-level hijack emergency supervisors into the Atlanta area—although there was no chance they could arrive before the deadline imposed by the bandits.

At a civilian field northwest of Atlanta, meanwhile, four National Guard helicopters took off, like gigantic brown spiders, their flashing lights clotted together as they rose over the south fence and headed for an area where their emergency orders told them to wait for further instructions. And farther west, in the green-blue-white maze of a military installation's runways, three Phantom jet fighters taxied for takeoff, the reflections of their own rotating beacons creating weird bright reflections on their sleek, shark-like hulls. They prowled in the shimmering distortions of their own heat, giving off a high-pitched scream of sheer power and readiness.

The expressways near the airport had clogged, and no traffic moved. As he banked sharply over the west end, Jack Abercrombie had a moment's glimpse of police cars in the melee, and officers on foot, trying to get cars onto exit ramps. The sun was a red ball on the horizon, and in another few minutes it would be dark.

Twilight would be a relief to Abercrombie's scorched eyes. But he dreaded it, too. The time was just about half gone now. Were they preparing to deliver, down there on the ground, or laying a trap? Had he and the others overlooked an angle? As he had so many times before, he tried to find out . . . failed.

It did no good to worry this way now. They were fully committed and had gone much too far for turning back. But this knowledge could not quite convince his mind.

Easing over on the yoke and rudder, he cleared the tower on yet another pass and hurled the Cherokee east and then southeast. He could see Keel out in front of him, turning over the far runway. A little close. Abercrombie touched the power, easing off perhaps 50 rpm; no time to look at gauges; it had to be all feel.

Behind him, Phil Lester had moved to the far back seat to try to avoid the fierce wind-blast from the open cargo door. Lester's AK–47 was on the floor of the plane in front, and so was the rest of the dynamite. Maybe they would not have to consider using it again. They had counted on using it only as a bluff. Despite the variety store Halloween mask, Lone Ranger style, worn by all of them as a hedge against the remote possibility of a super telephoto lens picture taken from the tower, Abercrombie felt nothing at all like a real bandit. Phil Lester, slumped against the remnants of the roaring wind, looked even less like one. He was a Walter Mitty figure trapped in a TV melodrama. If it came to using the gun or the dynamite, the masks would only make them more ridiculously aware of their own real shortcomings.

Of all the aspects of the operation, it was this one that

118

Abercrombie had never fully faced. If it came to *using* the guns or explosives, he simply did not know what he could do. He sensed that Lester felt the same, because they had walked up to the topic, in their conversations, and then just as rapidly walked around it.

Abercrombie did not think he could go through with it, if the situation eroded to a choice.

But what was he going to do if Donovan gave the order and then led the attack? What if Keel's plane, too, took aim on one of those fat, sleek, pathetic big jets parked below? Could a man go through with it, knowing there were innocent people below? Could he *refuse* to go through with it, knowing the rest of the team depended on him?

It was the old dilemma, the one that tasted faintly, acridly, of Nam. Would it be that kind of reflex here? Abercrombie didn't know. But he was soaked with sweat despite the loud, cool wind, and his whole body sang out with tension pain, and he was becoming more and more a part of, and one with, this airplane and Phil Lester's figure behind him and the tactical problem at hand, and the team. He did not want to think about doing it. He did not want to do it. He did not think he could. But he might. It could come to that. It had before, in Nam.

5:35 P.M.

In the cockpit of United Flight 396, parked fourth in the long line of jets on taxiway Delta, Captain Bill Roberts leaned back from the bank of instruments and switches before him and sipped his coffee disgustedly. "Even the damned coffee isn't right."

In the seat at Roberts's right, Charles Tabbah, his second-in-command, turned from peering out the tight side window. "They're still going around and around."

Roberts slapped his flattened palm on the yoke. "And we won't get to Milwaukee till morning. Jesus!"

The bulkhead door behind them opened and the chief

stewardess came in coolly, closing the thin door behind her as she stepped into the narrow aisleway. She was a leggy blonde.

Roberts turned in his seat. "How are they doing back there, Ruth?"

She sighed. "Well, we're serving drinks and snacks. They're nervous, but I think most of them are more fascinated than scared—so far."

"I'd like to have some new poop to give them, but the tower is still silent."

"When do you expect word?"

"Maybe when those clowns up there run out of gas. I don't know." Roberts was more worried than he was showing; all he was allowing out were the irritation and impatience.

"They're on their second drinks back there, some of them," Ruth said. "Do you think we could just go ahead and serve a third?"

Roberts exchanged glances with Tabbah. "Give them a third if they ask," he said, "and make it on the house. Just watch them. We can't have anybody getting sick or sloppy drunk if we can avoid it."

Ruth smiled stiffly. "They'll probably make you pay for the extra drinks, you know."

"Well, hard come, easy go." Roberts thought about it. "I think I might make another announcement, Ruth, if in your opinion it would settle them down any."

"Either that," she suggested, "or one of you could walk through, to show we aren't in any panic up here."

"We talked about that, but it's a little unusual and they might misinterpret it. Let me get my thoughts together and I'll come on with some friendly words in a minute."

"Yes, sir." She turned to leave, then turned back. "More coffee?"

"When you have time."

"Right."

The door closed firmly behind her.

Roberts told Tabbah, "Except for the one transmission, we don't have any real information. The tower can't talk. I think every plane in this lineup is in the same shape: we don't *know* anything, but we have to act like we do."

Tabbah nodded. "I guess you can say we're still holding, and hope to get going soon."

Roberts frowned and thought about it. Finally he reached for the microphone that connected him to the internal PA system in the jet. He paused, formulated his thoughts, and then pressed the button.

"This is the captain speaking," he said super-softly. "We are still holding here on taxiway Delta while the tower gets things sorted out. You can see from your windows that we have some unauthorized small aircraft over the field at the present time, and until the tower can get them landed safely, we're sitting tight here. There's nothing to be alarmed about, just one of those funny things that happen to you sometimes on the way to Milwaukee. We expect things to be cleared up shortly, and then we'll be on the way. In the meantime, if you have any questions, please don't hesitate to ask your stewardess. Relax, folks, and we'll make up this delay once we're in the air again. Thank you."

Roberts closed the microphone and snapped it back on its hitch. He looked at Tabbah.

"Very reassuring." Tabbah smiled.

"Who's going to reassure *me?*" Roberts countered quietly.

5:38 P.M.

As he walked back toward his office along a seldom-used overhead catwalk, Ted Kuhlman could look down into one of the main lobby areas. The broad, tiled area was much more densely populated than normal. There were long lines at the ticket counters, and other people milled out the exit doors. He saw servicemen, elderly couples, lone businessmen, and the inevitable families with small children. There was no sign of panic, and he hoped his announcement had helped.

I don't know how much longer you're going to be

121

penned up in here, he thought. *And I'm not sure what's going to be happening before we're through. But you do your part and I'll try to do mine. I'll try to take care of you.*

It was a conscious thought, and it had much affection and worry in it. Through the years—all the airports, all the crowds, all the problems, all the planes—these people had become the fabric of Ted Kuhlman's life. He realized how much they meant to him—the faceless crowds that one shoved through, taking them from comfortable family cars, insulating them from outside reality though the machinery of ticket counters and baggage handling and television scheduling boards and searches and departure lounge procedures, and then putting them into the big planes through the surreal moving tunnels. They were not only a part of his life; in many ways they had become his life. In a way—and this was embarrassing—he loved them.

They were very innocent in many ways. Right now they were depending upon him and didn't even know it. Just like the people out there in the parked aircraft, their well-being might depend to a large degree on how he could handle things in the next . . . he glanced nervously at his watch . . . thirty minutes.

Heading down the corridor toward his office, he met Rickman, the FBI agent-in-charge, hurrying in the opposite direction. Rickman stopped abruptly. "Good talk on the PA."

"I told them nothing," Kuhlman pointed out.

"Yeah, but you made them feel better."

"I hope so."

"I've been on the phone. None of your money is here yet, but all three airlines have it either on the way or being collected. It looks like they'll all make it."

"They'd better," Kuhlman said.

"Listen. I was coming to look for you. I need a master plan of this building and a detailed chart of the whole field."

"I've got a runway diagram in my office, on the wall."

"I know. I need something more detailed."

"There might be something in my office safe."

Rickman nodded. "Good. Can we check that out now?"

Kuhlman started on toward the office, the FBI agent beside him. "What do you need the plans and charts for, if I may ask?"

"We have to coordinate some things." Rickman said evasively. "You never can tell where all the best observation spots, et cetera, might be. Using a good chart, I can possibly get some better ideas."

"The airlines are sending the cash," Kuhlman said carefully.

"I know that."

There's no need, is there, for any kind of coordinated action by the law at this point? I mean, we give them the money and they get the hell out of here."

"Maybe so," Rickman said. "Maybe not."

"What do you mean by *that?*"

"I mean I'm waiting for more orders from Washington. The situation is unclear. In the meantime, my orders are to take all actions I think necessary to be ready to carry out whatever decisions finally get made."

They had reached the door of Kuhlman's office suite. He stopped and confronted Rickman. "Look. There are too many lives at stake here. I don't want to have any half-cocked actions against those Cherokees. We've already talked over a dozen possible courses of action, and all of them are too dangerous."

Rickman fished around for a cigar, found one, frowned as he lighted it, and blew smoke. "Look, Mr. Kuhlman. Better minds than ours are at work on this problem. Me, I take orders. In the meantime, I get ready in every way I can. That doesn't mean I'm going to do anything on my own. I'm not crazy."

Kuhlman tapped the agent's chest with his index finger. "I don't want any action without my knowing about it first. I'm responsible."

"You have my assurance."

Slightly relieved, Kuhlman pushed the office door open. "Let's go get to the vault and see what—" He stopped.

The outer office was empty except for Barbara and Saundra, still answering Christmas-tree telephones. "Where *are* they?" Kuhlman demanded.

"Who?" Rickman said. "Oh. My men, you mean?"

"Hell yes, I mean your men!"

"I've deployed them."

"Deployed them!"

Rickman gestured with his cigar hand. "To be in position. That's standard. Don't worry. They have walkie-talkies, and they're good men. They don't take chances and they don't do anything without precise authorization."

"Where *are* they? God, man!"

"Some are down in the lower baggage ramp area," Rickman said calmly. "Four others, with sniperscopes, will start moving out onto the field within the next few minutes, just as soon as we're sure it's dark enough that those clowns upstairs can't spot them crawling. But don't worry. Don't worry. We're not going to do anything on our own. We're not savages, Mr. Kuhlman."

5:40 P.M.

There were five men in the room in downtown Washington. Spread on the big table were charts of the Atlanta area, rosters of available personnel, and programs for several contingency plans. One of the men stabbed the big chart with a pencil.

"We'll have the fighters on top," he said. "The helicopters roughly here, here, here, and here. We may get six more in position in time, but we can't count on that."

"Radar is clearing all other traffic completely out of the area?" another man asked.

"If possible. They're having a bad time of it. So many flights from all directions, not to mention a lot of small civilian aircraft both under the tires of the TCA and outside its boundaries."

"It's important to have it cleared. If we can track them

on radar, assuming they get out of there, then we have an excellent chance."

"If they stay low," another man said, "radar might not be able to track."

"It's the best shot we have," someone else said.

"What about trying to take them when they pick up the money?"

"Assuming they land one at a time, which we can safely guess they'll do, the risks will be very great."

"We have people on the scene?"

"Yes. Crutchfield is at the downtown office, maintaining contact."

"Who's in charge at the airport?"

"Rickman."

"I don't know him."

"He's a good man."

There was a brief silence.

The supervisor said, "Rickman may be a good man, but Crutchfield is senior. He's been through something like this before in Miami. I'd like him at the airport so he can make judgment firsthand. There might be some close timing and split-second decisions to make. I'd trust Crutchfield's judgment in a situation like that."

"There may still be time to get him out there," someone said.

"We still have the line open to his office, don't we?"

"Yes."

"Well, let's order him to head for the airport personally, immediately. When he gets there, he'll coordinate our end of things." The speaker paused and looked around the room glumly. "If we have snipers on the ready, and all the rest of it, I want it to be Crutchfield who makes the final decision."

"I'll go talk to him right now, and tell him to get out there and take over."

"Good. Now, the rest of you. What do you have on that plane's range and performance data? And have we heard anything yet from the FAA?"

"—and so, at this very hour, a cloak of terror hangs over Atlanta's William B. Hartsfield International Airport," the car radio sang out. "Our man on the scene, Jerry Adams, reports there are three small planes, said to be Piper Cherokee aircraft. They are making continuous passes over the field at an extremely low altitude which may be dangerous in itself. That is a quote from Jerry Adams. Meanwhile, Atlanta police denied reports that one or more planes on the field had been damaged by an earlier explosion of uncertain origin. Police say the bandit aircraft are demanding ransom money. Stay tuned to this station for continuing coverage."

A singing commercial cut in. Hennigan reached out a burly hand and cut the radio off.

All around Hennigan's car, the tremendous traffic tie-up continued. His Buick was in the right-hand lane, and had not moved an inch for fifteen minutes. He was not irritated by this, because his spot gave him what he had come for: a perfect view of the airport from the east side. He could still make out the swooping little planes in the gathering gloom, and he could also see the great hulking shadows of the jets parked in the middle of the field, and the lights of the terminal area.

Hennigan was very angry.

The world was like this today, he thought. There was no more respect for law and order. And authorities did nothing about it. Right now, police should be shooting these little airplanes out of the sky. Instead, they were doing absolutely nothing. Each of the little white planes banked directly over Hennigan's position as they reached the easternmost point of their patch over the field, and he could have picked one of them off himself simply by getting the hunting rifle out of the trunk and finding a place to rest the stock for careful aiming. Why were the police taking it lying down?

It was part of today's permissive atmosphere, Hennigan thought bitterly. People did not care anymore. It was anything goes. Now it had gotten so bad that pirates—*flying pirates!*—could come right into a city like Atlanta and terrorize anyone they wished.

And where were the police?

Out having coffee somewhere, probably. Or directing traffic downtown. But they weren't here. They were never around when a citizen really needed them. Was it actually possible that they were *part* of the conspiracy? No. Hennigan rejected this view as too radical. But the fact remained that these air pirates were having it all their own way. No one was doing anything. And he and all these other law-abiding people were forced to sit here, helpless, in their darkened cars, waiting for the traffic jam to begin to break up.

Impatiently Hennigan turned the radio on again.

"—and this just in from the airport. Police say the pirates now circling the field have demanded a ransom in the neighborhood of 3 million dollars. That's 3 million dollars. The money is to be delivered within minutes, police added. In another development—"

Hennigan twisted the knob so violently that it broke off in his hand.

They were going to let the pirates get away with it. It was as simple as that. No one was going to do anything.

One of the small planes roared directly overhead, increasing Hennigan's rage.

He could shoot one of these planes down, he thought again. And probably one or two shots, even if the pilot were not injured, would be plenty to make the dirty coward turn tail and run for hiding.

And then Hennigan, as he often did out of frustration, translated the thought into fantasy and began playing it out in his mind. He would get the rifle from the trunk and go down the side of the road fill here. There was ammunition in the soft gun case, too. He could go through the big drainage pipe there to the far side of the culvert. He would be out of view of all the cars then. He could set up and wait. It was almost fully dark, but the planes were still quite visible banking overhead. They wouldn't see him.

But they would know when the steel-jacketed 30.06 slugs hit home.

Which would be beautiful. What they deserved. The cowards would run, then. And people would *see*. He would be a hero, the one man who had the guts to stand up for what was right, *done* something.

Of course it was dangerous. The gutless police would interfere, if they could. But after the deed was done, and he was proved right, no one could do anything.

It was a truly beautiful prospect.

Hennigan uncapped his fifth of Jim Beam and took another deep swallow.

5:43 P.M.

Tom Keel hauled the Cherokee through another turn. As he leveled, he shot another glance at the oil temperature gauge. It was a little higher. Still in the green, but inching toward the top end of the green now. In the advancing darkness with time running out, there was nothing he could do. Yet, if the needle went much higher something drastic might be required, and fast.

Some Lycoming engines ran hotter than others, Keel tried to tell himself. But while this was true, the engine was now running hotter than it had through any of the flight down, or the practices, or the short dispersal flight. It was not running correctly. It was showing signs of real danger.

Keel considered letting the others know. He resisted. Maybe it would be all right. It was not too hot yet. He would wait. He flew across the field, crossing over the parked airlines at an altitude of a hundred feet. His eyes kept going back to the gauge.

5:45 P.M.

Ted Kuhlman was alone in his office. Barbara came in without knocking.

128

"The FBI downtown just called," she said. "Crutchfield —the agent-in-charge for the area who called earlier—is on the way out here. He's in a radio car and he says he'll make it before six."

"By God," Kuhlman exploded with relief, "I hope so! If somebody else is going to take the responsibility, I want it to be the highest-ranking man we can find."

"What is the situation right now?" she asked worriedly.

"Static, as far as I can tell. All three airlines have the money on the way. But where the hell are they? We've got only fifteen minutes or so left!"

"The traffic is awful out there, from what I hear." Barbara was making him a fresh cup of instant coffee, for all the world as if it were a normal day around here.

"They're coming in police cars," Kuhlman reminded her. "If *they* can't make it, nobody can."

She brought the steaming cup to his desk. "They'll make it. There's time left."

"They'd better. My nerves can't take much more of this."

"And you don't act that nervous."

He looked up and met the quiet feminine admiration in her eyes. "Babe, I'm about to go bananas."

It broke some of the tension. She grinned at him. "I'll promise not to tell the rest of the help."

"If I had thought you would, I wouldn't have revealed it."

"You're an amazing man . . . the way you control your emotions."

"I don't control them. I just hide 'em. There's a big difference."

"People around here usually assume you have no feelings, except an occasional outburst of impatience. 'Our great stone leader,' they call you."

Kuhlman sipped the scalding black coffee. "Yeah. I know. I've heard 'em. That shows how much they know, huh?"

She was still leaning across the desk, watching him steadily. "Are you insinuating that I know any more?"

"You know me like a book, babe."

"Ha," she said.

"If anybody knows me, you do."

"And yet you've—never mind."

"No." he insisted. "Say it."

She nerved herself and almost glared. "And yet you hold me at arms' length, along with everyone else."

"I'm too tired to argue. But that's just good office management. You don't make friends too closely with anybody. Not when you're in charge."

"Are you every lonely?"

It was a straight question, no tricks in it anywhere, and a part of him cried out to answer straight—to say what he was feeling at this moment. But something held him back.

"I'm kind of lonely right now," he said. "Maybe you could get a couple more people in here for bridge?"

"You bastard."

The office door swung open again and Saundra stuck her head in. "Mr. Kuhlman, will you talk to Atlanta Center?"

It broke the moment between him and Barbara. She straightened, a careless hand touching up her hair.

"What line?" he asked.

"Four."

He punched a button. "Hello!"

"Ted?"

"Yes."

"Barclay here."

"What's up?"

"We've had some kind of a minor power surge here. It's knocked out the long-range scan on our radar."

"Oh, for Christ's sake!"

Kuhlman's reaction was immediate and instinctive, based more on the needs of the immediate future than on any instant complication. The radar facility had both close-range and long-distance scanning capabilities. This was because the Terminal Control Area centered on Atlanta was shaped like a gigantic inverted wedding cake. At its center, no aircraft off the ground were allowed to make a move without radar surveillance and permission. Five miles from

130

the center of the TCA, the "floor" was raised to 2,500 feet above ground level, to allow small aircraft to spook around, close in, below the level where the big jets' flight paths demanded positive control of all aircraft. Still farther out, the inverted-wedding-cake zone was raised again in terms of its floor, again to allow some maneuver below the altitude that demanded positive radar control. But the TCA required far-out contact, identification, and sequencing for aircraft at normal altitudes which intended to land at Atlanta. The TCA was the most stringent kind of control facility in the United States.

Now, with part of the radar out because of a damaging power surge, Atlanta might be handicapped in trying to get back into regular operation once the raid was over. Perhaps more important, Atlanta Approach Control would have little or no chance to try to track the attackers beyond thirty-five to forty miles.

"What can you do?" Kuhlman demanded.

"We've got everybody on it, Ted. Your tower has been notified. I thought you ought to be told personally."

"Okay. Thanks, I *think*. Keep me posted."

"Right."

Kuhlman hung up. "Radar is mostly out."

"Oh, my God," Barbara murmured in dismay.

"Yeah. Say it again. I'm—"

The telephone jangled, indicating Saundra had put another call through. Barbara deftly picked it up. "Yes?" She listened. Then she frowned and held the phone to her breast. "This is Wentworth. Several policemen have arrived. They came in on foot, I guess, like the FBI men did. They say they want to go out onto the ramp. They say it's dark enough now."

Kuhlman grabbed the phone. "Wentworth? Listen, damn it! You tell those cops to stay inside the building. I don't care what anybody says otherwise. You understand?" He slammed the phone down again.

"They're all trying to go ape," he said wearily.

"I think you stopped that one."

"Maybe."

"Shall I go see if any of the airline people have arrived yet?"

"No," he said. "Yes. Yes. Go ahead. They'd come here, surely. But go check. Also, make sure we have a couple of armed security guards up here. We'll stash the suitcases here momentarily, anyway. It would be really nice to get robbed right here in my office while we're waiting for our friends upstairs to finish giving us final instructions."

"I'll go see, and get two men, then."

He poured down the rest of his coffee as she hurried out of the room. She looked cool and unruffled, he thought, and the last glimpse was of decidedly nice legs. He wondered if anyone in his *right* mind would notice how attractive a woman's legs might be at a time like this. Maybe he *was* going crazy.

The telephone rang again.

"Hello!"

"Sir, this is Albright in the tower. We thought you ought to know. The Cherokees have just changed their pattern from a big oval to a figure 8."

"Why?" Kuhlman was mystified.

"Sir, we don't know. We can't figure it out. Maybe just to throw us off in terms of being able to predict their behavior."

"I'll be right up there."

The dim green lights had been switched on inside the tower, and beyond the bluish windows the world was almost completely dark. Off to the right, tangled traffic on the Interstate highways formed a glowing white snake with several arms extending out of the range of view. The sky had gone black.

After allowing himself a moment to let his eyes adjust, Kuhlman could make out the faces of the controllers sitting at the long, tiered console table. They had glanced around at him as he entered the steel doorway, now guarded by one of the airport security men, but they were watching the field again now.

The Cherokees, faintly visible at the same low altitude, had turned on their running lights and rotating red beacons.

132

Their new formation, a long figure 8, crossed over the aircraft parked on taxiway Delta. The new pattern did not bring the Cherokees quite so close to the terminal, but Kuhlman could see that the pattern allowed them surveillance as they passed nearest it. A very simple matter, to break off and still attack the terminal. The Cherokees had added to their element of unpredictablity by switching, and might change back—or to some new formation—at any time. Kuhlman had to admire their planning and skill.

One of the controllers got up from his swivel chair and walked over. "I'm Albright," he said quietly. "You can see how they've changed."

"Yes," Kuhlman said. "Unless this new pattern has something to do with the way they plan to pick up the money, I'd say they're just trying to keep us guessing."

"Is the money here yet, sir?"

"It's on the way."

Albright's youthful face set. "Then we are going to meet their demands."

"Was there ever any question in your mind, Albright?"

"I guess not, sir, actually."

"I notice they have their nav lights on now, too."

"That surprised me, but then I thought about it. I guess they have to be sure they can see each other, and to hell with whether it makes them more visible from down here."

Kuhlman considered it and saw that Albright had to be correct. "I think how well we can see them is the least of their worries."

Albright nodded. "I just hope, sir, they can't see those people crawling around out there in the grass."

"*What* people crawling around in the grass?"

"I assumed you knew. We could just barely make them out when they made their move a couple of minutes ago—I don't know if we can still see them or not—"

Kuhlman silenced him by grabbing his arm harder than he had intended. "*Show* me, man!"

Albright led him to the front glass, then peered down, frowning, at the vague gray pavement below and the nearly

133

invisible patches of grass beyond. Except for the areas immediately around runway lights, it was impossible to tell which was paved area and which was grass. It had gotten too dark now, and the whole area was a confusing maze of varied small lights, with blue taxiway lights predominating in a mixed pattern.

"I can't see them anymore." Albright said.

"What did they look like? Where were they headed?" Then Kuhlman thought he knew. "Did they have rifles—weapons of some kind?"

"Yes," Albright replied calmly, as if puzzled. "You *didn't* know?"

Kuhlman didn't reply. His anger was so great he could not trust his voice. He knew exactly what was happening. Rickman, as FBI agent-in-charge at the moment here, was exercising one of his options.

"There's one of them!" Albright said suddenly, and pointed.

"Where?"

"Beyond the taxiway. See him?"

Straining his eyesight along the line indicated by the controller's pointed finger, Kuhlman could make out nothing; only the confusion of brightly colored lights and a general grayness.

"Here, sir," the controller murmured, handing over some special binoculars. "These might help."

Kuhlman took them.

"Just beyond the taxiway."

Kuhlman moved the field of vision very slowly, fighting his impatience. The glasses seemed to add their own greenish-yellow illumination to the scene. He moved them along the edge of the pavement, and then he saw the man.

He was belly-down in the tufted grass that was allowed to grow almost wild between the runways. His clothing was dark, so he was hard to pick out, but he was moving slowly, crawling. He had a rifle or automatic weapon slung over his back. He was headed away from the tower—out toward distant runway 9L.

Kuhlman handed the binoculars back. "Jesus Christ. If those guys in the planes see him or his buddies—!"

"I don't think they can now, sir. It's really awfully dark, and they're busy flying their pattern."

"If they do, though," Kuhlman grated, "it means they'll attack."

"I thought this must be something you had authorized, as a contingency—"

"Do I look like the kind of fool who would send out infantry with rifles to fight a small air force?"

Albright was startled. "I didn't mean—"

"I know, I know," Kuhlman cut in bitterly. "Not your fault. You ought to be able to assume that the man in charge is . . . the man *in charge*. Unfortunately . . . well, God damn it, now we're in a mess. We've got to try to make sure those damned Cherokees don't spot Rickman's troops. But what can we do? Let me think a second."

He paced furiously. The Cherokees were lacing back and forth across the field in their figure-8 pattern. The chances were slim, as Albright had said, that any of the pilots would notice the FBI men crawling out. But it was possible. Something had to be done to divert as much attention as possible. What?

For a few moments, Kuhlman was crippled by the impotent rage going through him. Rickman had had no *right*. Of course he could reply that he was just doing his job. But that didn't mean he should have done it.

Again Kuhlman had that ugly feeling that everything was slipping out of control, like a wildly escalating international crisis where move brought automatic countermove, and that brought some new calculated risk of its own, and it built like a fire, feeding on itself—

But this wasn't doing any good. He had to deal with the immediate problem.

He made a decision. "Your transmitters are still on, of course?"

"Yes, sir."

Kuhlman strode around the desk to the nearest console,

shouldering the controller who was there out of his way. He pressed the ground control transmit button and spoke into the mike: "Cherokee leader, this is Kuhlman in the tower."

After an instant, the voice sang back over the loud-speakers, clear as before, a trifle high-pitched over engine noise. *"Go ahead."*

"Cherokee leader, we've got the money on the way. Repeat. All three airlines meet your demands. Money is on the way from downtown. It will be here in minutes. We would like to talk to the aircraft on the ground to give the captains information for reassuring passengers. Request your approval for this transmission on ground control frequency only."

"Atlanta, stand by one."

Kuhlman waited, his hand on the button. Console lights reflected dully from the dim illumination of the fixtures extending out on metal goosenecks from the top of the console.

They were taking no rash action, Kuhlman thought. Even this routine request brought consideration. He wondered if they were talking it over on a discreet frequency. Either way—discussion or waiting for their leader to make up his mind—he hoped they were slightly preoccupied by the information and the request, and would not scan the ground closely enough to pick up sight of the near-invisible FBI men.

The loudspeakers rasped: *"Atlanta, this is Cherokee leader. You will advise us when the money has arrived. You have fourteen minutes left. Do you understand? Over."*

Kuhlman's hand was slick with sweat as he pressed the button. "Affirmative. Do we have approval for single ground frequency transmission?"

"Affirmative, Atlanta. Make it brief. Any suspected trick will bring immediate retaliation. Out."

Kuhlman nodded in satisfaction and turned to the ground control microphone. He took a few seconds to try to compose his thoughts. A slip could mean disaster as serious as the results of spotting the FBI men.

"All aircraft on the ground," he said huskily, "this is

136

Atlanta tower. This is the airport manager speaking. Aircraft over the field have demanded payment. Their demands are in the process of being met. We anticipate their departure within fifteen, repeat, fifteen, minutes. Suggest you reassure your passengers there is no immediate danger. Continue to maintain radio silence. We will inform you when we have further word. Atlanta tower out."

Straightening up, Kuhlman felt the eyes of the other men on him. He hoped his voice had been firm.

"That's it for now," he said. "Keep me informed. I'll be back in my office—" He stopped as he turned because he spied Wentworth, his security chief, standing beside the stair door. "What is it?"

Wentworth gestured meaninglessly. "The Delta man is in your office. He has it."

"I'll go see him."

"He says you ought to tell the bandits that Delta's money is ready."

"That wasn't what they said for us to do. I'm to report when *all* the money has arrived."

"He says somebody may be late, and he wants to make sure no retaliation is made against Delta when—"

"I'll go see him now," Kuhlman said angrily, and headed for the door. This was all he needed: the airlines squabbling among themselves.

5:53 P.M.

Knowing that the expressways toward the airport were packed, Crutchfield left the FBI parking area and headed south on a familiar street route. The traffic was not so heavy once he had cleared the immediate downtown area, and he drove hard, often veering to the wrong side to make passes.

Crutchfield was feeling the pressure despite his years of learning to deal with pressure. Washington had made it crystal clear that he was in charge and should be on the scene. He had already known this, of course, but had thought it was too late to try to get to the airport before the deadline. Now he had no choice, under his orders: *get* to the airport in time, no matter how impossible it looks.

Crutchfield was not worried about Rickman. He was a good, seasoned agent and was not likely to do anything outrageous. But Rickman had not had training in this particular kind of situation; hell, *no one* had. It was all new, all a matter of playing it by ear. A mistake could be made under these circumstances, and if one was made, Washington wanted to be absolutely sure where the blame had to fall.

The thing to do, Crutchfield thought, swerving out into the wrong lane at 60 mph to pass a bus, was to keep everyone under wraps, make a few routine tactical moves, and hope like hell that the bandits would take their money and get the hell out of the area. There was no question but that the raiders would be caught sooner or later. They were flying new aircraft, which made it a little tougher tracking down their serial numbers, but the FAA in Oklahoma City would have this information momentarily, even if they had to go to the computers to get it. The planes could be tracked down, the pilots identified. It was just a matter of time.

Of course, in the back of Crutchfield's mind there was rancor about letting them get away with it even for a few hours or a few days. It would be nice to send snipers out onto the field to pick them off. Action like that tended to discourage others from trying the same thing. But with three aircraft it was a virtual impossibility. It was a clever operation.

—No, Crutchfield thought, swinging wide around a corner and drifting the specially sprung Plymouth into a new lane, the thing to do was play it cool. As soon as he got to the scene, he would make that clear. In the meantime, Rickman could be counted on to take the necessary preliminary steps.

What time was it now? God! He pressed harder on the accelerator.

Intent upon driving just as hard as he could, Crutchfield did not see the 1965 Buick sedan poke out of the alley until the very last moment. He was thinking about the need for haste, and the series of actions he would take on his arrival. He would definitely be the man in charge when he got there. There would be no confusion about that. It would be his baby, and he knew all the options that would confront him, and how he would deal with them. No one else would be forced to ad-lib anything. But he had to hurry.

His sedan was traveling at about 65 mph when it passed the city bus. It was at this point that the elderly woman in the Buick decided the coast was clear and fed her lovingly kept old car just a teensie bit of gas. This put the Buick directly in the path of Crutchfield's onrushing Plymouth.

Crutchfield saw her much too late.

He sawed on the wheel and got on the brakes fast. There was a slide and then some loss of control and then incredible impact. The Buick was knocked sideways half the length of the block, turning over and over. The Plymouth, shattered, vaulted into the air, inverted, and landed upside down on the sidewalk, crashing into a shop window. Onlookers screamed, as they had a right to.

5:55 P.M.

Traffic on the Interstate had moved a few feet, which had given Hennigan an opportunity to pull off onto the shoulder. The other motorists, not even bothering to turn on headlights in the grim confusion, had immediately healed the space where he had been in line.

No matter. Hennigan was much too excited about the prospect of taking the law into his own hands.

It was really a great idea, and he had no doubt he could get the job done. He was a crack shot. He knew the rifle in the trunk like a doctor might know his medical instruments.

All he had to do was take the weapon down the hill, crawl over the culvert, set up, find a rest for the barrel, load, and knock one of the bastards out of the sky.

Assuming he did this, Hennigan thought, one of two things would happen. Either no one would ever know he had done it—which was quite possible—or else he could admit what he had done, after the other two planes turned tail and ran. In which case he would be a hero.

Taking a last tug at his bottle, Hennigan considered the

139

possibilities of life as a local hero. He was better than most people and he knew it. But he had never had that one lucky break that a man sometimes needed in order to be recognized. Bad luck had always dogged him: in school when the asshole teachers picked on him and got him in trouble, and then in the service when sheer bad luck got him that stupid bad conduct discharge, for no good reason *at all*. He had had bad luck with all his jobs, too. He was sick of bad luck and being a nobody. You had to strike when chance provided something for you.

Hennigan's bottle was empty. He recognized that he could sit here and do nothing, or strike while the iron was hot.

Tossing the bottle onto the seat of the car, he got out on the driver's side and walked to the back. There were cars everywhere, but no one paid much attention in the dark. He couldn't even see well enough to insert the trunk key on the first try. He was a little drunk but not very, he thought.

Opening the trunk, he reached inside and got the rifle in its case. The ammo was in the side pocket of the case. Hugging the rifle to his body like a baby, he closed the trunk, stepped over the single-strand cable along the shoulder, and went quickly down the thick grass embankment. It was going to be great, he thought. Just great. Just great.

5:56 P.M.

Donovan's back and legs were afire with fatigue, and his eyes had that burning, sticky quality that close-attention flying sometimes gave them. Flying the lead Cherokee had become almost reflex now, and it responded beautifully to every command. Things had gone almost perfectly, but Donovan's nerves had begun to tighten painfully.

Below, things were the same as they had been for the last few minutes. Total darkness was almost upon them. He could still make out the vague outlines of the airliners on taxiway Delta, but they seemed dimmer each pass. The highways were now bright white blazes of light where they were moving, curiously dark in other long stretches, as on the east side where something had tied things up so thoroughly that drivers had extinguished headlights to wait it out. Donovan could see the dim light of the tower and the turning beacon on top and the brighter lights of the great scalloped windows of the terminal. He wondered what they were thinking.

Behind him, Fetzer yelled over the roar, *"Anything new yet?"*

"Not that I can tell!" Fetzer had heard the last transmission from the tower, saying Delta had caved in first; the radio receiver was turned full up to allow for that.

"Time's running out!" Fetzer yelled back.

Pulling the Cherokee through the X of the figure 8, Donovan took a slight, automatic pleasure in making the ball center perfectly, left aileron, left rudder . . . right aileron, right rudder, swinging out of one turn and into the other with proper synchronization. But his mind was on Fetzer and the slight tone of worry that crept through the man's voice even though shouting.

The panel clock was almost straight up. He was feeling the pressure, Fetzer was feeling it, and so the others had to be feeling it, too. It might be time to buck them up a little. It *was* time to buck them up a little.

Donovan pulled the microphone out of its plastic socket and held it close to his mouth. Then, remembering Fetzer, he signaled him to put on the back seat headphones so he could monitor. Fetzer complied.

"Ringleader to Falcon and Snoopy," Donovan said crisply, "go to channel three now."

Putting the mike in his lap, he turned the navcom radio to frequency 118.7, carefully counted to ten to make sure the others would have had time to switch, and picked up the mike as he banked the plane around the west turn, over the highway, heading east again.

"Falcon and Snoopy," he transmitted, "acknowledge frequency in order."

"Falcon standing by," came Tom Keel's voice.

"Snoopy here," Jack Abercrombie called up.

141

Donovan thumbed his microphone again. "We've got a little over five minutes left. Monitor tower frequency for later transmissions unless otherwise instructed. If they fail to meet our demands, my signal will first be for another channel. Then my signal will be to open attack. We'll hit the Eastern DC-9 at the tail-end of the line down there first. If I give the attack order, I'll make the first pass, followed by Falcon and Snoopy in that order. We will then immediately go to Formation Charlie. Acknowledge."

There was a moment's silence on the radio. Then:

"Snoopy roger."

Another slight delay—

"Falcon roger."

"Go back to tower frequency now. Out."

Donovan snapped the microphone back on the plastic hook with a feeling of angry satisfaction. The delay in acknowledgments proved that neither Keel nor Abercrombie wanted to face the potentiality of a real attack. Of course none of them did. But it was up to Donovan now to make them go through with it if they must. They had to see that there was no turning back. If they had to attack, they had to do it promptly, and well.

Although Donovan was secretly praying to God that an attack would not have to come, he was a realist. It *might* come. They might have to take one big jet to prove they meant business.

If so, he would do it. There was no choice. It was a matter of the other people or himself now. A coward had no chance of getting out of this situation they had created. Not alive and in one piece. So he would lead and Keel and Abercrombie would follow, because, from the start, a genuine attack had been their ultimate weapon, one they hated and did not like to talk about, but just as viable, under extreme emergency, as Washington's and Moscow's superbombs.

It did not escape Donovan's notice, either, that someone on the ground might have intercepted his instructions. If they did, it could only help.

At the FAA Center in Oklahoma City, one of the men scanning computer lists of recently registered aircraft found it easily.

"They're together," he said, furiously copying information from the list. "Here's the name of the registrant, an outfit in Nebraska. Get a TWX off to Washington with this information right now."

Another man looked at the list as the first still jotted notes. "What do you bet they're rental aircraft?"

"It doesn't matter. Somebody had to sign something. The FBI will get them from this."

5:59 P.M.

Kuhlman hung up the telephone and looked around the outer office. It was crowded again, and smoky, like a war room. Saundra was on the other line, talking to someone. Barbara was at the door, looking at a message someone had passed inside through the guard in the hall. The men from Delta and Northwest, as glum as morticians, stood beside the worktable that held their suitcases of money. Wentworth and the FBI agent, Rickman, were by the reception desk. Rickman had a walkie-talkie slung over his shoulder, and he looked gray with nervousness.

"That," Kuhlman told them, his voice tight with anger, "was Atlanta Center. They've got some special scanner receivers set up in tandem over there. They just picked up a closed radio transmission from our Cherokees on a frequency that no one uses in this immediate area."

"Who were they talking to?" Rickman grunted.

"The leader was giving the others instructions in case we don't meet the deadline. They're going to attack an Eastern DC-9 out there on the taxiway first."

"Oh, God," Barbara breathed.

Ebbets, the Delta man, said incredulously, "Eastern isn't even in this thing!"

"Eastern happens to be last in the line out there," Kuhlman told him. "He makes the most convenient first target."

"Where in hell is Southern?" Tonman, the executive for Northwest, asked complainingly. "Good Lord, we've got just a couple of minutes left!"

"We've got five minutes, exactly," Kuhlman corrected him.

"Well, where is he? You said he was on his way!"

"He *is* on his way. The police just called and said the radio car bringing him is stuck in traffic beyond our gates somewhere. He's walking in."

"*Walking* in!"

"In that traffic out there, it beats a car."

From the door, Barbara said, "There are some reporters outside. They want a press conference."

Kuhlman was thunderstruck. "How did *they* get here?"

"Maybe they walked, too."

"*Reporters* can get here, but the man from Southern can't," Tonman said.

"Tell the reporters to shove it," Kuhlman said. "No. Wait. Call PR. Tell him to get somebody down here to deal with the press. Tell him we aren't giving out anything but free coffee. Tell him to give out the coffee in *his* office, not around mine."

Rickman's walkie-talkie bleeped at him. He half-turned his back and spoke guardedly into the mouthpiece. Making sure no one else knew what was going on, Kuhlman thought angrily.

"What do we do," Ebbets asked, "if our man from Southern misses the deadline?"

"I don't know," Kuhlman admitted. He had the feeling of his back all the way to the wall. "I'm waiting another two minutes. Then we'll get to the tower. I'll stall if I can."

"How are those people going to pick up the money?"

"I don't know yet. They'll tell us when we say it's here."

"All I want," Ebbets said, "is for them to take the cash and get the hell out of here."

144

"Amen, brother," Tonman said.

Rickman put down the walkie-talkie. "My men are all in place now. The detachments of city police who managed to slip in on foot are being deployed under and around the airplanes you've got parked here by the building."

"What the hell do they think they're going to do *there?*" Kuhlman exploded.

"It's just preparedness," Rickman said. "Mr. Crutchfield is on the way and ought to be here any minute. Everyone understands he'll be in total command."

"Maybe he will and maybe he won't," Kuhlman shot back. "Nobody is going to start a shooting war around here if I can help it."

"He won't, he won't. He's a real pro, Mr. Kuhlman. You have nothing to worry about."

Oh, beautiful! Kuhlman thought. Nothing to worry about? Once again, his mind flicked over all the aircraft on the field, all the innocent people in the terminal building. At practically the same moment he thought again of all the alternative plans for thwarting the attack that had been briefly considered and then abandoned. Nothing was going to stop the Cherokees, short of an all-out attack that would end up taking more lives on the ground than in the air. Now city police were swarming around, probably falling over the FBI, and until Crutchfield arrived, there was no central control. No problems?

"Where *is* that Southern guy?" Tonman asked.

"What time is it?" Wentworth asked.

Saundra put the telephone on the counter. "Sir, this is the police downtown."

Kuhlman grabbed the phone. "Hello!"

"Mr. Kuhlman?"

"Yes."

"This is Tighlemann, special forces downtown. Have you seen FBI agent Crutchfield yet?"

"No. Don't you know where he is either?"

"He ought to be there by now. Have him call me the moment he arrives, ten-four?"

"If I see him, I'll tell him. Is there any new disaster we ought to know about up here?"

"No, sir." The detective sounded cheerful. "I just wanted him to know that we've managed to get our special snipers into your area now."

"*Here?*"

"Ten-four. We have a special drill that Mr. Crutchfield might want to consider, although the time probably is pretty short now. But our special unit is well trained, and we can command by radio. We could offer simultaneous radio-controlled sniper fire from about ten locations, and with some coordination on targets, I don't see why we couldn't knock out all three—"

"Christ!"

"Sir?"

"What if you *did* hit all three planes at once, Tigerman —or whatever your name is? Did it ever occur to you that a plane loaded with explosives might make a hell of a mess crashing through the side of this terminal building?"

"Well, sir, we weren't recommending it; we were only, uh, offering an option, there—"

"Listen! Don't do *anything*. Don't tell your people to do anything! Just sit tight, okay? If Crutchfield gets here in time, he'll call you. But in the meantime, *do nothing*. Understood?"

"Yes, sir." The detective sounded mystified by Kuhlman's shouting. "Just an option, you see, and—"

Kuhlman hung up on him. And glanced at his watch.

"Where in *hell*," Tonman complained again, "is Southern?"

"Where is Crutchfield?" Kuhlman countered.

"We've got three minutes by my watch," Barbara said.

"I should have gone into the grocery business like my father wanted me to," Kuhlman said, creating a small snowstorm of dandruff as he scratched at his scalp. "Or maybe an undertaker. I had an uncle who was an undertaker. Christ!"

146

6:00 P.M.

The oil temperature gauge was at the top of the green arc now, and Keel glanced at it every few seconds. The engine sounded fine, and he knew it could be a defective gauge. He rapped at it with his knuckles and got no response.

It might go at any time, he knew. If the gauge was correct, the Lycoming engine was getting dangerously hot. Possibly slow cruise would cool it. Possibly nothing could help it now. The engine might swallow a ring or lose a rod at any time. If so, at this altitude he had very little chance except for an emergency landing on the field itself, and into the arms of the law.

It was only half the worry.

In four minutes the deadline would be up. Donovan's radio call about contingencies had chilled him deeper, and more painfully, than any of the cooling night air that boiled through the open Cherokee.

He did not yet know whether he would be able to do it, if it came to that. He did not think so. If he couldn't, and Donovan led without support, Donovan would be betrayed.

But Keel did not think he could do it. Would the engine fail, and save him the choice by plunging him into something worse?

He thought of his brother and Cindy. This would change life for his brother . . . for Cindy . . . for him in other ways. There would be no more hurting and no more begging and no more lickspittle, ever.

He rapped the oil temperature gauge again, and again it remained just where it was, hovering on the danger zone.

6:02 P.M.

Officer Reilly pulled his motorcycle up behind the parked car and walked toward it. He expected to find another motorist who had run out of gas. In both lanes beside him, the cars sat mostly dark, mostly with their engines off, protecting against just such a contingency. Some people always goofed.

As Reilly reached the car, a motorist in the car beside it rolled down his window. "Hey, officer! What in hell is blocking things up ahead?"

"Somebody stopped to watch the airplanes and a truck tried to dodge," Reilly said disgustedly. "Jack-knifed."

"Across the whole damned road?"

"Just about. He was loaded with some kind of stuff in jars, and they're trying to clear about a ton of broken glass up there right now. It shouldn't be too much longer, though." Having done his best to be cheerful, Reilly peered into the parked car.

"You won't find him there."

"Oh?" Reilly turned to look at the other motorist, a graying businessman, for the first time. "Why not?"

"He just decided to take advantage of the delay and get in some hunting, I guess."

Reilly chilled. *"Hunting?"*

"Yeah. I was right here. He got out of his car a few minutes ago and got what sure looked like a rifle out of his trunk. Went down the ravine, there."

The businessman didn't know much about sports. You didn't hunt around here at all, much less at night. Not here by the highway. Reilly knew something had to be messed up here, some way.

Hurrying around the back of the abandoned sedan, he straddled the cable fencing and went down the steep grassy slope into the little ravine formed by various highway fills. It was dark in the ravine and he couldn't see much. But there was no one around.

Huffing for his breath, Reilly climbed the other side of the ravine. It was a high fill that then sloped down to airport property beyond. He had been through the area before the highway was widened, and he knew it well.

Reaching the top, Reilly could see the entire airport and the little planes with their flashing lights buzzing around. He wondered what was going on over there. But then, his back to the highway and all the snarled traffic, he reminded

148

himself about the man with the gun. Getting out his flash-light and his service revolver, he very cautiously began searching the weedy embankment.

He did not have to search long. And after his initial scare, Reilly was then not worried at all anymore.

Hennigan was halfway down the slope, in the high weeds, his unopened gun case nestled beside him. He was fast asleep.

6:04 P.M.

Ted Kuhlman stood in the Atlanta tower with the FBI man beside him. It was deathly still; the digital clocks had just ticked off the minute, and Rickman's soft walkie-talkie instructions to his agents sounded as if he were shouting.

"Hold your positions," he said huskily, trying to whisper but thwarted in his desire for secrecy by the quiet and by the gadget's volume requirement. "We're on deadline here. All agents and all Atlanta police on the frequency, hold your positions. No new word from airplanes. Expect orders within five."

Kuhlman, hearing the words, felt a growing, deepening sense of dread. The FBI snipers were scattered out there in the dark, along the runways. There were police somewhere below, and probably around the edges of the field. Some had heard Rickman's transmission, some probably had not. There was no ultimate coordination, and a wrong move meant disaster. *Where was Crutchfield? Where was the man from Southern?*

Out on the field, overhead, the moving lights of the Cherokees suddenly began to switch, change directions.

"New pattern again!" one of the controllers said.

One of the Cherokees swept wide, came around toward the tower, became blinking lights, larger and larger, until Kuhlman involuntarily ducked.

"They're back in their oval again!"

Kuhlman strode to the wall phone, which hung on its cord, the line open to his office. "Barbara?"

"Yes, sir?" She sounded frightened now, at last.

"Is the Southern man here yet?"

"No. We're trying to get through to the police, to see if they have radio contact with the car that was bringing him."

Kuhlman gritted his teeth. "I'm holding the telephone. When you have something, yell loud enough so I'll hear you even if the receiver is at my side."

"I'll scream if I have to."

"Yeah. Is Crutchfield there?"

"Not yet."

"Have Saundra call his office downtown and try to find out where the hell *he* is, too."

"Saundra has a call from Washington. She says she needs to tell you about it."

"Okay. I'll—"

The radio cut him off, the familiar voice from the lead Cherokee:

"Cherokee leader to Atlanta tower."

The controllers looked nervously around toward Kuhlman.

"Respond," he ordered, and then, into the telephone, "Hang on a minute."

Saundra's voice came over the line. "Mr. Kuhlman—"

"Hold on a second. Saundra!"

The controller leaned forward. "Cherokee leader, this is Atlanta tower. Go ahead."

"Atlanta, get the airport manager. Now."

The controllers turned again, their faces gray in the pale light.

Kuhlman grated, "Tell them I'm on the way up. Buy us a minute." Then, as the controller spoke into the microphone, he turned back to the telephone. "Go ahead, Saundra. Fast."

"The people in Washington have some experts on a military jet, on the way here now. They'll try to land at Dobbins Air Force Base before seven o'clock."

"That's too late."

"Atlanta, we'll stand by one minute."

"Roger, Cherokee leader."

150

Kuhlman turned to Rickman, who stood by with his walkie-talkie. "Your boss Crutchfield hasn't shown. Washington is sending in a new bunch, but they won't be here for an hour." Kuhlman's voice cracked with tension and he had to clear his throat. "No sign of the Southern Airlines man."

Rickman's face, in the side-lighting from the consoles, looked very old. For the first time, the pressures he was feeling were evident in his expression and especially in his eyes. "If those planes start an attack, I've got to order my people to fire."

"Hold them off, man! We might still get out of this!"

Rickman slowly shook his head. "If they attack, *we* attack."

Kuhlman hesitated, trying to make his splitting skull think straight. The options had been played out and none of them was any good. As another plane roared over the tower, rattling the windows, he saw what was going to happen unless he could somehow stall for time.

He handed Rickman the telephone. "My secretary is on the other end. She'll yell if she has word on anything."

The FBI man hesitated. "I've got to keep in contact with my men—"

"Take the telephone, you fool, or I'll knock your roof in!"

Startled, Rickman accepted the phone.

Kuhlman strode to the console. He leaned over a controller's shoulder and keyed the microphone. "Cherokee leader, this is Kuhlman."

"Go ahead."

"We've run into a small snag down here."

"Your time is up."

"I know that," Kuhlman agreed thickly. "Listen. We've got the Delta suitcase. We've got Northwest's. Southern is hung up in traffic or something. He's on the way. Repeat. He is on the way. Give us a few more minutes. We are doing everything we can to cooperate."

He paused and waited for a reply. How he hated the pleading tone of his voice! It was bitter for him. But it was necessary. He realized that he would run down Main Street

151

with his pants off if it could add even one percentage point to the chances of those passengers out there, and the people in his terminal.

The reply to his plea came over the speakers: *"Atlanta, stand by one."* Then: *"Falcon and Snoopy, go to channel one, now."*

"They're talking it over," someone said.

"I wish I could hear that!"

Kuhlman said, "Center may monitor it on their scanners, but it'll probably be too late by the time they can relay."

No one replied. He wondered if they were thinking what he was—that just about everything was too late, now. He turned toward the back stair door. Wentworth was standing there, mutely watching, and so were two controllers ordinarily due to come on duty. Each man, in his own way, was involved. Kuhlman knew that none was involved so deeply and passionately as he.

It was *his* airport. They were *his* planes and even his people. The legal papers and common sense might say something far different, but he had bought this responsibility, had worked for it all his life, starting with the flying lessons as a kid, when he had hiked eight miles to the airport for a half-hour dual whenever he had sold enough vegetables out of the garden or thrown enough papers, and through the years of flying commercial, and then the injury and starting over, selling tickets, then at Mansfield, shoveling snow in those blinding-cold Ohio nights when there would be no planes, and no passengers, but the book said to clear the ramp. . . .

Everything had led to this, and he could no more evade his feelings than deny his entire life, everything that had become the structure of his being.

"Atlanta, this is Cherokee leader."

He leaned forward again. "Go ahead."

"We see flashing car lights at your parking lot entrance. That could be your other money man. We'll give you five minutes additional time to check and see."

Kuhlman keyed the mike. "It has to be Southern, because—" But he stopped because the loudspeakers screamed at him, indicating a simultaneous transmission. The Cherokee hadn't stopped talking. He released the mike.

"—*no other delays. We will take action in four minutes.*"

"Understand," Kuhlman said.

Behind him, the FBI man called, "Your secretary says he's at the gate!"

Kuhlman turned from the console. He told the controllers, "Stall him if he calls again. Say anything. I'm going down to meet the Southern man and get his money to my office."

Rickman said, "I've got to hang up this telephone and make another call."

"Who?"

"The base. They've got some fighters up on top. If these people attack, we might have to bring the fighters down and see if *they* can do anything."

"And for every ten bullets they fire, nine will miss the target and hit whatever—or whoever—is on the ground!"

"We could be luckier than that."

Kuhlman didn't even argue. There was no time. With the feeling that the last bits of his control were disintegrating, he plunged down the steps, Wentworth hot on his heels.

6:07 P.M.

Powered well back, Major Sam Donaldby held his F-4 in a huge circular pattern at an altitude of 50,000 feet. His radar indicators showed the other fighter-bombers in similar patterns over the area. The throb of the jet engine pulsed through his body, and the instruments glowed on the complex tight-packed panel. Donaldby waited for word from the ground.

The sky overhead was brilliant black, with stars that seemed very close, very beautiful and cold. Below, a high scum layer partially obscured the ground, although he could well see the general sprawl of Atlanta.

153

As far as the airport was concerned, he could not see a thing.

6:08 P.M.

There was no need for Ted Kuhlman to go personally down into the main area of the terminal to meet the man bringing Southern's money. But there was no way he could leave it to anyone else. He had to be in action of some kind at this moment, whether he was really needed or not.

The terminal was densely crowded, as bad as it sometimes was around holidays, when the weather would not cooperate. In the thirty-minute period bracketing the time when the Cherokee Sixes had first appeared and frozen everything in place, Atlanta had been scheduled for twenty-nine regularly scheduled commercial airline takeoffs and landings, plus training flights, bizjets and private aviation craft. Passengers had disembarked from many of these flights now stuck at the gates, while arriving passengers and friends anticipating either an arrival or a departure had also piled into the building before the parking area shut off their way out again. The result was contained chaos.

The main ticket areas were jammed. Long lines had formed at all the counters. Along the rows of benches and attached chairs in the waiting areas, there was no place to sit. Smoke from cigarettes, pipes, and cigars made the vaulted ceilings hazy. Although no arrivals or departures were being called, there were plenty of notices for incoming or outgoing passengers to meet someone somewhere, or for general information. The PA system's tinny voice echoed over a continual din of voices, movement, wonderment.

As he descended the escalator toward the front doorways, Ted Kuhlman was surprised that the scene was not even more abnormal. He could see one or two of his security people in the crowds, but otherwise it was just as if things were shut in for weather. No panic, no overt anger. It crossed his mind to wonder if the people knew what was

154

going on, but then he remembered his own guarded announcement; of course they knew in general terms, and that was why the observation areas were so packed.

Passing near a TV area where passengers could lounge and watch shows from downtown, he noted that this area, too, was jammed, with more travelers sifting in to stand at the outskirts of the area. He got a glimpse of the color TV screen and saw a distant, fuzzy picture of the terminal itself as seen from highway side. An announcer's face filled one corner of the scene and he was reading from notes. So the Atlanta media had gotten as close as they could, and the people here were now learning about their own plight by remote control. Would seeing it on television make it more real for them when they were already unwilling bystanders in the actual thing?

With Wentworth still following, Kuhlman reached the front doors. The automatic equipment swept them wide and he strode out into the cool night.

Cars were doubled up everywere along the entry area. The skycaps were ticketing some luggage while the passengers talked excitedly among themselves. Cabs had piled up as well as limousines. Three Atlanta policemen stood nearby. Out beyond the immediate area, parking was a blaze of lights, and beyond that, the entry and exit gates appeared thoroughly blocked.

Wentworth finally caught up with him. Out of breath, he muttered, "They'll never get through all this."

"No," Kuhlman said. "Look."

Coming across the pavement was a clot of men, mostly uniformed police with riot guns. With them was a short, rotund executive whom Kuhlman vaguely recognized from some dinner or other airport function. The man had a suitcase.

"Ted," he gasped, holding out his right hand. "We got blocked in traffic, then we had to run for it from the gates—!"

"Is this it?" Kuhlman asked, pointing at the suitcase.

"Yes, it's all here. What's the situation?"

Kuhlman took the bag. "We're late and maybe in trouble. I'll talk later. Go on up to my office. I've got to make tracks with this."

One of the police officers put a heavy hand on his shoulder. "Just a minute, sir. Do you have any word about deployment?"

Kuhlman paused, then understood. "Yes. You and your men are to remain right here and secure the area in front of the terminal."

The policeman nodded and turned to his men. "All right, men. Fan out along the front here." They began to move off.

Kuhlman turned to Wentworth. "Go to my office and get the other bags. Bring a guard with you and get to the tower as fast as you can."

Wentworth's face furrowed. "They can't pick up from the tower—"

Of course he was right. Kuhlman was not thinking quite straight. He responded by thrusting the Southern bag at Wentworth, who almost dropped it. "Okay. Right. Take this one to my office with the others. Stand by there. I'll get to the tower for instructions."

"Just generally, how are we doing? My boss—"

"We haven't lost anybody yet. Go with my man here. He'll fill you in."

With that Kuhlman headed for the entry doors before anyone could ask anything further. He bolted inside and had to restrain the impulse to run through the milling crowd. He needed to hurry, yes, and desperately. But if he ran he might frighten people in the crowd. You always remembered your public relations. It was part of your life.

6:11 P.M.

One of the controllers, the one named Albright, was hunched over his desk, talking with grim calmness into a microphone, when Kuhlman burst into the tower hopelessly

156

out of breath. It was clear in an instant that Albright had been trying to buy additional time.

"Just a minute," Albright said, turning to see Kuhlman. "The airport manager is back."

The loudspeakers rasped. *"Go ahead, then, Atlanta manager."*

Gulping for air, Kuhlman dropped into one of the vacated chairs at the control table. His legs were afire with fatigue from running the last stairs and corridor.

"Cherokee leader," he said, "this is Kuhlman. Southern has arrived. Your three bags are ready."

"Roger, Atlanta." Was there a breath of relief in the crisp voice? *"Each bag contains one million dollars, unmarked, small and medium denominations only. Affirmative?"*

Kuhlman had not checked. He could only pray the orders had been followed downtown. "That's affirmative."

"Okay, Atlanta. Here are your instructions. The three bags will be placed on an open cargo-handling vehicle. The vehicle will be marked by its headlights and taillights and its warning flasher. All will be operating at all times. The driver will be alone on the seat. He will proceed from the baggage area to the intersection of runways 3 and 35. He will place the three bags at the west corner of the intersection nearest taxiway Delta. He will then proceed immediately back to the baggage area. Confirm these instructions so far. Over."

Kuhlman mopped sweat from his face and closed his eyes to concentrate. "A single baggage truck, lighted up. Only the driver. Bring the bags to the 3–35 intersection, place them on the west side nearest Delta. Drive back to the terminal." He released the key.

"Affirmative, Atlanta. We will pick up the bags at that point. Only one of our aircraft will be on the ground at any time. Any trick or attempted attack on us will result in instant retaliation. Is that understood? Over."

Understanding far better than they might think, Kuhlman wearily pressed the transmit button. "Understood, Cherokee leader."

"Get moving. You have two minutes."

"We can't get it down there in two minutes!"

He waited. The loudspeakers were silent.

"Christ!" Kuhlman jumped up and ran to the telephone that still held a line open to his office. "Barbara!"

"Yes, sir?" she said instantly.

"Get Wentworth on the extension."

The security man came on and Kuhlman carefully and quickly repeated the orders. "You're to drive the bags out there personally, Wentworth. If anybody hassles you in any way, take whatever action is necessary. Move!"

"I might be needed up there, sir. If we could ask Jones—"

"You do it, Wentworth! And do *exactly* as I said, understand?"

"Yes, sir." The man still sounded dubious.

"Get someone to help you carry the bags, and hurry! We've got about a minute or two left, or hell might still break loose." Kuhlman broke the connection, then wished he hadn't. Turning, he saw FBI agent Rickman huffing up the stairs with his walkie-talkie.

"I heard on the monitor," Rickman panted. "My men are out in good position, I think. Explain to me what they're doing exactly. I want to be sure."

Kuhlman pointed to the airport diagram on the wall, tracing the length of the two runways that formed an X across the long parallel runways that ran east and west. He explained. Putting the bags at the intersection adjoining taxiway Delta—where all the big jets were stacked in line—provided maximum protection from the possibility of sniper fire directed at the Cherokees from the ground; stray bullets could go right on into the airliners. Also, the orbiting planes could be in the best possible position to watch both the pickup and the helpless, hapless big jets nearby.

Frowning, Rickman looked closer at the two long runways forming the X. "Which way do you think they'll land? Which runway?"

158

It was so obvious, to a person who knew airports and aircraft, that Kuhlman was startled for an instant. Then he pointed. "It can't be on 35. The jets parked on the taxiway are blocking it in the center. The Cherokees will land on 3, taxi to the intersection, pick up in the shadow of the jets, and take off again right toward the ramp area."

Rickman nodded slowly, showing the pressure in the slow working of his jawline. "My men can pick them off when they taxi."

"And shoot into the *airliners?*"

Rickman's eyes became opaque. "My men hit what they aim at."

"The guy on the radio already said only one plane will land—or at least they're to land and pick up one at a time. You can't get more than one plane with your snipers. What about the other two? The other two will demolish the airport! You can't do it, Rickman!"

The agent's face changed as the truth dawned. He licked his lips. "Crutchfield. He ought to be here."

"Call somebody else, then," Kuhlman argued. "Call downtown. Call your superiors in Washington. They've been on the line ten times in the last hour already. Tell them what's happening. Let me talk to them. Jesus God, man! You can't fire on one of those planes now!"

Rickman studied his face for a moment. Kuhlman wanted to reach out and shake the stolid agent, to make him make sense.

"I'll call," Rickman said. He turned to the wall telephone.

Kuhlman hurried to the tower windows, looking down to see the baggage carrier. It was not yet in sight. He gritted his teeth. The Cherokees flashed over the center of the field in their low, deadly pattern.

6:14 P.M.

With a sense of unreality, Tom Keel spotted the lights of the baggage carrier heading out from the terminal area. The

159

truck, little more than a high-speed little tractor for pulling luggage carts, moved quickly, and, according to instructions, it was lit up like a Christmas tree. Elation tried to break through Keel's foreboding. He tried to hold both emotions back because it was too early for either.

"Here he comes!" MacReady yelled from the back. *"Look at him come, boy!"*

Keel nodded but gave no other sign. He was still very busy with the aircraft. Involuntarily he reached forward and rapped the oil temperature gauge with his knuckles again. No response. It remained on the edge of the red.

"Lookit him come!" MacReady continued to whoop. *"Here comes our fortune, baby! Yow!"*

Coming out of the bank, Keel had another brief look over the nose at the spot where the pickups would be made. The baggage truck had almost reached the brightly lighted X of the two runways.

Keel was savagely tired, and so much was still to come. He could not keep his eyes off the temperature gauge. Yet everything else was perfectly normal and the engine sounded fine. It would be typical of his luck, he thought, if the money were right there, the trick a success, and then his engine broke on him.

The overhead loudspeaker blasted, *"Falcon and Snoopy, go to channel two. Now."*

Keel quickly switched the receiver to the new frequency. As he hit the right slots on the dials, he heard Abercrombie already checking in: *"Snoopy here."* Keel quickly got the mike and gave his own ready signal.

Donovan's voice sang back instantly, excited and jubilant. *"On my signal, we go in the order we set. Wait for my order. Confirm."*

Keel hit his microphone button. "Falcon roger."

The loudspeaker echoed, *"Snoopy roger."*

Donovan came back. *"Stay this frequency."*

Keel understood. Donovan had dual navcom receivers and could monitor both frequencies simultaneously. But he and Abercrombie were to await orders which would come on this same channel.

160

It meant that only Donovan now had communication with Atlanta tower. For a few seconds, this made Keel feel oddly isolated. But then he saw that of course there was no more need for him or Abercrombie to listen to the tower. All that was over. It was down to the pickup now, and—if that worked—getting away.

If the engine did not break in the meantime.

Anxiously he rapped the gauge. His knuckles were getting sore.

6:15 P.M.

Lying flat in the cold, wet grass, agent Wilson Good looked down the blue barrel of his sniper rifle at the sight of the cargo tractor stopping on the runway less than a hundred yards away. Even without use of his special sniperscope, Good had perfect vision of everything: the seat, the three suitcases tied loosely on behind him, the way he reached for a handle as he braked the tractor and came to a halt.

His stomach tight with readiness, Good watched the man climb down from the tractor seat, untie the bags, and hurriedly carry them to the edge of the broad paved area, very near a cluster of raised white runway lights. Near the lights it was almost as bright as daylight, and Good could even see the dark stains in the man's coat-back from nervous sweat and exertion.

Very carefully, Good turned his head slowly to his right. He could not see Jackson over there but knew he was less than fifty yards distant. And another of his fellows was an equal distance on the right. They had ideal position. It could not have been better. The big airliners behind the pickup point were of no serious concern because Good knew that neither he nor his associates would miss. They never missed.

Inwardly, however, Good was steeling himself for this. All his shooting with the special rifle and scope had been under controlled training conditions. There was always that remote chance that this, being real, shooting at a living man, would be different enough to enter an imponderable into all

161

the training equations. He had to be sure he did not, at any level, flinch from killing. Because if the order came on the little receiver at his side, he must kill as he had been taught.

He was glad it was not his decision to make.

The driver of the tractor hurried back to the vehicle, engaged gears, and turned in a broad, fast circle, heading back for the terminal. Good trained the rifle on the suitcases and looked at them through the special scope. He trained the reticules on the center bag and studied it. Beneath the handle were two half-inch gold initials. He could read them easily: *J.M.* He wondered who J.M. was, then decided it probably didn't matter. He waited.

6:16 P.M.

On the telephone, Rickman had been listening for what seemed an agonizingly long time. His face was now the color of dirty cotton. "Hang on," he said finally, and held a hand over the mouthpiece as he turned to Kuhlman. "Crutchfield had a wreck. They're on the way to a hospital. He might be dead."

Kuhlman had been standing beside the FBI man, watching the Cherokees continue their endless circling as the baggage truck trundled out, waited, then started back. It had all had a curiously dreamlike quality, as if a play were being acted out automatically, beyond anyone's control. But now Rickman's words jolted him.

"You're in charge, then?" he said aloud.

Rickman blinked at him. Instead of replying, he raised the receiver again. "We've got it on the field. Yes. That's right, they're in position. . . ." He listened, scowling with concentration. "I don't know. Play it by ear, I suppose." He listened again. By now, Kuhlman could see the baggage truck almost back to the terminal. "Yes. Right, sir."

Rickman hung up. He looked at Kuhlman. There was absolutely no expression on the agent's face. "We decide," he said flatly.

So there was nothing else left. There would be no Crutch-

162

field to save the day by taking it out of their hands. Seeing it, Kuhlman knew that he had been yearning for a Crutchfield, because that would place the ultimate responsibility upon someone else's shoulders. But there was no one else. And no escape from it.

Rickman mopped his face with a splotched handkerchief and picked up his walkie-talkie off the table. "All agents," he said thickly. "This is Rickman, agent-in-charge for this emergency. Stand by for immediate action."

6:17 P.M.

"Ringleader to Falcon and Snoopy, acknowledge."

Keel, going east on the top side of the tight flying circle, had the mike already in his slippery hand. "Falcon here."

"Snoopy here, too."

There was a slight pause, then: *"Falcon, go. Now."*

Keel was already approaching the turn that would take him south, along the east boundary of the field. He had no time for much besides automatic technique. He would land on runway 3, running generally north and a slight bit east, so he had only one broad turn, about two hundred degrees, to set up the landing.

"Get ready back there!" he yelled over his shoulder.

Swinging into the right turn that put the Cherokee roughly parallel with runway 3, headed in the wrong direction, Keel went through bits of the mental checklist without conscious thought. The fuel pump had never been turned off and the mixture was full rich. Looking out ahead to the right, he gauged the end of the runway and the turn he still had to make, and backed off the throttle more by feel than reference to the manifold pressure gauge. Touching right aileron and rudder, he moved the prop knob fully forward, giving maximum rpm. The Cherokee obligingly began to settle.

At such an extremely low altitude, he had nothing like a normal approach. Feeding in additional power, he yanked in one notch of flaps, then a second, touched up the power

163

again, and banked into the turn that brought the plane around in a sweeping turn from south to north, lining up the nose down the jewel-glowing brightness of the lights along both sides of runway 3. He was low and got on more power, stabilizing the shallow descent. The big jets were much closer on the immediate left now, and he was coming in from the south, aiming at the huge white numeral painted on the threshold of the runway; he pulled in the third notch of flaps, touched the trim, and came in over the number.

He was stiff from the hour-plus of maximum tension. The slightest crosswind tried to turn the plane crabwise. He corrected and flared a shade high, corrected for this, too, eased off the power.

The plane settled slightly, seeming to enter the glare of the lights themselves. He saw the pavement rushing by and eased back on the yoke another fraction, and the wheels squeaked on.

"Come to momma, baby!" MacReady yelped in the back. "Come to me!"

"Get ready!" Keel snapped, and he dumped the flaps and got onto the brakes as the Cherokee rolled past the enormous jetliners, slowing. He could see the suitcases just ahead about thirty yards. MacReady was already in the open cargo door, waiting to jump just as soon as the plane could be brought to a standstill.

6:18 P.M.

The pale green lights inside the tower gave Rickman's face a ghastly pallor under its sickly film of sweat. Every man in the enclosure was watching the Cherokee roll slowly past the big jets, coming closer and closer to the X where the bags had been placed. Into the walkie-talkie, hunched against his shoulder like a violin, the FBI man muttered, "Good, Jackson, Cole, stand by for order to fire. Others hold position."

Ted Kuhlman grabbed his arm. "You can't open fire!"

"There's nothing left to do." Rickman had binoculars

164

fixed on the scene, and he was as still as a statue. But his voice quaked. "This is the last chance here."

"The other planes will retaliate."

"I can't help that. Washington put me in charge. I've got to do what I think is right."

The Cherokee was almost stopped, and Kuhlman's desperation peaked. He had to stop it. He knew what gunshots would mean. "You *can't* do it! I've told you that! Think of the lives that can be lost!"

"Let them get away with it?" Rickman asked. "Is that what you want?"

"No, it isn't what I want. But it has to be that way."

"No, it doesn't. I can stop it."

"Against my wishes?"

"If it has to be that way." But Rickman's eyes wavered.

"Do you want another Tallahassee here?"

"What?"

"Tallahassee! It was a skyjacking. The gunman ordered the plane to land for fuel. The FBI was waiting. The pilot—"

"The pilot wanted it stopped," Rickman said.

"The hell the pilot did!"

"My information—"

"The pilot asked authorities not to do anything. The FBI intervened anyway—shot out the tires. Result: the gunman killed the pilot. He killed the co-pilot. Then he killed himself."

Rickman's hands trembled, but he clung to his belief, his sense of duty. "This situation isn't like that."

It was a nightmare. He would not yield. Out on the runway the plane was coming slower and slower, like some dream sequence in which everything was horribly slowed down.

"It's a matter of lives," Kuhlman said. "Forget the money. Forget everything but the lives."

"If we don't get them now," Rickman retorted, "we might not get them at all."

"You've got planes up on top. You've got helicopters. You've got radar. And agents all over the country. You can catch them later. You even know where the planes were bought or rented. This isn't your only chance! *Don't* give the order to fire, man, for Christ's sake!"

The Cherokee, its little lights blinking, was a small white speck on the distant runway. It had almost stopped. Time was gone. Rickman licked his lips, and a tic appeared in his cheek as he swung his eyes to Kuhlman.

"Let them get away with it?" he repeated. "Will that save lives? If these guys get away with it, then someone else will try it. Some other airport will be hit. There's no defense against this, they'll say. It will be like skyjacking. It will go on and on until some people get killed. If we don't stop it now, *more* lives will be endangered!"

"My business isn't other airports and other people. It's *this* situation. Here. Now."

"I've got my job. It's different. I worry about *all* of them."

Kuhlman had the agent's arm in a steel grip. *"Don't fire."*

The Cherokee out on the runway had stopped. A figure darted from its side—a man running toward the suitcases.

Rickman raised his hand to the walkie-talkie for transmission.

"No!" It was a shout from Kuhlman.

Rickman's nerve broke. "You can stop me, damn it. Yes, you *can.* Our orders are to listen to the civilian authority. That's you. Do you want to let them go? It's your decision. I'm saying *fire,* now. Are you going to countermand that? Are you going to take it all on *your* back?"

For the smallest fraction of a second, time froze for Ted Kuhlman. He saw with a sense of incredulity that it had all been coming to this. Not only the last hour, but his life.

There was no easy decision. A part of him wanted very badly to turn away, let the FBI man take charge and issue his order. After all, that would be the easiest, right? He could say later, if things went badly, *"The FBI did it. They took it out of my hands."* It would be easy that way, and no one ever had to know.

But it was *not* that easy. Even wanting to stop the pirates as much as he did, he knew that shooting at the single Cherokee now was not the right thing to do. It would bring chaos—everything he feared.

He knew, too, however, in this agonized instant, that *he* was taking the responsibility by thwarting the gunshots. It was *his* choice now. If he spoke, he was accepting full responsibility. If the planes got away and the airlines lost three million dollars and other bandits struck other fields, with terrible loss of life, it was all on his back.

He had to choose, and not only his job but his life's work and reputation were hanging here on a decision that paralyzed him.

Out on the runway, the figure had reached the bags—picked one up—turned toward the waiting Cherokee with its propeller silvery in the cone of its landing light.

"I'm going to fire," Rickman said. "I've got to." He raised his hand again.

"No!"

"It's on you! You're going against my recommendation!"

"I don't give a damn!" Kuhlman yelled at him. "Let them go. *I'll take it—all of it.*"

The man on the distant runway was running back toward the plane. The sniper rifles had to be trained on him. There were only seconds left.

Rickman took a deep breath and keyed the walkie-talkie. "Hold," he said. "Do not fire. Do not fire. Hold."

6:19 P.M.

MacReady hurled the suitcase in through the open cargo door with a hollow thud and threw himself in after it. "Go, baby!"

Tom Keel released the brakes and fed power to the engine. The Cherokee inched away and began to pick up speed. He had a world of runway remaining, about four

167

thousand feet or more, and the takeoff would be even easier than the landing. A glance at the oil temperature gauge showed no change. Or had it inched *down* a hair?

The plane was now going *50* mph, indicated, now *60*, now, rapidly accelerating and becoming light on its feet, *70*, and Keel fed in slight back pressure, and the nose wheel flew. The Cherokee Six lifted off as the airspeed indicator moved through *85* and to *90*. Keel craned his neck to see where the other planes were in their pattern. The terminal building dropped away on the left side as he began to level and bank right.

In the rear, MacReady had gotten the suitcase open for a look. *"We got it! Look at it! Tons of it! Tens! Twenties! Fifties! They did just what we said! Yow!"*

Keel had no time to look, or even to feel elated. He reached for his mike. *"Falcon to Cherokee leader. Pickup good."*

Donovan's voice sang back from the aircraft just ahead, winking through a far turn to the south of the runways. *"Roger, Falcon. Snoopy, go."*

Abercrombie's plane broke from the pattern and started its short, sharp, curving descent to runway 3.

6:20 P.M.

The FBI agent had turned and bolted from the tower within seconds after reluctantly calling off the snipers. Now, seeing the second plane waft in for landing, Kuhlman saw that each of them would pick up one bag, and that this would promise separate escape routings, which was sure to complicate life for pursuers. He had a flat, empty sensation in his gut, as he had had once after playing in a high school football game that his team won at the cost of serious injury to a good friend. Some victories left a man the acrid aftertaste of loss and regret.

Kuhlman walked to the controllers' console. The supervisor, a new one, looked bleakly at him but said nothing.

"They'll clear the area after picking up," Kuhlman told him. "You can sort things out after a while, I suppose."

The supervisor nodded. "We have extra men, and I've talked to Approach Control. We'll be screwed up most of the night, but we have a plan started."

Kuhlman pointed his thumb over his shoulder. "I'm going to my office. Keep this line over here open, and let me know what happens next, right?"

"Right, sir."

There was more that needed to be said. Kuhlman felt a deep-down need for something, some kind of reassurance, the slightest grim smile that said *You were right.* But there was nothing from this man, a veteran who knew better than to commit himself, and the others in the tower were watching the second Cherokee landing.

So you made your decisions alone and you lived with them that way, too.

Kuhlman turned and headed back downstairs.

The outer office was in crowded turmoil. More FBI men were there, some police, Wentworth, a couple of men who looked like reporters who might have slipped in, Barbara, Saundra, another girl from a steno pool, the airline executives. Rickman was trying to talk on two telephones at once, and the police had some elaborate electronic gear spread out over a table. Charts had been spread on a section of the floor. It was smoky and loud. Kuhlman realized, as several faces turned to him, how tired he was.

"Mr. Kuhlman—" one of the reporters said, starting toward him.

"What's the report?" one of the airlines men asked. "Have they—"

"I've got Washington," Rickman yelled at him.

Kuhlman ignored them. He burrowed straight through to his office door and slammed it behind him.

Inside the office, in his den, it was quieter. The fluorescents buzzed slightly, and except for the Christmas tree effect of the lighted phones, things looked normal. He walked to his desk and looked down at a bronzed model of a DC-3 the people at Indianapolis had given him when he left there. Unaccountably, his emotions broke.

The door opened behind him, quietly. He kept his back turned. This was all he needed, someone to see him like this. "Get out!" he yelled.

The door closed, but there were light footsteps. Barbara came to his side. He tried to keep his face from her.

"Coffee?" she asked.

Well, hell.

He turned and faced her. "Yeah. Great."

She did not flinch from the tears on his face. She looked at him very straight, very calm, very strong. She held out his mug with coffee already in it.

He took it and went behind the desk. He sat down gratefully, looking at her over the clutter of papers and memorabilia on the desk. "Thanks."

"You did the right thing," she told him.

He blew his nose. "Big airport executive chokes up like a kid."

She smiled. "You spend too much time being tough. Maybe this is good for you."

He did not answer. The night's tension had moved them closer together than might otherwise have been possible. Now she had seen him at his worst, with his defenses gone, shattered, and yet she was smiling at him with much in her eyes. He did not know how to react. He knew he might be frightened of this woman.

"Good coffee," he said over the rim of the cup.

She sat on the edge of the desk, swinging a leg. "Sure."

"A lot of people are going to be after my scalp, babe."

"So what else is new?"

"I don't even know if I did it all right!"

"How many people ever do, you big dummy?"

The intercom box flashed. He pressed the button.

Saundra's voice said, "Second plane is off and the last one is landing, the tower says."

"Okay."

"Some of these people want to talk with you right away."

170

"In a minute." He cut the connection, gave Barbara a rueful look and honked into the stupid hankie again.

She asked, "How long do you suppose it will take to get back into normal operation?"

"Hours."

"Those little planes are going to get away."

He shrugged.

"I'm hungry," she said.

"You can get out of here soon, Barbara. We can handle it."

"That's not what I meant. What I meant was, I wonder if I could persuade you to buy me a steak a little later?"

He looked at her, unable to read her strange, smiling expression. "I'll be here half the night."

"I can wait," she told him.

"No need for that. I've asked quite enough of you."

Very quickly she came around the desk; she stood there a moment, looking down at him.

Then, startlingly, she turned herself and plopped down on his lap. She was a big girl and she felt nice.

"I've wanted to do that for about a hundred years," she murmured.

"Get up," he said. "I mean, you can't *do* that. I'm supposed to be—"

"Human, you big dumbbell," she whispered. And with a solemn, lovely intensity, she pressed her mouth against his.

Ted Kuhlman did not react exactly as he would have predicted he might. So much had happened in such a short time that he had no emotional defenses left. He held her, and the need started pouring out. He had denied it for so long that it shocked him. How had he *not known?*

The door of the office flew open, and Wentworth barged in. He was so intent upon his message that his wide eyes did not even react to the unexpected sight of his boss holding a pretty secretary on his lap.

"Last plane just made its pickup!" he said hoarsely. "He took off and the three of them broke formation, right over the tower. The tower says they're headed straight for downtown Atlanta!"

171

ESCAPE

With rotating beacons and running lights now turned off, the three Cherokee Sixes fled northward over the city of Atlanta at a ground speed of approximately 155 mph. Bunched in a close V, with Donovan on the forward point, they held altimeters on 1,600, m.s.l., or a little over five hundred feet above the level of the ground. At this extreme low altitude, their speed seemed much faster: below their wings, streets, cars, intersections, buildings and shopping centers flashed by almost too swiftly to register.

Packed in this low, they were masked from aircraft above by the continuous glare of the city's lights. Their greatest enemy now was radar. They had to remain low, in the ground clutter on the screens back in Approach Control.

Near the heart of the city, on the preselected frequency, Donovan keyed his microphone without words for five seconds. On the signal, the three aircraft veered slightly to the west, taking them to the vector that would let them pass to the left of Atlanta's tangle of tall radio and TV towers on the northeast side. There was a slight haze of smog over the city, but the pilots could clearly see the flashing red beacons that marked the jungle of towers.

Still packed densely together, the Cherokees picked a path midway between Fulton County airport, on the left, and DeKalb-Peachtree on the right. Both fields had been warned by the Atlanta International tower and were holding traffic against a possible midair, and to try to help pursuers.

With the lights of Dobbins Air Force Base nearing on the left side, Donovan again keyed his microphone, producing a loud break in the normal channel hiss on the other planes' overamplified ceiling loudspeakers. Again the signal was recognized and the three aircraft veered back toward true north, hugging the ground. They clung to their formation for what seemed like another few fleeting seconds but was actually about four minutes. Then, without further signal, Tom Keel applied light right aileron pressure and banked off to the east, moving rapidly away from the other two. Within seconds, Jack Abercrombie's aircraft broke off from Donovan on the other side, sliding out into the dark to the west. Donovan's Cherokee bored on northward, and the space between the planes rapidly widened.

The major sprawl of city lights was now behind them, and below was black countryside punctuated by outside farm lights, here the twin cones of a car's headlights on a road, there a lonely service station. Very busy with his flying, Keel looked back to see if he could still make out the ghostly outlines of the other two aircraft. The sky had swallowed them up. Keel knew he would not see them again.

At approximately 6:34, Abercrombie turned his low-flying plane almost directly south for about one minute, then did a 180-degree turn to the north for two minutes, then swung back to a heading of 250 degrees, almost directly west. Two minutes later, and almost simultaneously, although they did not know it, Keel and Donovan broke from their first headings; still very low, Keel turned to a heading slightly south of due east, while Donovan, some twenty-five miles away by this time, swung to a northwesterly direction.

At this time, Atlanta Approach Control was scanning its near-airport radar screens, looking at an electronic circle that extended out between thirty-five and forty-five miles, depending on ground obstacles and atmospheric conditions. Already, with the immediate emergency lifted, several commercial airliners were calling in for sequencing into the

173

landing pattern, and three of the long-delayed flights had lifted off from runway 9L. Except for these targets, well highlighted by transponders, Approach Control could not spot a thing.

Atlanta Center, with its more powerful long-distance scopes, was still operating on its backup systems because of the power surge that had broken some equipment earlier. Built-in redundancy made the backup system adequate, but there were more than a hundred targets all over the long-distance screens, many of them private aircraft passing through the area under Visual Flight Rules, with no radio contact required, and there was absolutely no way to know whether any of the blips might be the Atlanta raiders.

F-4s, on top, could not see a thing. The Guard helicopters, barging about at low altitudes, were just as helpless.

In Washington, D.C., the lights were all ablaze in the suite that they called the "Hijack Room." Actually a series of conference rooms connected by sliding doors, it was the nerve center for any hijacking or other major unlawful incident affecting public transportation, airlines in particular. The central room, some forty feet long and equipped with the finest communications facilities that could be packed into a ten-foot, floor-to-ceiling console, was often referred to as "the pit." There were some dozen experts in the pit now, some on telephones, some on special radios, others huddled over charts. In one of the smaller rooms adjoining, the two men at the center of the capture operation stood looking glumly at a ten-foot map of North America.

The shorter of the two men, with balding, crinkled hair and a brown suit to match, was holding a pencil attached to a length of string. His name was Joe Bishop and he was thinking worriedly out loud.

"You say those Piper specs show a range of maybe nine hundred miles for a Cherokee Six of this type," he muttered, fingering the string. "But that doesn't mean they had that much range remaining to them when they bugged out."

The other man, D. C. Granger, looked up from the papers he held in his hands. He was almost six feet five, incredibly lanky, with shaggy graying hair. He was wearing

174

Levi's and a flannel lumberjack shirt because he had been at home when his FAA superior ordered him out on the double to act as adviser to the FBI on the case.

"They won't have the full eighty-four gallons left," Granger said. "That's certain. They were over the field for more than an hour, and prior to that they had to take off and rendezvous. They were flogging those Sixes over the field, too, and they had another takeoff. Do we know yet where they originated?"

Bishop scowled. "You mean for figuring how far they had flown before they showed up over the field?"

"Right."

"No. That's just one of the things we don't have yet."

Granger nodded. "Okay. Figuring their probable range is problematical at best, because we don't know what power settings they'll use, or at what altitudes, or even what kinds of winds they'll face."

"I'm looking for a ballpark figure."

"Okay. Give them three-fifths of their fuel remaining when they left the field area." Granger pulled a flat leather case from his shirt pocket and took out a small E6-B type flight computer. He spun the front dial. "Figuring seventy-five percent power, zero wind, properly leaned . . ." He read the dial. "Yes, that checks about right."

Bishop leaned against the big map and placed his finger, holding the string, on the pin marking Atlanta. "How far out do I draw the circle? That will indicate how far they might run, the area we have to give strongest concentration."

"Make it six hundred miles," Granger said.

Bishop frowned with concentration as he marked off the string against the scale on the map. Then, holding the appropriate length on Atlanta, he swung the pencil out at maximum extension, scribing a large penciled circle on the map.

"God," he muttered disgustedly as he did so.

Then he stepped back and took a better look. His beat-up features seemed to shrink, all the lines turning down in dismay.

"God almighty damn," he said.

175

The circle touched the southern tip of Florida's Keys, extended through much of the Gulf of Mexico, and entered the United States again around Houston, Texas. From there the curving line ran up through, or near, Dallas, Tulsa, Kansas City, Cedar Rapids, Milwaukee, Saginaw, Buffalo, and New York City before going out to cover a huge piece of the Atlantic.

"They can fly to half the God damned country!" Bishop said in dismay.

"Almost," said Granger, who was very literal-minded.

By 7 P.M., Tom Keel was more than sixty miles east-northeast of Atlanta on a heading to the southeast that would have eventually taken him to Jacksonville, Florida, if he had remained on it. His altitude was now 11,500 feet, m.s.l., one of the normal altitudes for routine VFR flight, and he had the beacon and running lights back in operation. Except for the battering wind entering the rear cargo opening, it was now almost a normal flight, proceeding—for the radar boys—from a point that certainly would not appear suspicious on the scopes.

MacReady had climbed up into the front right-hand seat and sat there beside Keel, his teeth chattering from wind chill despite his leather jacket, gloves, and cap.

"Farther south we go, the warmer it ought to get, right?" MacReady said loudly over the noise.

"We can hope so," Keel agreed.

"We can be a little cold for this kind of payday, right, mother?"

"Let's get it down before we start bragging too much."

"We've got it made! What could happen now?"

Keel shrugged and did not comment. It irritated him to concede that MacReady was probably right. *Probably.* The oil temperature had subsided now, indicating that all might be well, and only the wildest chance could bring another aircraft close enough now for the missing cargo door or their registration number to be noted. It was a very big sky.

Keel also knew, however, that they had another three hours of flying ahead of them. Then would come the wait, and then finally would come one of the trickiest maneuvers

176

of all. They were not clear yet by any means. Perhaps it was superstition, hating to start any congratulations until *all* of the escape plan had been completed.

So far it had all gone almost exactly according to plan. There was no real reason to anticipate otherwise in the hours ahead. But Keel knew that the final phases of this particular escape plan, involving MacReady as it did, could still turn sour. He had given much thought to this, and figured he was ready for all eventualities. But it was no time to count any chickens. Not quite yet.

"What are those lights out on your side, way out there?" MacReady asked, nudging him.

Keel did not have to look out his left side to know. "Augusta."

"We're already going back south, huh?"

"Southeast."

"Then we get down below Macon and hook it back southwest, right?"

"That's right. According to plan."

MacReady slapped his arms against his sides. "I'm cold!"

"It's the wind-chill factor. The air temperature is—"

"I don't care what it is, man! I'm cold!"

Keel did not reply. The air was very smooth, and overhead the stars shone with brittle intensity. Light patches of haze momentarily blacked out some of the scattered ground lights below them, but it was a perfect night. Keel could feel aches and pains as some of his tension momentarily slackened.

He was very tired already. The work over Atlanta had been harder than he had expected, the nervous energy draining him fast. Now the chilling did not help. The time had about passed when there was really much chance for any kind of aerial intercept, and with this fading threat, his emotions were slumping to allow his body the luxury of discomfort.

Tapping MacReady's knee, he pointed to one of the thermos jugs on the front floor. MacReady nodded, uncapped the bottle, and shakily poured each of them a plastic cup of coffee that steamed heavily because of the altitude.

"Wonder if the others remembered java," MacReady said, leaning back.

"I imagine," Keel said, correcting course ever so slightly to keep the VOR needle centered.

"Wonder where they are by now."

"I don't know."

"I wish we had a way of knowing what's going on!"

"What could be going on?"

"I mean I'd like to *know.*"

"Maybe we can do something about that."

Aware of MacReady's intent look, he leaned forward to the controls of the ADF, a device capable of "homing in" on low frequency radio sources, including commercial radio stations. As he flicked the knob on, the needle turned and tried to point at something. He turned the selector switch to *audio* and there was a burst of static from the overhead speakers.

"What's this all about?" MacReady demanded.

Keel twirled the dial. Loud country music blared in.

"Hey! Hey! All riiight!"

Keel kept tuning and got an announcer's voice. He stopped and listened.

"*—no further developments on the brazen attack at Atlanta's major airport,*" the announcer clipped. "*Apparently there were no injuries. The three small private aircraft demanded, and got, three million dollars from a trio of the country's major airlines, Northwest, Delta, and Southern.*

"*While the planes circled the field at low altitudes, the airlines delivered the money in the suitcases. These were placed on a runway, and, while helpless law enforcement officials watched, the planes took turns landing and picking up a suitcase each.*"

"You better believe it!" MacReady chortled.

"Listen!"

"*After the money was picked up, the three airplanes headed over downtown Atlanta. The last visual sighting was reported by a farmer north of the city, who said he saw the three planes heading west, according to unofficial sources.*"

"West!" MacReady echoed in amazement.

178

"At the present hour, there is no word on the three planes. The FBI and state and local authorities have thrown a tight ring of security around their investigation. It appears, according to one source, that the planes escaped the immediate area."

MacReady yodeled approval and tossed his empty coffee cup on the floor. "You better believe it!"

"In other news at this hour—"

"How does this work?" MacReady asked, reaching for the dial.

"Just turn it."

MacReady turned it. In again came a country girl singer, backed by fiddles and guitars, lamenting her honey who left her on a lonely country road. MacReady grinned, lit a cigarette, and leaned back, tapping his hand on the instrument panel cowling. Keel wondered about Donovan and Abercrombie—where they were and how they were going—and yearned for more news. But he did not argue.

They flew on into the night, the western music blaring in the windy cabin.

It was only 6:30 in Nebraska, and Cal Reveloff was still in the office at the airport when the FBI came.

There were two of them.

Reveloff took one look at their identification, one at their faces and started to get that paranoid feeling. He reacted by being overly hearty. "What's it all about, gentlemen? Are you sure you've got the right airport? Ha ha."

The taller agent took out a sheet of paper on which he had carefully penciled three aircraft registration numbers. "These aircraft belong to your outfit?"

Reveloff glanced at the numbers, recognized them. "Yeah, I think so. I think they're three of our new Sixes." He turned to the counter. "Let me check my book here." He thumbed a few pages quickly. "What's this all about?"

"We'd like to know who you rented these planes to, and when. Also any other information you might have."

Reveloff found the proper entries. "Here you go. Smith-

179

Peterson Aerial Survey. Out of Memphis. They picked up one on the uh . . . let's see . . . October 12, and then one about a week later, and the third one on the twenty-first. What's going on?"

The one agent leaned over the ledger book. "Do you have an address?"

"Sure. Here it is."

He copied it carefully. "How did they pay you?"

"Check, I think."

"On what bank?"

"I don't remember. Say, what is this?"

"Was it a Memphis bank?"

"I imagine so. I think it was. Yes."

"Can you describe the man who made the arrangements?"

"I didn't handle it myself," Reveloff said. "My manager did. Say, what is this all about? Have my airplanes been stolen or something?"

"Something like that," the shorter agent said. "Will you call your manager? We need to talk with him right away. It's important."

By a little after eight, Donovan had the lights of Memphis off his starboard wing. He was listening to Memphis weather. Ahead, the sky was vastly opaque, sure sign of the frontal system they were fast approaching. Already a few light streaks of rain showed on the windshield. The altimeter showed 10,500.

Beside him in the right-hand seat, Fetzer looked like a frozen Indian in his close-wrapped blanket. His breath puffed steam as he spoke anxiously. "What do we do now?"

"Go on through it," Donovan replied calmly.

"You can't."

"Why can't I?"

"That means IFR. You've got to file a flight plan and give our number. They're bound to have our number."

Donovan grinned at the young mechanic. "As long as we stay on a VFR altitude, the chances of meeting another plane are millions to one. We'll just go down low, to make sure we aren't on someone's radar, and bore right through it on instruments."

"That's against *all* the regulations—!" Fetzer began, and then saw how stupid the remark was, and shut up.

"Get in the old flight bag, there, and hand me a sandwich," Donovan suggested, still smiling. "Have one yourself, if you'll promise you don't get airsick."

"Is it going to be that rough up there?"

"Oh, I don't know. Maybe a little. But I don't see any lightning, do you? It might be a little rough, but nothing too bad."

Roughly a hundred miles south of Donovan's position, and slightly farther west, it was indeed a little rough. Abercrombie was already in the weather, flying illicit IFR just as Donovan was going to do. The Cherokee was continually buffeted by gusts, and rain hammered against the thin metal skin and swept in through the cargo door opening. Abercrombie leaned forward in the pilot's chair, his eyes intent on his instruments, the only things that could tell him, now, whether he was right-side up. It was not supposed to be a very thick line, and he hoped that was so. He did not like this.

The clock in the alcove off the pit in Washington jumped a notch, and it was exactly 9 P.M. Seated at the narrow table that faced the wall chart on which Bishop had drawn his range circle for the escaping planes, Granger sipped bitter black coffee and tried to figure out what was bothering him.

As far as he could tell, everything in the world was being done. All towers, radar facilities, airport operators, and Flight Service Stations had been notified, even those within the maximum possible range beyond Bishop's circle. The Cherokees had to come down somewhere, and soon. If they tried to land at any manned airport anywhere near the edge of the circle, or within its confines, there would be somebody nearby on alert.

Granger knew as well as anyone that there were also thousands of tiny grass strips that were seldom manned. These too were possible landing sites. He knew Bishop had given orders to send priority messages to law enforcement agencies everywhere within the circle, asking maximum possible help in keeping these smaller fields under surveillance until the time when the three aircraft had to be out of gas.

By Granger's best calculations, out-of-gas time had to be around ten o'clock. Even if the pilots of the Sixes cruised at fifty-five percent power, they couldn't get much beyond Bishop's pencil lines in range and much past ten o'clock in flying time. So within an hour or so they had to be coming down . . . if they were not down already.

It all made good sense. And yet something tickled at the back of Granger's mind, as it sometimes did when he forgot a minor appointment, and compounded that error by forgetting to check his appointment book so he could remind himself. It was a feeling that there was something he had overlooked. With all the possibilities floating around in his brain, he could not pinpoint it.

Bishop, looking haggard, came back in from the crowded pit. "Well, it looks like Atlanta is getting back on its feet. They say incoming flights are being held about forty minutes now. No casualties down there; that's verified."

"Any news on the Cherokees?"

"Nope, nothing. Some kids up near Charlotte called the police and said they saw a small plane land in a field near town, and the police found the plane, all right. It wasn't ours. Some clown ran out of gas."

"No possible connection?"

"I don't think so. They're holding the guy temporarily, but he was in a Cessna 150 and he checks out as living right in that area. He was on his way back from up in Ohio someplace and that checks out too."

"Have you gotten anything from the outfit that rented the planes?"

"Yeah, they rented to people in Memphis. We've got

men on the way to work that angle now. The way things have gone so far, I'm not very hopeful."

"Did you get descriptions on the men who picked up the planes?"

Bishop made a wry face. "The one guy they can give a good description of, I'd say he was probably set up. We've got his name out there and somebody is tracking him down. Your people in Oklahoma City say he recently got his commercial license. He told the Nebraska folks this was one of his first jobs. My guess is that these guys hired him to pick up two of the planes and he didn't know from nothing."

"Even so," Granger pointed out, vaguely enjoying playing detective, "he can give you descriptions of the people we *really* want."

Bishop snorted. "Judging by what the Nebraska man said, I dunno. My guess is that one of the real guys picked up the extra plane. Man out there describes him as long-haired, obviously a wig, dark glasses, some face hair, dark pants, dark shirt, medium height, medium build. Obviously the guy was hiding behind the shades and the hair. It makes a zilch description to work on."

"Maybe you'll be luckier with this young commercial pilot," Granger said.

"I'm not counting on it. These people were careful. They didn't leave us any autographed pictures."

"How about their office, if they had one?"

"They had one. Don't count on anything." Bishop sat down and got out a cigar. "I'm beginning to get a picture here. I can't say I like what I'm getting. Some guys move into Memphis. They set up a dummy company, a telephone, an address, a bank account, the works. They contact the Nebraska people by phone, make a deal to rent the planes, trick a kid pilot into flying the planes back for them, except for the one they have to get themselves, probably because of time pressure. But even there they look ahead to our investigation, and go in a disguise that messes up memory just enough to make it impossible for us. Then they set up and reel off a perfect quasi-military operation over one of the biggest, busiest airports in the country. Then they break out of there and show every sign of getting away clean."

Bishop paused and looked at Granger with eyes that drooped from fatigue. "Do *you* think we'll find diaries and fingerprints in that office in Memphis?"

"It sounds like you won't get much."

"We probably won't get a damned thing." Then, however, Bishop seemed to cheer up with an effort. "Of course we've got all sorts of techniques the general public doesn't know much about. We can go over that office with an electron microscope, if we have to. There are all sorts of things we might get lucky and find."

"Or get unlucky and not find?"

Bishop ignored the remark. "We're probably going to start going through your organization's lists of pilots tomorrow, if we don't get them tonight."

"I told you how many names are on those lists."

"Yeah," Bishop said. "I know. I used to be a cop in Little Rock. When I saw the number of people that are licensed pilots, it gave me a shock. It really did. My God, is everybody a pilot? I thought there might be a few thousand, but this is ridiculous. I was thinking we could take that list of pilots and start checking them out, working from a narrowed field, you know. But I feel it's like it would have been in Little Rock if somebody had told me the field of suspects had been narrowed to a local man." Bishop rubbed his forehead. "It isn't that much help."

"And, of course," Granger pointed out, "they don't have to be licensed pilots."

"*What?*" Cigar ashes fell on Bishop's shirt front.

"I'm sorry to tell you, but there are a lot of people out there capable of flying who aren't licensed pilots. Plenty of military pilots never change over when they get out. And an advanced student pilot might pull it off. Or a pilot's wife, who had flown with him a lot, and learned it all, but never got up her nerve to take the test."

"I *hope* that's not too damned likely."

"It's not too likely," Granger conceded. "But it's possible."

184

Bishop got back to his feet. "I'll go see if they've got anything new. Why don't the bastards just land at some big field and let us catch them? Don't they have any consideration?"

Granger grinned as the FBI man strode out of the room. But the grin did not hold. Granger was still not satisfied that he had considered all the possibilities. Things were eluding him. He frowned at the chart, studying it, trying to put himself in the place of a hijacker.

At 9:45 P.M., Abercrombie had the lights of Texarkana off his starboard wingtip at a distance of about thirty miles. He had broken through the front and was in clear air again, although the wind had turned unfavorable. He was lagging behind his planned times now, using up precious fuel.

"Is there any way to tell exactly how much we've got in that thing?" he asked Phil Lester.

Lester yawned and turned to look at the lashed-down 55-gallon drum behind the seats. "I could take the top off, but we're bound to have a bunch left."

"We'd better have. We've got more than two hours to go."

"We figured it and figured it, Jack. We're okay."

Abercrombie subsided. He knew it was absurd to worry now. He should be feeling elation. They were far from the main search area and had not been challenged. He knew he could put the Six into the area they had selected in West Texas, and nobody could possibly have found the two dirt bikes they had hidden under the charred planks of the old burned house. By midnight they would be just a couple of motorcycle nuts, going their separate ways, tooling along back roads with little camping packs. By the time the plane could be found, or what was left of it after they blew up the dynamite, they would be long gone.

It had all worked well and it all would work well. He felt strangely confident about that now. His worry was based not so much on fact as on longstanding habit.

Touching up the trim, Abercrombie let the plane practically fly itself. He allowed himself the luxury and the agony of looking ahead.

He was glad that some of them, at least, had decided against the earlier plan of assuming new identities. This had been the subject of considerable debate at their last impromptu meeting, held after the second delay for weather.

At first the new identity had seemed the perfect plan. But as Abercrombie had worried about it, as he worried about everything, it had begun to dawn on him that some of them might be traced more easily by the fact that they had so suddenly dropped from sight. He had mentioned this worry and had learned that some of the others had been thinking the same thing.

Donovan had argued that hundreds of men dropped from sight every year. Nothing was easier than to move to a new locality and assume a new identity, he had said. But Lester had chimed in with worry, and regret, of his own: he wanted to go back to the Houston area and resume his life. He said he wanted all the time in the world to go around the country at his leisure, passing the money off in small doses.

Finally it had been decided that changes of identity, like escape plans, would be left to the individual. Each escape route had been a matter for a two-man team, up until the time the plane was landed. But after that, Abercrombie, for example, did not know exactly what Lester's plan might be. Nor did anyone know his. It was better that way, he thought.

He needed no new identity, and no excuse for his absence the past days. By the end of the week, after quick trips to Minneapolis, Chicago, and St. Louis to change money in quick sweeps through shopping areas, he would be at the clinic in Temple with his excuse for work absences very obvious in his throat.

Abercrombie knew it was cancer. That had already been confirmed. The only question was whether it might be halted. The doctors had been reasonably hopeful . . . weeks ago.

Now the hoarseness was worse, and the soreness. No

186

one would question the way he had left his last job. They knew. And there was nothing about the operation that was bogus. No one would suspect that a man in his condition could have carried off a part of Operation Nightfall.

Thinking about it, Abercrombie felt the usual bitterness mix with his fear. He thought he wanted the cancer to be arrested. There were times when he was not so sure.

His larynx, the doctors said, had to go. They would slash out his voice, poke a hole in his throat, and possibly save his life. He might learn to talk with a new device, or by using the older method of swallowing air. His days of normal speech were at an end. But with luck he might live a long time.

He might even fly again someday.

Abercrombie was trying very hard to convince himself that he wanted a life like that. Half the time he succeeded.

Looking at the brighter side, he thought bitterly, a man in such a position was expected to liquidate belongings in order to help cover expenses the insurance overlooked. There would be mountainous bills, and large amounts of money going through his checking account on the way to various doctors and technicians. Ruinous checking transactions were the norm for a cancer victim. This would all help screen the influx of Atlanta money, as he made trips around the country, getting rid of more of it for clean change.

But there was no way he would ever enjoy any of the cash the way some of the others might, he thought. This was not really self-pity but merely a factual evaluation of circumstances. If the cancer had gone too far, he was a dead man, and soon.

He thought about the others, especially Donovan and Keel. Had they landed by now? Were they all right? What about MacReady, the weak link in the chain?

For a moment, Abercrombie almost regretted his part in this. He thought about his ex-wife and how things might have been different.

Beside him, Phil Lester fished out a harmonica and began playing softly, low, despite the deepening cold. It was a lonely sound and it touched things in Abercrombie, and, paradoxically, he felt better.

It occurred to him suddenly that he might die very soon, but even if he did, *they could never take this away from him.* Not the planning, not the work and worry, not the agonizing delays, not the high adventure over the airport, not the storm, not this moment, now, high over the piney woods of East Texas, with a buddy playing a slightly sour harmonica in the icy wind.

As long as he lived, short time or long time, this was the high point of his life. He would always look back to it as the peak. And it was mighty fine, this peak. Many never had one.

Abercrombie swallowed with some effort, grinned at Lester, and asked—a little hoarsely—if he knew "Yellow Rose of Texas." Of course Phil Lester did.

At the time the FBI agents broke into the little office in Memphis, Keel was over Mississippi, letting the well-trimmed plane go its own way as he double-checked VOR bearings for his turn south toward Gulfport. He had finally persuaded MacReady to turn the ADF off, and the relative quiet was very nice. Donovan, meanwhile, had the lights of Tulsa behind him and to the south, and was drinking more coffee because he knew he had almost three hours yet to fly, and an extraordinarily difficult landing at the end of it.

The FBI men, a team of five, had the janitor call the building manager, but by the time he reached the scene they had already broken into the Smith-Peterson offices.

"I don't understand this!" he protested. "Why are you doing this?"

Agents were walking gingerly around the offices in their stockinged feet while one of their fellows carefully vacuumed the floor around them with a small, battery-operated cleaner. One man was dusting things for fingerprints, another was taking photographs, the others were very carefully going through desk drawers and wastebaskets.

"What do you think?" one of the agents asked another.

"I think," the other said, "this place is clean as a whistle."

"That's what I think, too," the first agent said.

Things were not much more hopeful in the pit in Washington. There the major work of notifying other authorities had been done, and there had not even been a false alarm to stir things up in over an hour. Some of the experts in the larger room had allowed themselves a coffee break down the hall. Bishop and Granger remained in the smaller room, where Bishop had been having the finer points of aeronautical charts explained to him.

"If they're anywhere in this damned circle," Bishop said now for the third or fourth time, "it looks like somebody ought to spot them!"

"Agreed," Granger said, glancing at the clock. "But they've got to be out of fuel within the next ten minutes. There's just no way. We have to face the facts. They must have all landed without being seen."

Bishop balefully eyed the clock, which showed about 10:30. "You'd think somebody would see some damned thing."

Granger said nothing. He was still listening to the tickle in his mind. They had picked Cherokee Sixes for their range and capacity, obviously, and the fact that the cargo door could easily be removed for use by gunners. The Six was a nice, forgiving, stable airplane, ideal for the job. It had good short-field capability. There were a million places to land one in an emergency.

"We only got to get one of them," Bishop said half to himself. "You catch one, he'll crack and tell where the others went. It stands to reason they scattered, but if we can just catch one, we can get the rest too."

"What if they land and get away from the planes?" Granger asked. "Then what?"

"We'll still get them. It will just take a lot longer, maybe."

"By the money?"

"Huh?"

Granger clarified. "You'll catch them when they try to spend the money?"

"Eventually," Bishop said. "Or by checking every damned name we can come up with. Or from the composite descriptions, even if they aren't too good. Or with something from the lab."

"Then catching them when they land is not a matter of life and death."

"It's nice to get 'em fast."

"Well," Granger said, staring at the map once more, and at Bishop's penciled circle on it, "we've got to face the fact that our chances are just about gone."

"Yeah, I suppose they're almost out of gas."

"Yes."

"I thought," Bishop said, standing and jamming his hands in his back pockets, "we might have a chance, having that circle to concentrate in. I mean, at least it narrows it down."

Granger nodded silently, noticing how the FBI man's hands made the back of his pants bulge. Back pockets, he thought randomly, were not built to carry weight.

Then Granger's mind made some strange little jump.

The back . . . weight!

He looked at the map again, and at Bishop. Granger's pulse fluttered with excitement and dismay. Why hadn't he thought of it before?

"You know," he said, amazed at how calm he sounded, "I'm afraid we've overlooked something very elementary."

Bishop turned. "What?"

"Extra fuel."

"Extra fuel! You said those planes carry eighty-four gallons!"

"Yes. But listen. Why would they pick the Six, rather than, say, an Arrow? We assumed it was for the cargo door. But a window could be knocked out of other aircraft. *What if they used the Six because it provided so much space for a special extra fuel tank?*"

190

Bishop looked stunned. "Can you do that? Just throw on an extra tank of gas?"

Granger was thinking about his time in Cherokees, and what little he knew about their layout, and he was on his feet now. His mind was satisfied because he had found the absurdly simple item they had been overlooking.

"It could be done," he muttered. "I don't even think it would be very hard. Just get some kind of a big container, say a fifty-five-gallon drum, tie it or bolt it down in the back, there, run a hose up front. I think you could probably hook into the fuel selector valve, or maybe into the floor . . . the lines ought to go right through the middle of the plane there. . . ."

"You mean they might have had more range than my circle shows?" Bishop demanded angrily.

"A lot more," Granger said. "I should have thought of this. I was stupid—of course it's just a possibility, but—"

"Indulge me," Bishop snapped, and went to the wall and retrieved his pencil and string. "Show me how far those bastards could fly if they *did* have some extra fuel."

"I don't know how much they might pack on there. My God, they might stow a hundred gallons, they could be overgross, but—"

"A fifty-five-gallon drum," Bishop said. "Like you said. Would that make my circle much bigger? Would it mean that maybe they've flown clear and the hell across the country while we were only alerting people in this smaller area?"

"It could. I've been stupid—"

"Show me," Bishop ordered, handing him the pencil and string.

Granger knew, even before he pulled out his E6-B for a quick, simple calculation, that it was going to be bad. He translated the figures into some shrewd educated guesses, and looked at the map. It *was* bad.

"You're not going to like this," he said, and fitted the string to the board.

He carefully drew the new circle outside Bishop's. This one went far south of Florida, reached a part of the Yucatan peninsula, swung through most of Mexico, included much of New Mexico, Colorado, Wyoming, Minnesota, a huge portion of Canada, all of New England, an incredible area of the Atlantic.

He stood back and looked at his circle, comparing it ruefully with the one Bishop had drawn earlier.

"God," Bishop said. His face was slack, beaten.

"It means they might still be flying," Granger said, trying to be stupidly helpful. "I mean, there might still be a chance . . . somewhere."

"Yeah. But it means a little more than that, buddy."

"What?"

"It means we've had it. We've lost them."

Making sure to remain well north of Mobile, Keel tracked inbound on the Picayune VOR until he had the distant lights of Gulfport-Biloxi somewhat to his south and east. He had been descending steadily, and when he made his turn south, to a heading of 170 degrees, the altimeter showed 2,500 feet. Everything was according to plan.

It was much warmer at this altitude and so close to the Gulf, and MacReady had perked up again. "We're getting there, right?"

"Not far now," Keel agreed.

"How far is the island from here anyway?"

"Not far." Keel was busy.

In a little while, with the panel clock showing almost 10:40, they slid over the spangled highway that marked land's end. Off to the distant right was the starry sprawl of New Orleans, with only a little low haze to obscure portions of it. The Cherokee was now over the dark water of Mississippi Sound. Keel held his course, practically knowing the way by heart now.

His nerves were at high tension once more despite familiarity with the area. Aircraft skylarking around in the night, in this area, were not so common, and he feared radar. The landing, assuming all went well in the next few minutes, would also be a little tricky.

"Hey," MacReady grunted, looking down. "What are those lights?"

"Fishing boats, probably," Keel said.

"Are we going to have fishing boats around *us*?"

"I damned well hope not."

"What do we do if we—" MacReady stopped. "Oh, yeah. I remember."

There was a contingency plan. Keel knew of three lighted, unattended little airports in the immediate area. If the island appeared to have people on it at this time, or if there were fishermen around, if the weather had been foul, or if something was wrong with the boat, they could try one of the inland fields and hope for the best.

As the last minutes ticked off, one possibility after the other was eliminated. Once he had the light on the north end of the island clearly in view, Keel guided toward it, swinging in a broad, gentle arc but seeing no lights of boats. Descending further, he had the island itself in view and could see no campfires or other illumination. There had been times in the past when he had had one of those islands entirely to himself during the night. It had been romantic then. Now it was simply mandatory.

He was very, very tired, but the adrenalin was flowing again. Swinging around from north to east, and then back toward the way he had come, Keel flew along the narrow length of the island's central section. Lights of cities were faint jewels on the far horizons, but close at hand the water of the Sound was dark and smooth. He could see, at low altitude, the slightly rolling swell of the water and the gentle breakers on the long beaches. The island itself, low, sandy, covered with knee-high shrubs and brush, appeared to be deserted. Except for the navigation light on the northernmost tip, there was no other telltale gleam.

Keel reset throttle and propeller to landing settings and banked to the right, beginning his descent. With the light as it was, there was no need to accept the marginal risk involved in slipping into the cleared strip. He would land on the beach itself.

"Buckle up," he reminded MacReady. His companion

nodded and obeyed. Was MacReady just the slightest bit afraid in an airplane? It had not appeared so earlier, but now Keel wondered. His silence was uncharacteristic.

Then, however, another explanation occurred to him. MacReady might be thinking the same possibilities that were in his mind: division of the money and the steps they still had to take. There were places for treachery just ahead. Did MacReady see this, and, if he did, was he worrying about treachery on Keel's part or planning some of his own?

No time now to think about it. Keel swung the Cherokee around to the north, got the flaps down, and descended toward the sandy strip between coarse vegetation and the surf. He kept some power on and wafted over the irregular sand surface at a height of about a foot. With fingers that sensed every turn of the engine, he bled the power off in minute fractions, simultaneously easing back the yoke in almost imperceptible degrees. The stall light winked red at him. The right main gear touched down with feather lightness, followed by the left. The plane veered a hair and then was down firmly, kicking up dust. They were down.

Wind and sun had baked the sand surface hard, and the plane taxied nicely enough as Keel got the flaps dumped, the landing light off and the other lights doused. He fed in some power and turned around and taxied back the way he had rolled on the landing, searching for the place he had spotted dimly from the air. He was soaked with nervous sweat.

"That was perfect!" MacReady said too loudly over the idling engine. "What're we doing now?"

"Looking for the boat."

MacReady pointed. "Just ahead there. See where the stuff is thickest? I saw it when we touched down."

Keel spotted the place MacReady was pointing toward. Then, as he taxied a few more yards, he saw the gray canvas covering against the darker coloration of the scrubby vegetation. He swung the plane a little to the right, nearer the brush, then swung it back the other way to have a takeoff roll in a hurry if that should become necessary. He cut the radio, bled the engine and flipped off the other switches, leaving the key in the mag starter switch.

194

The prop swung through another few revolutions and then stopped, and it was almost frighteningly quiet after the hours of racket. With ears that continued to ring, Keel heard the ripple of the surf on the sand fifty feet away and the call of some lone night bird. For a few seconds, the transition left him mighty disoriented.

Then he unhooked his harness. "Let's check it out."

MacReady popped the door open and climbed out onto the wing, then to the ground. Keel followed on legs unsteady from sitting so long. He felt a little dizzy following MacReady to the covered boat.

It was aluminum, fifteen feet in length, with a big Johnson motor bolted on the back. Inside, under the canvas cover, were an extra gasoline can and some cheap fishing gear and the half-dozen slender wood rods MacReady had used to roll the thing out of the water and into cover. Even using the roll-rods, Keel thought, he had done a hell of a job getting it this deep into the brush.

Checking the boat over, they found no sign of tampering. Keel found it hard to believe this good luck. He had been emotionally prepared for the disappointment of vandalism or an outright theft, even on this deserted island. These eventualities—or bad weather—would have forced them to one of their options mainland. These would not be necessary.

"It looks all right," he said finally.

MacReady stood with hands on his hips. "Want to get this baby into the water?"

"I think we'd better. Then we can wade it out far enough to put the motor down and make sure we can start it."

"We can start it." MacReady grinned.

"I hope you're right. Assuming you are, all we have to do then is try to get some rest before morning."

"*After* we divide the money," MacReady corrected him.

"If you want to do that now," Keel said coldly, "fine."

"I want to do it before you get back in that airplane, I'll tell you that."

"Do you think I'd take off and leave you?"

"I ain't saying you would and I ain't saying you wouldn't. I just want my half under my seat in that boat, that's all."

Keel looked at him, feeling the hate that flowed in both directions. It could all go up in smoke right here, he thought. If he let it.

With considerable effort he smiled. "I don't care how the money is handled, friend, as long as we both get our share and we get the rest of our plan taken care of."

"Then things are going to be just dandy," MacReady said sarcastically.

"Let's get the boat in, shall we?"

They got on opposite sides, used one of the wood roller bars to get started, and manhandled the boat down the gentle slope to the water's edge. MacReady had such tremendous physical strength that it was surprisingly easy. They walked it out to knee-deep water and MacReady deftly climbed aboard, rocking the craft dangerously. Keel held the front steady to keep it from turning sideways to the beach, and MacReady went to the back, squatted on the back seat, and lowered the motor.

"It's hitting bottom," he said, raising it again.

"Want me to walk you out farther?"

"Let me get the gas on and ready and then you can just give me a shove."

Keel waited while MacReady fiddled with lines and valves.

"Okay. Give me a good shove out."

Keel complied, almost falling over. The boat slid silently backward through the gentle wavelets. MacReady lowered the motor again, bent to check something, and gave the rope a hard pull. The engine farted but did not respond. He hauled on the rope a second time and it fired, tried to die, caught, and began throbbing smoothly. Turning, he sat down on the back seat, swung the motor to one side, fed it some gas, and took it out away from shore in a small circle.

Keel stood where he was, the boat's waves splashing

coldly against his thighs. MacReady knew how to handle the boat; of course he had had practice getting it out here, pulling the smaller boat he had used to get back. He swung out away from shore, turned left and then right, headed away from the island and gave the motor full throttle for a few seconds, reduced power, turned, and came back.

He came directly toward Keel. Keel backed up and got onto firm dry ground. MacReady cut the motor, raised it, and expertly slid the boat right up onto the beach.

Together they pulled it up a little higher, beaching it firmly.

"Now," MacReady grinned, rubbing his hands together, "let's count that money, huh?"

East of Lubbock, Abercrombie and Lester landed in a hill valley shortly after 11:45, eastern time. The night was vast and still, with a characteristic immense Texas sky overhead. They waited beside the plane for almost fifteen minutes, making sure no one had seen them from the distant country road.

Abandoning their earlier idea of blowing up the Cherokee, they left it standing there in the eroded field, where it might not be found for a week or more, and hiked the half-mile to the burned-out old farmhouse. There was a minute of panic when they found that someone had camped nearby in the last few days. But digging under the charred planks showed that the two light motorcycles had not been discovered or bothered in any way.

Lashing their camper packs on the back, they fired up the two bikes. The two-stroke engines popped and banged in the vast stillness. Forking his machine, Abercrombie leaned across and silently shook hands with his partner. Then they put the machines in gear and took off across the fields, headed for the distant section-line road. When they reached it they gave each other the slightest final salute and turned off in opposite directions, Abercrombie heading north, Lester south. They left behind them on the dirt road a slowly dissipating haze of oil smoke, and after a while the sound of their cornpopper engines was gone, and the night slept.

Wednesday, November 13

Warm in his sleeping bag, Tom Keel lay under the broad white wing of the Cherokee and listened to the soft sound of MacReady's snoring. Keel was fully awake, as he had been the entire hour or so since his companion had quickly fallen off to sleep. He envied MacReady a little, and hated him too. Too much could still go wrong. How could the man blissfully sleep?

Staring at the lines of flat rivets under the wing, Keel thought about the beating he had given this bird in the last few hours. It was, he thought with a flier's affection, some tough little bird. He hated what he was going to do to it.

The wind under the protection of the wing was very slight, occasionally stirring little tufts of weed that brushed against the sleeping bag's coarse surface. The breakers made a gentle, continuous rippling sound. Beyond the coverage of the wing, the sky remained brilliantly starlit.

Keel licked scummy teeth and thought about the others. It was possible that they were all still flying, he thought, glancing at the luminous dial of his watch. By careful leaning, they might have another thirty minutes or so. He did not imagine that either Abercrombie or Donovan would elect to cut it that close, but he had no way of knowing.

They might still be flying, or down.

They might have been caught.

The last possibility was one he did not like to consider. They had discussed what would happen in such an eventuality: the authorities would want all of them; the first caught would surely be offered some kind of plea-bargaining position—tell us what we want to know, and your own sentence will be lighter.

Keel thought Donovan had had the best answer: "Look,

boys. If we get caught, they aren't about to let anybody off lightly. The only question is whether you take your own medicine, and give the rest a chance, or drag us all down with you to the same federal prison."

It had been the subject of some sleepless nights for Keel. He hoped to God if he got caught he would not tell them anything. The others, he thought, probably told themselves the same.

But you didn't know what you might do. If anyone had told him even a few months ago that he would be here, now, in these circumstances, he would have suggested a padded cage.

Knowing he would not sleep, Keel considered quietly climbing up into the airplane and listening to a commercial station a few minutes on the ADF. He was hungry for news. He didn't *think* either of the other planes had been tracked, and he knew the odds against capture, once they were clear of the immediate area, were not that strong. He wished for reassurance.

But he did not make a move. He wanted a perfect battery before dawn for starting up again. Even a few minutes' operation could make a small difference, a crucial one if by some fluke he had starting trouble.

So he would just have to wonder.

A puff of stronger wind rustled the brush against his bag.

The work of the next few hours gnawed at Keel's consciousness. He made an effort and closed his eyes and willed sleep to come. It would not. There was too much of the past and the present and the future all mixed up and going around in circles in his head. The vibration and noise of the Cherokee still buffeted his senses. He could see, with his eyes closed, those planes on taxiway Delta and the lights of the terminal and the rows of runway lights. Simultaneously, a part of him was looking just ahead, and then to getting ashore, getting to the car, going to the bus station, where he would at least be free of MacReady and *that* worry, for the time being.

On Thursday he would be in Kansas City, on the Kansas

199

side. He intended to rent a car and buy just as many groceries and small appliances as he could load into the thing, changing twenties and fifties at every stop. He would give it a maximum of four hours, park the car downtown in a lot with all the goods still inside, take a taxi to the train station, and head for Chicago. On Friday he would make a heavy sweep, making clothing purchases he could immediately hock. He hoped to be in Utica, New York, Saturday morning, and on Sunday he would make his first guarded contact with the man in New York City who might be able to get him fifty cents on the dollar in a trade for as much as $100,000 of his split.

In some ways getting rid of the money was the riskiest part of the entire operation. But Keel was determined to be very patient. If necessary, he could take years to change all the cash. With or without the man from New York, he knew he could clear a few thousand dollars within a week's time. This clean money would be enough to change his brother's debt situation, if not his entire life.

In about ten days, Keel would begin his new life in the Pacific Northwest. He intended to go to a photography school first, and then perhaps back to college. It was not too late. He could start over. If he missed flying too much, he could take lessons all over again, making all the stupid early learning errors he had seen his students make. His new identity could eventually earn new ratings, if he chose to go that way.

But he had to be so very careful. Always.

The wind puffed weeds against his bag again.

He turned and idly watched the little breakers coming in on the beach. He noticed that one of them came up and splashed slightly against the back of the boat, although he was sure MacReady had manhandled it completely out of the water earlier.

Keel watched the waves coming in and then he suddenly chilled.

He turned and looked out beyond the tip of the wing at the starlit sky. But now the stars were mostly gone.

"Jesus Christ!"

200

"What?" MacReady was instantly awake, alert.

Keel tore at the zippers of the bag. "Come on. Get up. Hurry."

"What's going on?"

"The weather is changing. The sea is trying to come up. We've got to do this right now." Keel got out of the bag and fished for his wet shoes.

"You said yourself we had to wait till the first light of morning."

"We can't do it at all if the wind gets strong and the waves get high. Hurry!" Keel jammed his feet into the shoes, rolled up the sleeping bag, and hurled it into the back of the plane.

"If it's going to get bad, maybe we ought to just leave the airplane—"

"No. We can do it now if we hurry."

"Are we going to have time to get back to shore?"

"Plenty of time—if we hurry."

MacReady threw his bag into the plane, pulled out one of the two small satchels, and hurried toward the boat. He tossed it inside and hurried back, hopping a little because he was barefooted and hitting weed stobs. "What of your stuff do you want in the boat?"

"The overnight case," Keel snapped. "And my satchel."

MacReady stared at him. "Your half of the money?"

"My half of the money," Keel repeated meaningfully.

"I figured you'd want to keep that with you."

"It's safer in the boat."

"You . . . trust me?"

"I have to. Just like you've had to trust me."

MacReady grinned crookedly, unable to believe. "I've never trusted you or anybody else. I take care of number one."

This was necessary. This was important and had to be said now. "If you want to," Keel told him, "pull my sleeping bag back out. You'll find a .38 Smith & Wesson down inside the lining."

Staring at him, MacReady said nothing. His face worked.

"You went to sleep," Keel said, pressing the point home. "If I had wanted to dump you, I could have dumped you fifteen minutes ago."

"You ain't a killer. You didn't—"

"All I would have had to do was slug you and take off with all the money. Or put a nice little hole in your head."

"If I lived, I would've got you. Or told the pigs."

"We're both in that spot, MacReady. We have been all along. We've trusted each other because we had to. And we *still* have to."

MacReady swayed silently, watching him. Keel could tell his words had had the desired shock effect.

He said, "Hurry it up. My money in the boat too. And my little bag. And don't forget the flashlight, for God's sake."

MacReady broke off his stare, grabbed the bags, and hustled.

By the time he came back, Keel was inside the Cherokee, the front door latched. Keel leaned over to the little flap window on the left side and looked down at him. "You know what to do. Take it right out there. Give me the light signal. It's deep there. When I come down, don't get in the way, but don't wait too long, either."

MacReady's face was pale. "I won't. I'll be ready."

"Have we left anything there on the beach?"

"I don't see anything—"

"Get going, then. *Clear!*" Keel hit the starter. The engine whined, and fired.

MacReady ran for the boat.

Quickly checking instruments and controls, Keel forced himself to do it properly, including cycling the prop control twice to loosen the oil. The sea was definitely on the rise; the clouds had slipped in closer, blacking out the stars, and the deep water here on the east side of the island was now gentle, long rolling currents with a touch of froth here and there. A freshening wind rocked the plane slightly. He had no time to spare, but the last thing he needed was a takeoff crash because he had not used thirty seconds for something vital.

Everything checked.

Turning, he saw that MacReady was in the boat, had it fired up, was tooling out away from the shore.

Keel fed power to the engine and started his takeoff roll. The wheels jounced along as if reluctant to do so. There was plenty of beach, but Keel agonized as the plane began rolling so slowly. He had been stupid not to watch the weather more closely, he thought. Now he had to hurry and do this at the worst time, the dead of night.

The Cherokee began rolling faster. Brush off the left side blurred by. As the plane accelerated, it became more efficient in some sort of geometric progression; the wheels began to skip and it felt ready to fly, and then, with the yoke well back for the soft-field technique, Keel felt it lift off. He eased forward pressure, holding in the ground effect as he gained speed, and then it was all right and he began climbing.

The instant he was in the air, he could see that the storm was a whopper, and closer than it had appeared on the ground. But there was still time.

Leveling off a few hundred feet over the beach, he banked to the right, swinging out over the water. He could not pick out MacReady's boat and felt a second of panic. If MacReady had elected to run for it, there was damned little he could do but fly to the mainland, put down—with all the risks that involved—and accept his beating.

He banked back toward the island a little, adjusting power and continuing to look for MacReady's flashlight. Panic tried to take hold of him. He fought it down.

Then, continuing the bank, he saw it: a bright white flash, repeated, then steadying. He saw that he had missed it before because MacReady had stayed somewhat closer to the island than he had expected.

Relieved of one fear and facing another, Keel turned downwind and hauled his straps tighter. A glance over the gauges showed everything normal. He turned a base leg, losing altitude, and swept along the surface of the water at a height of about one hundred feet, showing MacReady the course he intended to fly. As he applied power and started his final go-around, he saw the boat quite clearly for an instant. MacReady was coming out to the proper place, having read the signal.

Keel gained a few hundred feet, scanning the water on all sides for signs of life. There was nothing. Visibility was markedly lower now in several directions, and the sea was gently rolling, with longer waves that promised worse to come within minutes.

Keel reached the far end of his circuit and came around a last time. With loving care he reduced power and let the Cherokee waft downward toward its final landing. The water was going to be black and cold, he thought, and he was afraid. He had kicked off his shoes, and the rudder pedals felt cold under his socks. The ax was wedged between the seats where he could get it quickly.

Up ahead, over the long, slowly rolling water, MacReady was waiting in the boat with the light directed straight toward him.

The plane came lower, very slow now. Keel began holding it off as the water came up.

In the boat, MacReady clutched the flashlight with a hand suddenly slippery with cold sweat. The motor was in idle and the boat pitched gently in the swell. He watched the airplane come in from right to left, very low, nose up, propeller seeming to turn slowly, quietly. A swell tried to rise up and catch the plane at the last instant, but the nose was too high to be touched and the tail made a little furrow in the swell, and then the plane settled softly and there was an enormous watery woosh. The plane hit and stopped very rapidly, water flying everywhere, hiding the scene for a moment. Then the splash subsided and MacReady could see the plane, floating low in the water, turning around halfway.

There was a movement in the cargo opening. Tom Keel appeared, however, out of the far front door, stepping gingerly out onto the wing. The plane was awash but staying up.

MacReady fed the boat motor some power and moved in closer.

Standing unsteadily on the wing, Keel swung the ax. With a light metallic rending sound it broke a hole in the metal covering of the wing. He swung again. Moving in, MacReady could see the fuselage filling with water, and now the sea was rushing into the wing cavities through the holes made by the ax.

Keel straightened up. The one wing was sinking fast. *"Come on!"*

MacReady gunned the boat up, bumping the half-submerged wing. Keel, white-faced, scrambled on board, bringing the ax with him. He had gotten soaked and his teeth were chattering.

"Around to the other side," he panted.

Obediently MacReady gunned the boat around the sinking front of the plane and to the other wing, which stood crazily atilt out of the water.

Standing unsteadily in the boat, Keel swung the ax, bashing a large hole in this wing's metal covering. Water rushed in, bubbling. Things were making cracking, straining sounds all over, and the engine was hissing and steaming.

Keel tried to swing a second time, but lost the ax. He almost fell in. The second blow was not necessary anyway. With a great sighing sound the aircraft went under in a chaos of bubbles and hissing.

Keel sat down with a plopping motion and took a deep breath. "She was a good old bird," he said softly.

MacReady turned the boat, gave it full throttle, and headed for the light at the north end of the island, and the mainland beyond.

In the tight box canyon, swirling snow carried by a high Colorado wind reduced visibility sharply. The coyote, working along the edge of the woods where the snow was not so deep because of wind protection, paused suddenly, its ice-crusted muzzle twitching, at the first sign of the unfamiliar sound.

Out of the snowstorm along the length of the canyon, about three hundred feet away, suddenly appeared a ghostly aircraft, white with red markings. It was extremely low and slow, with flaps down and landing light yellow in the pelting snowflakes. Its sound was a subdued murmur in the wind.

The coyote watched.

The plane drifted lower, was jostled by the wind, touched its gear to the deep, piled snow, skipped, touched again, and then plowed in. It skidded along, hurling great dense white clouds into the blackness, rotating as it skidded and bounced along. Then it caught something under its shattered propeller and, almost as it had stopped, started to tip over, tail over nose. The tail came up in a spray of white and hung there for a split second and then went on over. The aircraft lay belly-up in the snow.

The coyote ran for its life through the woods.

Moments passed. The aircraft was still.

Then there was a movement in the rear cargo door area. One man crawled groggily out into the deep snow and managed to get to his feet. He sank in almost to his hips. He reached up and a second man handed him out some small parcels. Then the second man crawled out and joined him beside the upside-down airplane.

"Well," the one man said, "not the best landing I ever made, but under the circumstances it will have to do."

They turned and struggled off into the night, and the snow came down, covering the airplane.

AFTERWARD

It was spring in Dallas and the trees in the park downtown were coming into leaf. The two men met at a bench under a maple, shook hands warmly, and sat down to talk.

"You've lost weight," Donovan observed.

Keel smiled thinly. "All this travel, changing money."

Donovan, who looked absolutely the same, except that his mustache was a little fuller and perhaps more rakish, paused to light a cigarette. Then he asked, "It's going well?"

"My New York thing didn't work out, as you know. But otherwise, yes."

"What happened in New York?"

"It didn't feel right. I pulled a disappearing act."

"You always were a worrier, but I'd say in this case you probably were right. A man can't be too careful, I always say."

"It looks like we've all been careful."

Donovan leaned back, extended long legs, and sighed. "Well, of course that was a bad time when our friend Mac-Ready got himself arrested on that stupid statutory rape thing."

"Evidently he didn't tell them a thing."

"No. My guess is that he has the money well hidden. He'll ride it out. With that lawyer he has, he'll beat it, too."

"Unless he tries to pay the lawyer with the wrong money."

Donovan looked at him. "You *are* an idealist. What better place could you put your money than into the hands of an expensive lawyer?"

"You think MacReady—!"

"Yes. And I think the lawyer will probably have most of it in fees by the time he's finished. Then MacReady will be free—but broke—and disposing of it will be the lawyer's problem."

"Which might be a problem for us."

"That lawyer has been paid in a lot of illegal things, I hear. There's no problem for any of us if he takes poor MacReady to the cleaners."

"Do you hear from Abby?"

"Yes. The operation was a success, as far as they can tell."

"I heard that," Keel said.

"He wrote me. He was low. No voice now, you know. But I daresay he'll learn to talk that funny way those people have. He's a fighter. And I'm not worried about his making any mistakes."

Keel digested the information. "I talked to Phil Lester."

"Oh?"

"He's spent hardly any of his share yet. Scared. But he did say Fetzer's mother died. There was a small estate to settle. Fetzer got what there was. So he's passing a little money now and then, and no one can suspect anything because he's supposed to have some money from the sale of the house and everything."

Donovan chuckled. "So we are home free."

"It's still a little hard to believe. I still feel like I'm being followed sometimes. They haven't stopped looking for us, you know."

"I imagine not, the way we continue to spend their money!"

"No. They'll keep looking and keep looking."

"But they won't find us, will they? Any more than they were able to pin responsibility for anything on that poor Atlanta manager in that stupid hearing they held."

Keel had watched news reports on the hearings with considerable interest and irritation. There had been elements set upon placing blame for the entire operation on the manager, Kuhlman. But in a little impromptu speech that was now a part of contemporary folklore, Kuhlman had iced the Congressional investigators with an explanation of the factors involved in the attack and his decisions.

Kuhlman had made a hell of an impression nationally with that blunt, fighting speech, sitting there at the witness table with his beautiful new wife at his side, and public sympathy had been immediate and direct. The probers had backed off, the airlines had stated their support for all decisions made, and Washington had announced "new and sterner procedures" for handling all such cases in the future.

A stupid little attempt upon Miami International—two Cessna 150s in a driving rainstorm that damned near blew them into the ocean—had helped calm the public, too. Both of those youthful pilots were in jail now. No one else had tried it since.

"So is your new life all right?" Donovan asked now, watching Keel closely with those intent eyes.

"I'm in school," Keel told him. "It's going all right. I suppose I'm happy enough."

"And your brother? I know you were concerned—"

"He died a month ago."

For a minute Donovan said nothing. Then he put a hand on Keel's shoulder. "I'm sorry. I truly am."

"At least he didn't have the worry right there at the end. Cindy and the kids are taken care of. At least I have that."

"Yes."

They sat there on the bench awhile in silence.

"I can't say I regret doing it, though," Keel said thoughtfully.

"Of course not."

"We got away with it. That's what counts. Right?"

"Would you do it again?"

"I don't know," Keel said. "I was a different man then. It seems a long time ago already."

Then he realized that Donovan was watching him very closely.

209

He turned and met his old friend's stare.

"What is it?" he asked finally.

Donovan's eyes were filled with pleasure and excitement. "If you think that one was good, wait till you hear the idea I have now. And this one will just take the two of us."